Red Team Alpha
A Crimson Worlds Adventure

Jay Allan

Also By Jay Allan

Marines (Crimson Worlds I)
The Cost of Victory (Crimson Worlds II)
A Little Rebellion (Crimson Worlds III)
The First Imperium (Crimson Worlds IV)
The Line Must Hold (Crimson Worlds V)
To Hell's Heart (Crimson Worlds VI)
The Shadow Legions(Crimson Worlds VII)
Even Legends Die (Crimson Worlds VIII)
The Fall (Crimson Worlds IX)
War Stories (Crimson World Prequels)
MERCS (Successors I)
The Prisoner of Eldaron (Successors II)
Into the Darkness (Refugees I)
Shadows of the Gods (Refugees II)
Revenge of the Ancients (Refugees III)
Winds of Vengeance (Refugees IV)
Shadow of Empire (Far Stars I)
Enemy in the Dark (Far Stars II)
Funeral Games (Far Stars III)
Blackhawk (Far Stars Legends I)
The Dragon's Banner
Gehenna Dawn (Portal Wars I)
The Ten Thousand (Portal Wars II)
Homefront (Portal Wars III)

www.jayallanbooks.com
www.bloodonthestars.com
www.wolfsclaw.com
www.crimsonworlds.com

Red Team Alpha

Red Team Alpha is a work of fiction. All names, characters, incidents, and locations are fictitious. Any resemblance to actual persons, living or dead, events or places is entirely coincidental.

Copyright © 2016 Jay Allan Books

All rights reserved.

ISBN: 978-1946451002

Author's Note

For readers of the previous books of the Crimson Worlds series, I wanted to offer a bit of guidance on placing Red Team Alpha in the overall timeline. The setting is in the years preceding the outbreak of the Third Frontier War, which places this book 3-4 years before the beginning of Marines. It is therefore, somewhat of a prequel, though it is more of a standalone adventure set in the universe (and using some of the same characters).

Prologue

Roderick Vance stared at the intelligence report. He was sitting in the study—his *father's* study—reviewing the pile of work that had fallen on him. The room was dark, lit only by the flickering light of his workstation's screen and the dying embers of the untended fire in the hearth behind him.

It had been barely a month since he'd gotten the call in the middle of the night telling him his parents where dead…just over thirty Martian days since he'd inherited the responsibility for one of Mars' largest conglomerates, a sprawling enterprise involved in trading, manufacturing, and finance. One that employed thousands and accounted for just over two percent of the Confederation's GDP. It was overwhelming, but right now it was the least of his concerns.

His father had bequeathed another job to his only son, a position far less public than the other, one that had been held by a Vance since the early days of the Martian Confederation. Roderick's father had spoken to him only a few times about his role as the director of Martian Intelligence, and he'd done almost nothing to prepare the younger Vance for a job he hadn't been expected his son to fill for several decades.

The Council had almost selected another director, fearful that Vance was too young, too unprepared. But Roderick felt the call of family obligation, and he resolved to follow in his father's footsteps. He began his new career by teaching himself a central tenet of his new craft…lying. He stood before the Council, assuring them with unchallenged sincerity that his father had schooled him in espionage since he'd been a child. It was a wild bluff, and he held his ground, hiding his nerves, completely unprepared to answer any incisive questions. But Martian society was based heavily on tradition, and a Vance had always run Martian Intelligence. Roderick's confidence, the stone cold nature of his performance, had silenced his doubters. There had been no questions, none at all. He'd been confirmed in his new role almost at once, the necessary security clearances approved moments before he was sworn into the job.

Now he faced his first great challenge. The report displayed on his glowing tablet was disturbing to say the least, even stunning…but it was not conclusive. It would be a few days before he had more information…a period he was sure would seem like the longest of his life. If the find was what it appeared to be, it was impossible to overstate its importance…to the Martian Intelligence, to the Confederation, even to history itself. Things would never be the same again.

If he did get the confirmation, he knew he had to move quickly…and quietly too. There was no time to spare. It appeared that the precious information had already leaked. One of his agents was on the detention level even now, suspected of passing the news to Alliance Intelligence. Vance wasn't sure, but he knew finding out would be another baptism of his new job. He'd trembled slightly as he signed the order authorizing level one enhanced interrogation on the suspect, but he knew there was no choice. He simply had to know for certain if the news had been divulged. And, if he'd ordered the torture of an innocent man, of a loyal agent, the part of him that was already older in spirit than his years realized that, too, was part of the job, as was living with the guilt from his actions.

He put such thoughts out of his mind. He had to decide what to do, how to inspect the mysterious site, and how to get there first. His first urge was to mobilize the fleet, to send every bit of force he could scrape up. But he knew that wasn't possible. A massive operation would destroy whatever secrecy remained. No, he couldn't mount a large expedition. A small group could move faster, maintain tighter secrecy. He wasn't comfortable yet with all the various specialized assets and resources available to the head of Mars intelligence, but he knew of one, small but also the very best. A secret force, operating under the direct command of the intelligence chief. A unit with an unbroken record of success Twenty men and women—warriors, veterans, killers.

Red Team Alpha.

Chapter One

From the Personal Journal of Alex Vandenberg

The Scotch had a bite to it as it slid down my throat. I'm not much of a drinker, usually only a glass of wine with dinner, if that, and almost never hard liquor. But a promise is a promise, even when decades have passed…and one made to brothers standing with you in hell is sacrosanct. We swore to each other that night, and I have not missed a single year since then. Not one.

I am wearing my uniform, as I have every year…even in the near decade since I retired from active duty. The style is much the same as the one I wore on that night so long ago. The jacket just a bit longer, with a wide gray stripe down each side the earlier design lacked. The brightly gleaming, brand new lieutenant's bars of that evening have been replaced by two platinum stars, older and, I ashamed to say, far less polished than that young officer's insignia. I was all excitement and dash back then, obsessed with the drive to gain acceptance, to go into battle against the enemy. Any enemy. To prove myself. To show I was as good as those who came before me.

Now I am old, and I have seen more death than any man should witness, fought deadly struggles against enough enemies to last a lifetime and more. Now I seek only quiet. Peace. But I still remember that mission, every agonizing moment of it, my first and only one with Red Team Alpha.

This is the fiftieth toast I have drunk, the fifty-first counting the one I made will all my comrades that night. I had to crack open another new bottle to make it, and I am fortunate indeed to have it. I long ago ran out of what we had set aside, and now it is getting difficult—no, damned near impossible—to find more. I wouldn't even have this one if Roderick Vance hadn't given it to me. Since the Fall, old liquors, like most of the luxuries we once took for granted, are extremely rare, and almost beyond price. Certainly beyond the means of a retired general's pension.

I don't know how Roderick knew...or how long he has been aware of my ritual. It was a secret oath, only between the members of the unit, and I certainly never told anyone else...not friends, not my wife, nor my children. But I long ago realized it was pointless trying to understand how the head of Martian Intelligence—and now the effective ruler of the Confederation—knew the things he did. Roderick Vance is the most gifted spy I've ever known...save perhaps for one, whose name I have tried with all my ability—and little success—to forget.

I held the cut crystal glass up to the light, admiring the amber liquid for a few seconds, remembering the first toast, the one we all drank together. We were all still alive then, comrades in arms, though my entry into the Team hadn't been without its bumpy moments. I'd come to those brave men and women as an unblooded rookie, and to them I seemed a privileged elite, excused from the years of combat and suffering they had endured to gain their places. I can't blame them, not really. I doubt I, a veteran now for many decades, would feel any differently in their position. I had hoped to gain their acceptance without divulging the full truth of who I was, but in the end I could only find my place among them by sharing my legacy.

I drank again, deeply. I hated it, the Scotch, not the toast. But I forced it down. I didn't like it any better fifty years ago, but I'd had enough trouble fitting in, and once my comrades had finally begun to accept me, I wasn't about to do anything to lose what I had gained. I would have tossed back a glass of battery acid if that's what they'd been drinking, but there was no way I was going to stand out as different, as I had so starkly in the weeks leading up to that moment.

We knew the mission would be a dangerous one, even more so than the usual disasters the Team was called upon to handle. The mood was somber that night, hours before we were scheduled to land, and we all agreed to the pact, then and there. Once a year, the survivors would gather together and drink a toast, one to those who didn't make it back…and to comrades the Team had lost on other missions too. And that oath has been kept, for half a century and through three cataclysmic wars the eighteen men and two women gathered in that room so many years before couldn't have imagined. It has been kept despite combat, disasters, and mass death, through the struggle against the First Imperium and the final wars leading to the Fall.

Even if it is now kept only by one man, a tired old veteran, worn out by a lifetime of war and ready to join his comrades.

Martian Intelligence HQ
50 Years Earlier

"The Team isn't going to like this, sir. They're all veterans. There's never been a rookie assigned to our ranks. Never. And so soon after we lost Colonel Warren…" Colonel John Reginald stood at attention, despite the fact that he'd been told to relax and take a seat. His tone had been firm, unwavering… until he'd mentioned Colonel Warren. Then his voice cracked a bit. The Team's longtime commander had been killed on the last mission, and the loss had hit them all, and none harder than Reginald, who had been forced to step into his friend and commander's shoes. "How can we give the colonel's roster spot to a rookie, sir? That's what it is, after all, isn't it? His spot?" There was a pleading quality to his words now.

"I understand your concerns, Colonel…and I know you're still getting used to command, that the men and women are still mourning Colonel Warren. That is only fitting and proper. But I assure you, Lieutenant Vandenberg is an extremely capable soldier, and a *very* appropriate replacement for the colonel. He just graduated from the Officer's Academy with the highest scores, not just in his class, but in Confederation history. He is intelligent, enormously fit…in every way, one of the very best we have ever had." Roderick Vance sat behind a massive wooden desk, his posture perfect, his voice firm. There was only the slightest hint, easily overlooked, that he was uncomfortable, holding something back.

"I have no doubt about his abilities, sir…and I'm sure he will have a long and distinguished career. But he's not there yet. He has no combat experience. There has never been a member of Red Team Alpha who was not a combat veteran. You know that." Reginald paused uncomfortably. "That was your father's rule, sir."

"Yes, John…it was *his* rule." Vance paused, his shield of cold logic failing him for just a few seconds. The Team wasn't alone in suffering a recent tragic loss. Vance's parents had both been killed only weeks before, when their landing craft lost power and crashed in the open Martian desert. It was still a mystery, one he suspected someone had tried very hard to make look like an accident. Vance didn't believe the stories about instrument failure, not for an instant. There was someone out there to blame for his parents' murders, and one day he would find out who.

That will be a bloody day…

The new head of Martian Intelligence had inherited his post—and control of the massive Vance business interests—suddenly, decades before he'd expected the burden to fall on him.

"*His* rule," Vance repeated. "If my father had the chance now to give me one piece of advice, I know it would be to use my own judgment, not try to figure out what I think he would have done. And this is my decision to make." He paused. "Though I suspect my father would have agreed in this case. He was a man who knew when to break a rule."

Reginald shifted uncomfortably in his chair. "What if he

panics the first time we get into a nasty fight? It's not like a battle, with thousands of other troops in the line. If one of us bolts, or even hesitates at the wrong time, we could all get scragged. There's a reason combat experience is a requirement for acceptance into the Team. No matter how good a soldier looks on paper, you never really know until you see how he handles himself under fire."

Vance held back a sigh. He understood Reginald's concerns, even sympathized with them. But he'd made up his mind. "Again, Colonel, I understand everything you are saying. Indeed, I would agree with you in most circumstances. But this is an exception. We have never had a fresh graduate with Lieutenant Vandenberg's capability." Now Vance paused and looked thoughtfully at his desk, as if trying to decide what he wanted to say, how much to divulge. "And I have other reasons, Colonel. You will just have to trust me…and leave it at that."

Reginald stood still for a moment, clearly struggling to hide his surprise. Vance knew he'd made an impression on the colonel, the same one he did on everyone, at least all save those very few close to him. The new head of Martian Intelligence was considered a bit of a cold fish, even a bit awkward, and he knew those around him were watching, waiting to see how well he would fill his father's massive shoes.

Vance watched as Reginald nodded grudgingly. Vance knew the colonel still disagreed, but he was also sure the officer realized there was nothing more he could do. He suspected Reginald had been prepared to argue facts, to make a case for enforcing the experience requirement for admission to the Team. But the spymaster's last statement had made the facts irrelevant. He'd asked Reginald to trust him…and there was no way for the veteran soldier to say no. Not without openly challenging the new intelligence chief.

"Yes, sir," he said, clearly hiding as much of his doubt as he could manage before adding, "But I can't control the Team's reaction." He paused, and a frown pushed its way through his discipline and slipped onto his face. "I'll be surprised if they don't give him a hard time. A very hard time."

Vance nodded. "You're probably right, Colonel. They will be rough on him. But Alex is tough. He says he can handle it, and I believe him. And he's on the Team." The last sentence was spoken with a cold firmness that left no doubt the conversation was over. Whether Reginald liked it or not, the valedictorian of the Academy was now a member of Red Team Alpha... in all his unblooded glory.

"Understood, sir." There was an edge to Reginald's voice, but he said nothing else. He stood up and snapped off a salute and stared at Vance with a look nearly devoid of emotion.

Vance glared back. "Very well, Colonel. You are dismissed." He turned his gaze to the screen on his desk, but an instant later his eyes rolled up, taking a last look as Reginald turned and walked toward the door. "Thank you, Colonel," he added, a touch more warmth in his voice than Reginald had yet heard from Martian Intelligence's new chief. "And good luck."

"The Rock"
Red Team Alpha HQ
Three Days Later

"Let's move it! I've seen better from a bunch of schoolkids back in the Metroplex." Sergeant-Major Tyrell Jones stood in the center of the massive gymnasium, watching eighteen men and women struggling to complete the grueling interval training session he'd devised for them. They were all in excellent condition, the very best Mars had to offer, but Jones knew his job was to challenge them, and he had a sadistic streak in his mind, at least when it came to creating training regimens.

Jones was the senior NCO on the Team, indeed he was practically the ranking non-com in all of the Martian armed forces...though the roster of the Marine Division, where he'd spent most of his career, listed him as retired. That was true of everyone present in the room. Every one of the nineteen warriors gathered in the training hall was listed as retired or discharged. They had come from different services, served before in a number of capacities…but they had all been invited to join a truly special unit, and each one had answered that call. They had been Marines, army, navy…but now they were Red Team Alpha, every one of them.

All save one, perhaps. Jones watched the new kid moving through the course. Vandenberg was good, as good as anyone else out there, he had to admit. But he was still skeptical. He'd trained more young recruits than he cared to remember, and he'd never seen one like Alexander Vandenberg…but his doubts persisted, and he knew the rest of the Team felt the same way. He hadn't discussed it with any of them, but he was sure all the same. He could see it in their expressions, in the way they acted. And he knew that was trouble waiting to happen.

The Alphas were all veterans, experienced men and women who had completed some of the most dangerous and vital missions imaginable. They had done it out of loyalty to Mars, and because they were the best, and they were driven to excel, to push themselves to the ultimate. There was no glory for Red Team Alpha, no parades and medals…only secrecy and danger. They worked mostly in the shadows, facing threats the civilians of Mars never knew existed.

They had two covenants, unwritten promises they relied upon as they marched again and again into the fire. First, they were deployed only on missions of the highest importance, matters vital to the security of the Confederation. And second, the members of the Team, the men and women at their sides as they charged into hell, would always be combat-tested veterans.

Jones didn't have anything against Vandenberg—he seemed like a good kid. But he was the living, breathing embodiment of the breaking of that covenant. The sergeant-major didn't understand why they were being forced to accept an unblooded rookie into their ranks…and he didn't think any of the others did either.

"Alright, enough bullshit over there!" Jones's head snapped around, and he jogged forward. There was a scuffle on the course. O'Reilly had gotten into it with Vandenberg, and the two were wrestling on the floor. The rest of the Team had stopped their training and gathered around the disturbance. Most of them watched quietly, but more than a few were cheering O'Reilly on.

Jones shook his head as he moved toward the fight. O'Reilly was a hothead, there was no question about that, and Jones didn't doubt the high-strung corporal had started it. But he still couldn't understand what the colonel had been thinking when he'd taken Vandenberg into the Team. The Alphas were more than a military unit, more even than a family. Each member was attuned to his comrades on a level no outsider could comprehend. The trust between them all, at least in battle, was total. And it wasn't realistic to expect that camaraderie to extend to a twenty-two year old just out of the Academy, with his honors and awards, but not so much as a scratch on his brand new combat armor.

"O'Reilly, on your feet now!" Jones's command boomed like a clap of thunder.

"But, Sarge, this fucking cherry…"

"I don't wanna hear it…you got me?" The sergeant-major's voice was like an elemental force. "Don't make me get into this fight, Ian, or I shit you not, I will send your insubordinate ass to the infirmary for a month." The sergeant-major's tone was like ice, and he stood less than two meters from the struggling men, his fists clenched. No one in Red Team Alpha—no one—wanted to go toe to toe with Tyrell Jones.

O'Reilly shoved hard against his opponent one last time, and he slowly rose to his feet, turning and standing at something like attention before Jones. "Yes, Sergeant-Major," he said grudgingly, spitting a spray of blood from his mouth as he did. The fight had been far from one-sided, Jones realized with a good bit of surprise.

Jones stared silently, his eyes panning up and down the battered corporal's body. O'Reilly had been a troublemaker in the Marines, winning and then giving back his stripes more than once. His temper would have gotten him bounced out of the division, save for one fact. Ian O'Reilly was one hell of a fighter…and he was fearless in combat. He'd saved the lives of so many comrades under fire—including more than one of his officers—none of them had the heart to send him packing with a dishonorable discharge. And when Collin Vance went looking for the best warriors for the new Red Team Alpha, he picked O'Reilly, despite half a dozen warnings and suggestions he pass on the troublesome corporal. Along with Jones, O'Reilly was one of the eight originals still on the Team, and while he remained a hardcore pain in the ass between missions, absolutely no one had anything bad to say about having Ian O'Reilly at his side once the shooting started.

"You look like shit, O'Reilly," Jones snapped. He could see Vandenberg out of the corner of his eye. The young lieutenant had climbed to his feet and was standing at attention about a meter from his opponent. Vandenberg actually outranked Jones...everywhere except in the training center. Here, during sessions, by both custom and regulation, the Team sergeant-major was lord and god, even over the officers.

He turned to face Vandenberg. "I do not tolerate this kind of bullshit in my training hall," he snapped, his voice sharper than he'd intended. He paused, pushing his own resentment aside. He wasn't any happier about having a cherry on the Team than anyone else, but if there was one thing Tyrell Jones knew how to do, it was follow orders.

He felt a wave of surprise as his eyes wandered over Vandenberg. The kid was banged up, there was no question about that. But it was also clear he'd held his own. Jones snapped his gaze back to O'Reilly. If anything, the grizzled corporal had come off the worse for the short struggle. That was a surprise. There weren't many in the Martian military who could go toe to toe with Ian O'Reilly and come away on top...and to see the Team's young puppy lieutenant manage it was a bit of a shock.

"Lieutenant," Jones said, the edge gone from his voice, "Corporal O'Reilly struck you, sir. Do you wish to press charges?" Jones struggled to keep his voice even. The idea of a fighter like O'Reilly getting bounced out of the service—or worse—over something this foolish was hard for him to imagine.

But no one told the stupid son of a bitch to go after an officer...

"No, Sergeant-Major." Vandenberg spoke calmly, whatever anger he felt toward O'Reilly deeply hidden. "Nothing happened here. The corporal and I were just…doing some extra training."

Jones felt a wave of relief. He'd imagined that a freshly minted officer would conduct himself 'by the book,' and go running to his superiors demanding punishment for the NCO who dared lay hands on him. And the book was clear about what happened to corporals who assaulted officers. O'Reilly was a pain in the ass and a hothead, but Jones didn't want to lose him to some cherry lieutenant's righteous rage.

Vandenberg just stood there, calm, his fatigues rumpled and torn in several places and his left eye swollen almost shut, but otherwise looking like he was on parade. He stood silently for a few seconds then he turned toward O'Reilly, his expression neutral, not a hint of apparent anger at the man he'd just been fighting. Then he extended his hand.

O'Reilly didn't move, he just stood at attention with a scowl on his face…at least until Jones's eyes found his. The Sergeant-Major's stare was as cold as space itself, and it communicated a clear message, one even Ian O'Reilly didn't have the guts to ignore. The corporal stared back at Jones for a few seconds, but Jones's glare was too much for him. He turned to the side and shook Vandenberg's hand, grudgingly, looking all the while as if he'd tasted something bad.

Jones turned slowly, sighing softly to himself as he did. *This is going to be just great*, he thought. *We're still in the training hall, and we're already having trouble. What's going to happen when we get into the field?*

But he didn't really want an answer…so he pushed the thought aside and focused on the men and women standing around staring at him.

"Alright," he growled, the training master inside him taking control. "Nobody told any of you to stop working. Let's start over…back to the first station."

The groans were audible, but everyone in the room, officers and non-coms alike, turned and walked back to the starting line.

Sergeant-Major Tyrell Jones's voice was like the word of God to all of them, at least in the confines of the Team's training hall.

Chapter Two

Martian Intelligence HQ
The Next Week

"I know why you're doing this, Roderick…but are you sure now is the time?" Andre Girard sat across from Vance's massive desk, gesturing toward the data chip he'd just placed in front of Mars' top spy. "This one is serious, even by the Team's standards. If that intel report is accurate, it's the most important mission the Team has ever drawn. Why don't you just come up with a reason to keep Alex behind? Nothing dishonorable… nothing even permanent. Just something to get him off this operation. If Alliance Intelligence is really onto us, this could be a hell of a first fire experience for any warrior, no matter how talented. You'd be doing him a favor. And the Team too…they really don't need any distractions on this mission." He paused, twisting around in the plush leather guest chair, his hands absent-mindedly straightening his uniform as he did. Girard was a military officer as well as a spy, and he was dressed in the garb of his more public career…though this conversation was undoubtedly a function of his other, more clandestine, profession.

Vance leaned back slightly in his chair, trying to force his bolt-upright frame to relax, at least a little. But he gave up a few seconds later and snapped back to the erect and uncomfortable looking posture that was so natural to him.

"Nothing dishonorable, Andre?" Vance's voice was cold

and unemotional, as it usually was. But the man he was speaking to was one of his oldest friends, a trusted confidante of his father's who had transferred that allegiance as the son took charge of intelligence operations. "Ordering him to stay behind while the rest of the Team goes on a mission this dangerous? Exactly how can we make that honorable? How could we convince him it is anything but a lack of faith that he can handle it?" He took a deep breath. "You know why he's there, Andre. If I'd known about this mission in time, perhaps I could have delayed his appointment. But how can I pull him from the Team now?"

Girard stared across the desk looking like he was going to say something, but Vance beat him to it. "No, Andre, I can't do it." A pause. "I won't. We discussed all of this before, we had these arguments with ourselves. Alex is an extraordinary young officer. He'll be fine in battle…and he's an asset to any force that counts him in its ranks."

"Yes, Roderick…except for one thing. They're not accepting him. Oh, Colonel Reginald will follow your orders…and the officers will follow his. But the others are having a tougher time with it. Battle experience is almost a cult with these men and women. You know the kinds of things they've been through. Alex has been in three…incidents…since he reported. Can you imagine how that affects the trust and comradeship a unit like Alpha relies on?" Girard was shaking his head as he spoke. "And they just lost Colonel Warren. Reginald is still settling in as their new commander…and they're getting used to seeing him that way, learning to trust him as their leader." Girard hesitated. "Are you sure about this, Roderick? Now?"

Vance sat for a few seconds, staring back with a noncommittal look on his face, as if he was considering what Girard had said. Then he shook his head. "Andre, I understand everything you've said, and I appreciate your insight. But I have to do what seems right to me. Alex Vandenberg is part of Red Team Alpha…and the others will just have to accept that." A strange feeling passed through Vance's mind. For all he was regarded as cold and calculating, his first controversial command hadn't had anything at all to do with logic. He'd put Vandenberg on the team for reasons that had nothing to do with raw logic, and everything to do with loyalty, emotion. About what *felt* right.

Girard nodded. He knew when an argument was lost. Roderick Vance was young to be the head of Martian Intelligence, but Girard had known him since he was a child. There was no immaturity in Vance, no emotional weakness. Collin Vance had been a brilliant man, but Girard's instincts told him his old friend's son was even smarter, more capable. The younger Vance expressed barely any emotion at all, save a basic sense of honor. But when Roderick Vance decided something was right, nothing changed his mind.

"Then perhaps you should tell them...explain to them why he is there. I know you wanted to respect Alex's privacy, but if you send them into action now, with this unresolved..." Girard paused. "They'll accept him then...you know they will."

Vance hesitated, a thoughtful look on his face. "We'll see, Andre. I promised Alex I wouldn't...and I understand why he wants his privacy in that way. I truly do." Vance took a deep breath before continuing. "But if there is no other way...I won't jeopardize the Team or the mission. I will tell them if I must."

"Very well, Roderick." Girard paused, his eyes dropping again to the data chip. "Should we go over there and brief them in person? They've got to ship out tomorrow...there's no time to waste. This is the big one. The one that can affect history."

Vance nodded, and then he slid his chair back and stood up. "Yes, let's go," he said, reaching down and grabbing the chip off the table. "And you're right...there's no time to waste."

"The Rock"
Red Team Alpha HQ
An Hour Later

"Why do you want to be here so bad, cherry? Why the hell you want to go and die?" O'Reilly was standing over Vandenberg, having gotten the better of his opponent through the simple expedient of jumping him from behind. It was the third fight between the two—and Ruiz and two of the other corporals had taken shots at the kid too. Every time the officers weren't around, one or more of the non-coms tried to convince the new recruit to quit. But none of it—fights, threats, persuasion—had worked. Vandenberg put up a hell of a fight every time he was attacked...and even when he got beaten down he refused to give in.

"You can't keep me from being on this team, Two Gun...no matter how hard you try." Vandenberg had been calling O'Reilly by the nickname the rest of the Team used, and it clear it was just pissing off the big, bad tempered soldier even more.

O'Reilly pulled his foot back and delivered a savage kick to Vandenberg, just as the lieutenant was trying to get up. The rookie didn't shout—he didn't make a sound—but he crumpled back to the ground with a thud.

"Just quit, cherry. Go down to HQ and put in for a damned transfer. We got no room here for a fancy officer who ain't even had a shot fired at him. If you want to go get yourself blown to bloody chunks, I guess that's your business. But you ain't gonna get the rest of us killed. We lost enough of our own without worrying about wiping some kid's nose. I been here since the beginning, and I buried eighteen friends. You think I'm gonna sit here and watch you get more of 'em scragged?"

"You can't force me out, you big dumb piece of shit. No matter what you...ooph." Vandenberg didn't manage to hold in the groan this time, as O'Reilly kicked him again.

"You got some kind of death wish, boy? You think it's all glory and honor, don't you? Bands and bugles and shiny medals? Well it ain't. It's fucking blood and death out there, but you wouldn't know that...'cause you ain't never been there. You never watched your friend bleed to death on some miserable rock, moaning in pain, calling out for his mother while he holds his guts in the best he can with two hands. Why you want to go and die...and maybe take half of us with you?" He pulled his foot back to deliver another kick.

"O'Reilly!" The rafters of the building seemed to shake as Jones's voice filled the room. The sergeant-major walked in from a back corridor. "I've had it with you, O'Reilly…you've just had your last chance. You wanna fight a comrade…bring it over here you worthless piece of shit, and show me what you got. 'Cause I'm gonna beat your sorry ass like you never been beat before." Jones threw down the small 'pad he was carrying, and it hit the ground, the screen shattering. He held his arms out in front of him, hands balled into massive fists.

"That won't be necessary, Sergeant-Major." Colonel Reginald stepped into the gym. He'd just walked through the far door with a small cluster of companions. He turned toward the disheveled corporal. "You're going to be lucky, O'Reilly if you get out of this without a court-martial. I should save us all the time, and put a bullet in your head right now." The Marine walked forward, his boots echoing loudly on the hardwood floors of the training hall. His right hand rested ominously on the holster at his side.

"But, Colonel…why'd they have to send us this damned rookie?" O'Reilly's voice was angry, but there was uncertainty in it too. It was clear he'd gone too far this time. He'd managed to get caught in the act right in front of the colonel…and a pair of grim-looking figures still standing behind the CO. One of them wore an army uniform, with a single brigadier's star on each collar…and the other he knew, even though the two had never spoken to each other. Everyone on the team knew Roderick Vance, the new head of Martian Intelligence. Even if he could have convinced Reginald to let him slide, it wouldn't matter. Word was, Vance was as cold blooded as they came…and not one to give second chances easily.

Vance stepped forward, his face frozen, unreadable. "Corporal O'Reilly, I'd have you dragged out of here right now and taken to the north polar region to dig out terraforming tunnels for the next twenty years…but I need this team complete and ready to go."

O'Reilly stood at attention and stared back at the head of Martian Intelligence. His looked sick, like his stomach was doing a few flops as he stared at the man who could have him shot with a word.

"Complete and ready to go...do you understand that?" Vance looked around the room, his eyes pausing for a second on each Team member present. "That means you, O'Reilly... and it means Vandenberg too. This foolishness stops now." A pause. "*Now.*" He stared over at Reginald. "Colonel, if Corporal O'Reilly...or any other member of the Team, behaves in any way inappropriately, either in this training hall or in the field, you are hereby instructed to shoot him immediately." The room fell silent with Vance's words, every eye focused on the spymaster. He hadn't been in his job for long, but now they were getting a taste of what he was made of...tougher, even, than his legendary father.

"The Team is on a war footing as of now," Vance continued. It's time to think of the mission, and to forget any grievances." His eyes moved to Vandenberg, and the rookie looked back and nodded, as if he knew what Vance was about to do and was giving his assent. Then Vance turned and stared at O'Reilly again. "And I'll tell you why Lieutenant Vandenberg is here, Corporal...why he wants to be part of Alpha...why he's willing to risk death serving beside you all and why your pointless abuse has not driven him away."

There was an edge of cold anger in Vance's voice, an uncharacteristic display of emotion. "Because Vandenberg is his mother's name, the one he used to apply to the Academy, the one he has gone by all his life, for security...and for a number of reasons. His father is dead, a Marine killed in action. Recently. You all knew him. His name was Warren. Colonel Travis Warren." He paused, allowing his last sentence to hang in the air.

"That is why it was so important for him to serve on Alpha... and that is why I approved his assignment, despite his lack of combat experience. I think it is appropriate that the founder of this Team bequeath his spot to his son, especially when we are talking about a young man who has excelled in every measurable way." The anger was still sharp in his tone, and he stared at O'Reilly and the others, greeting their stunned expressions with a disgusted look on his face. Then he turned and started to walk back to the door, pausing only for a moment to turn back toward Reginald. "You have your orders, Colonel. The Team is to be ready to embark at 0600 hours tomorrow." And, without another word, he turned again and continued on his way.

"Yes, sir!" Reginald stood silent, stone still, watching as Vance and Girard walked toward the door. Then he turned and glared at his assembled troopers. "I hope you were all listening to Director Vance, because, you can bet your ass I *will* shoot the next one of you who behaves in any way beneath what I expect from a member of this Team." He paused, letting his threat sink in. The expressions in the room suggested no one doubted him.

"And wherever Colonel Warren is, he's looking down at all of you with shame." He started to move forward, to help Vandenberg up, but he was too late. O'Reilly and Ruiz were already there, reaching down and gently pulling the young lieutenant to his feet, holding him up when his legs gave out and he stumbled. Neither of them apologized, not in words. But they carried him back toward the door, heading toward the barracks. And that was the last of the rift in Red Team Alpha. When they boarded their ship the next day, they were twenty men and women…and one unit. Ready to face whatever was waiting out there, as they always had before.

Chapter Three

**MCS Westron
Approaching Gamma Epsilon Warp Gate
Five Weeks Later**

The wardroom was small, barely large enough for the twenty men and women gathered there. Space was always at a premium aboard ship, and on a military vessel like *Westron*, every ton used for recreational facilities was that much less devoted to energy generation and weapons. Even the Martians, accustomed as they were to tight quarters in their domed cities and subterranean passageways, found extended service aboard a naval vessel tended toward the claustrophobic.

The Team was used to travelling by ship, but this had been a long run, and that, combined with the realization that the mission itself promised to be difficult and extremely dangerous, had them all on edge. And all the time in the tanks hadn't helped. Lying there drugged up and bloated, getting squeezed by the pressure all around…it wasn't something that made the time pass any faster. But Roderick Vance's orders had been clear. The mission was beyond urgent. There was reason to believe that Alliance Intelligence forces were also on their way to investigate…and it was absolutely essential the Martians get there first. And that meant spending most of the trip crammed into the tanks, while *Westron* accelerated and decelerated with a lot more gees than her crew and passengers could have handled

Red Team Alpha

outside the protective units.

Now they were approaching the target. It was the eve of the mission, and the Alphas had gathered together. They had rearranged the room with an abandon that would have unsettled the more fastidious naval crew if any of them had been around. But *Westron* had ferried Red Team Alpha before, and her crew knew enough to stay out of the way of the elite warriors. Cleaning up the mess afterward was much easier than trying to tame twenty of Mars' deadliest fighters.

The chairs had been pushed into a rough circle and the three small tables were set aside, stacked one on top of the other. Tomorrow the men and women of Red Team Alpha would climb into their armor and bolt into the landers that would bring them to the surface of Gamma Epsilon II…and whatever awaited them there. But tonight they were comrades, and they were together…to recount past battles, to talk of lost friends. It was a Team tradition on the eve of battle, one started by none other than Vandenberg's father during the eight years he'd led the unit after founding it.

"Do you really think we've made first contact with an alien race?" Lieutenant Elise Cho looked out at her comrades as she spoke. Cho was the smallest member of the Team by far, standing just a touch over 1.5 meters and weighing in at 44kg. But her size didn't detract from her deadliness in a fight, and she was generally considered to be the best shot on the Team, with a list of kills so long, impressive wasn't a strong enough word to describe it. She'd saved a number of the people in the room with her precise covering fire, and she was one of the most well-liked members of the Team.

"I don't know, Elise. It looks that way…at least if everything checks out how Mr. Vance expects it to." Clark Dawes was a captain, and the Team's new executive officer. It was obvious he was still feeling his way into his new role, just as the colonel was adjusting to command. Also, like the colonel, he tended to cling to the traditions and procedures instituted by Colonel Warren…including the informality of these pre-mission gatherings. Tomorrow the diminutive sniper would again be Lieutenant Cho, and he would be Captain Dawes. But tonight they were Clark and Elise.

Beneath the good-natured camaraderie Colonel Warren had instilled in the tradition, the meetings were always somber, serious occasions. Alpha's missions were always dangerous...and the Team rarely went in without someone getting wounded or killed. There were a lot of ghosts in the air, Alphas who were gone, but not forgotten. Never forgotten.

But there was something else this time, more than just the fear, the caution, the tribute to lost friends. This mission would be the first without Colonel Warren, and the wound from losing their longtime commander, the only one the Team had ever known, was still fresh, painful. His absence in the room was tangible, and it was clear they all felt it.

There was something else too. This time they weren't taking on terrorists or enemy infiltrators. It wasn't a rescue mission or a hostage extraction operation. They were going in to investigate a crashed spaceship, one Martian Intelligence was fairly certain had not been built by humans. Mankind had encountered alien plant life on most of the habitable worlds it had colonized, and animals too on many of them. But this was the first sign of intelligent life ever encountered, and the enormity of the situation pressed down on them all. Fiction had dealt with the subject for centuries, but the reality of it all now lay heavily on the room. Friendly aliens come to solve mankind's problems were a pleasant image, but every member of the Team was well aware the likelihood of a hostile encounter was very high. Humanity couldn't get along with itself—five thousand years of bloody history attested to that. What chance was there of peace with a totally different species?

The door slid open, and Colonel Reginald stepped through, carrying two cases in his arms. "Sorry I'm late," he said softly as he walked toward the single vacant chair in the room. "I had some last minute things to attend to." He sat down, setting his burden gently on the floor in front of him.

The others turned and looked over at their commander, most of them nodding silently as they did. They knew why he was late, of course—all of them—and it had nothing to do with last minute details. Colonel Warren had always arrived midway through the meeting, giving his people some time alone, without the commander sitting in the room...and John Reginald was following through with his predecessor's ways, acting almost as if Warren were still there.

"Don't let me interrupt the discussion," Reginald said, waving his hand for them to continue. His was doing a good job, projecting confidence and seeking to create a feeling of normalcy in the room. But anyone listening closely to his voice could detect a slight wavering. Stepping into Colonel Warren's shoes was a monumental task, and it was clearly taking all John Reginald had to manage it.

"We were just talking about whether this is actually our first contact with intelligent aliens...and what that will mean." Dawes looked across the room as he spoke, his eyes settling on Reginald. "And if they're hostile..."

Reginald nodded. "Yes, that's the big question, isn't it? And judging from the preliminary reports on that ship, it looks pretty advanced. The drone didn't catch any activity outside the wreck...it's possible everyone on board is dead...or that the ship is old, that it has been there for years, maybe even centuries. We may just go in and secure the site. Indeed, that's probably the likeliest scenario." He paused. "Still, we can't be sure, and if there is anything alive down there we might have our hands full on this one...which is why I'm going to cut the get together short tonight. I want all of you to get a solid rest before we launch in the morning."

Dawes returned the nod. "I think you're right, John. Maybe we should wrap things up now, get some sleep." There was an odd tone to his voice, doubtfulness, perhaps. It was common to speak of getting rest, but Reginald was well aware the combat veterans in the room all knew that was far easier said than done on the eve of battle. They'd all had their sleepless nights, lying in their bunks, staring at the ceiling, waiting for H-hour. And this time they were going up against the unknown. It would be a miracle if any of them got an hour's sleep. Still, lying in bed was better than pacing the corridors of the ship…

A rustle worked around the room as the others nodded their agreement and began to get up.

"Wait." Reginald held his arm out in front of him, gesturing for them all to stay seated. "Before you all go…" He leaned down and opened the case at his feet. He reached inside and pulled out a bottle of amber liquid. "This is Scotch…not just any Scotch, but eighteen-year-old Scotch. The real thing, imported all the way from Earth, from Scotland.

"Colonel Warren bought it," he continued. "He was planning a…a celebration for the ninth anniversary of the Team's founding." Reginald paused, his voice cracking a bit with emotion. The Team's lost commander was still a difficult topic, and everyone present knew they had let the unit's anniversary pass unheralded in the wake of their leader's death. None of them had been in the mood for any kind of celebration. "I thought we could put it to good use…something the colonel would have liked." He started pulling small racks of glasses from the second crate. "Bring over one of those tables." He gestured toward O'Reilly and Ruiz as he continued pulling out glasses.

The two corporals jumped up and started pulling down one of the tables, and Vandenberg followed, reaching up and helping them drag the heavy metal object to the center of the room. They set it down and each took a step back, watching as Reginald and Dawes carried over the glasses, and two of the bottles of Scotch. They set out twenty of the small glasses, and then they opened the bottles and filled each one about halfway.

Reginald took a glass in his hand and stepped back. "Okay, everybody get one. It's time for a toast." He nodded and watched as the members of the unit moved forward, each taking one of the glasses and stepping back in turn. Vandenberg was last. The Team's newest member paused, but only for an instant. Then he reached out and took the last glass, turning to face the colonel as he did.

"First, I want to tell you that the colonel would have been proud of you all." Reginald tried to keep his voice firm, but he stumbled a few times. "He created this unit…and he picked every one of you. And believe me, I picked most of you with him, and it was a long and tortuous process. So, if you are here, know it is because one of the best warriors Mars ever produced decided you too were one of the very best."

A small wave of nods moved around the room, and more than one of the grizzled soldiers looked close to tears.

"But Colonel Warren always knew the Team he built was bigger than any of its members, even himself. The fact that we are embarked, and about to execute yet another mission without him…that is the ultimate validation of all he believed." He paused and took a quick breath. "So tomorrow, when you're all strapped in and ready to go, take a minute to think about that, and to realize that your readiness to do what must be done is the greatest tribute you can pay the colonel."

He glanced over at Vandenberg. "And you, Alex…your father would be bursting with pride to see you here, part of Alpha just like he was." Reginald stopped for a moment. Then he just said, "I am sorry that you had a hard time at first…but now you are where you should be, right where you belong."

"Thank you, si…John." Vandenberg looked a bit uncomfortable as the center of attention, but he just smiled and looked around the room. "I am glad to be here. Proud to be here."

Reginald nodded slowly. He paused for a moment and held up his glass. "Then let us share a drink together, a toast, first to Colonel Travis Warren, in more ways than one the father of Red Team Alpha…and truly the father of its latest member. We salute you, as our commander, as a hero of Mars…and as our friend. To you, and to all the other comrades we have lost in battle. You will live forever in our hearts and minds." He put his glass to his lips and drained it about halfway, and he waited as the others did the same.

"And now, one last toast, not to the past, but to the future. To Red Team Alpha, and to each man and woman in this room. Though we work in secret, and enjoy no glory or open gratitude for what we do, it is important that we not be forgotten. The nature of our work mandates that only we can do that…only the members of this Team will remain to pay tribute to the fallen."

He looked around the room, his eyes settling for a few seconds on each man and woman present. "There are four more bottles of Scotch in that case. I propose we save it, store it somewhere safe and secure. And on the anniversary of this date, hours before our most difficult and dangerous mission, the survivors of Red Team Alpha will gather…and they will drink a toast to those no longer there…to lost friends."

The room was silent, not a sound save the distant humming of *Westron's* reactor cutting the stillness. The Alphas just stood still for a moment, moving only enough to look around the room at their comrades. Finally, Captain Dawes raised his glass. "Yes, Colonel," he said softly. "I will swear that oath here and now. Each year, to come back, to gather together and drink a toast to the fallen."

"To the fallen." Lieutenant Cho was the next to repeat the toast, but the others soon followed until each of them had said the words and emptied their glasses. They stayed together for a long while afterward, saying nothing, just standing where they were, in the company of their comrades.

Finally, Colonel Reginald said, "I think it's time to call it a night, everyone. We have a serious mission ahead of us…and I want everybody at their absolute best."

The colonel stood and watched his unit file slowly toward the door and out into the hall. Alex Vandenberg was the last to move, and he nodded toward Reginald and started toward the door.

"Stay, Alex…" Reginald's voice was soft, gentle. "For a few minutes if you don't mind."

Vandenberg turned back. "Certainly, sir."

"No…no 'sirs.' Not yet. I'm John here. Just sit with me for a while." Reginald slid one of the chairs next to another, and then he sat down.

Vandenberg walked over and sat next to his CO. "Yes, si… John." He sounded nervous, and far more uncomfortable with the informality than he had been when the whole unit had been present. Now the others were gone, back to their quarters, presumably to get some sleep before H-Hour. At least Vandenberg assumed that's what they were doing. This was his first mission, and he likely didn't realize yet how difficult it was to sleep on the eve of an attack.

"I know some of the guys were hard on you at first, Alex… before they knew who you were." Reginald was clearly uncomfortable. "That shouldn't have happened. And Mr. Vance shouldn't have been put in a position where he had to give us your true identity. It was your right to stand on your own, and I respect you for wanting that."

"Thank you, John. They didn't make it easy on me, I'll admit that. But I know it came from their own loyalty and dedication. They were giving me a hard time, but to them they were protecting the unit…the unit that was my father's pride." Vandenberg paused. "I have no hard feelings about it. I think they've accepted me now, and that's enough. As far as I'm concerned none of it ever happened." He twisted in the chair and put his hand behind his neck, grimacing. "And I'm glad Ian O'Reilly's on my side now and not standing against me."

Reginald nodded. "I hope he knows how much he owes you. He could have been shot for attacking an officer, but at the very least his career would have been over, and he'd be shoveling shit wherever he could get a job after a dishonorable discharge."

"Please, let's not even speak of it anymore. I'm here with all of you, and that is enough for me. I know that is what my father would have wanted."

"Your father was a great man, Alex." Reginald's voice was strange, distracted. "I am very happy his career doesn't seem to have interfered with his relationship with you."

"Well…" Vandenberg replied, his tone sounding a bit doubtful. "I can't say it was easy. He was away most of the time. I can't remember a birthday when he was around, even years before he founded Alpha…and I know it was difficult for my mother. It would be a lie to say I never resented it, that it didn't' affect our relationship. But as I got older, I began to understand. It wasn't like he could tell me much…you know how classified most of Alpha's missions are. But I started to understand how important his work was. Then, when I went to the Academy,

I realized he was a hero, at least within the service. I began to understand he wasn't just choosing to be away so often. He was out there…protecting us all. Saving lives."

Reginald sighed and looked down at his feet. He was silent for perhaps half a minute then he looked up at Vandenberg. "Your father was my friend for a long time, Alex. We were comrades in arms for more than twenty years…but I never knew anything about you, other than the vague knowledge that you existed." He paused, taking a deep breath. "And he never knew my wife…my daughter. We set those ground rules a long time ago between us. In the field, on the base…we were brothers. But we swore we'd keep our other lives separate, live like we were each two different people. We talked about it one night, early in the Second Frontier War. We were on the front lines on Beta Chronos III. The fight there had turned into a stalemate, and we were entrenched along a ridgeline. We were young, both of us, and committed to lives in the service. I think even then we realized how difficult it would be to have personal lives, to get married, raise children."

Reginald paused. "I'm not sure any more which one of us came up with the idea, but I remember sitting there that night, during a pause in the fighting, talking about it all. We would be brothers in the field, comrades in arms…but when we were away from duty, we would be different people. We wouldn't bring the blood and hell of the battlefield home with us, not even in the guise of a close friend. We'd seen too many soldiers distracted by thoughts of home…who ended up getting themselves killed as a result. We would avoid all that, we agreed. When we were in the field, we would have no home life…we would leave that side of us behind, speak nothing of it. And when we left on leave we would bid each other farewell until we returned."

"That sounds like a good idea." Vandenberg's tone suggested he thought anything but.

"No it wasn't. It was stupid, an idiotic idea two scared kids came up with on the battlefield…and never had the good sense to admit was a mistake. Your father was my friend…the best one I've ever had. And I didn't even know his son when he walked into my barracks." He looked at Vandenberg, his eyes full of pain. "Maybe your father could have helped me handle my own family...since he seemed to have done better with you than I managed."

"Family, sir?"

"Yes, Alex. My wife, who couldn't take the constant absences, the loneliness, the secrecy of my service. She tried, I truly believe she did...but she just couldn't do it. And I wasn't any help. I was full of self-righteousness about what I did then, insensitive to the emotional toll on my family." He took a deep breath. "She left fifteen years ago. I've only seen her three times since."

"I'm sorry, si...John." Vandenberg's voice was slow, halting. "My mother and father weren't together either. I think they both tried too...and I know my mother realized that dad's work was important. But I guess someone can only be alone so much before a relationship dies."

"But your father managed to hang on to some kind of connection with you, didn't he?"

"Yes, I suppose...some kind..." Vandenberg's tone was sad, somber. "...I guess..."

"You didn't hate him, at least. You didn't act like he was dead."

"No...but we didn't have a close relationship, not really. Part of me respects what he did in his life...but part of me feels like I didn't even have a father." Vandenberg stared at his commander-in-chief, clearly seeing the pain in Reginald's eyes. "But we're not talking about me, are we?"

Reginald didn't answer right away. He just sat quietly for a few seconds, staring down at the floor. Then he looked up at Vandenberg. "I have a daughter, Alex. Her name is Lina."

Vandenberg maintained the colonel's gaze, but he didn't say anything. It was clear Reginald just needed someone to listen.

"I haven't seen her since she was thirteen. I was gone for years at a time when she was younger...and she hardly knew me when I came home the few times I did." His voice was straining, the emotion clear in every word. "She was too young to understand why I was away, what it took to keep Mars safe. And then when she was thirteen she told me she never wanted to see me again, that she hated me for what I'd done to her mother... and that she didn't need me, that I wasn't a father to her. I was nothing. I can remember it like it was yesterday...she said it, and then she turned around and walked out of the room. And she never spoke to me again."

Vandenberg sat silently, clearly unsure what to say. Finally, he just reached out and put his hand on Reginald's shoulder.

"So you see, Alex?" Reginald said, his voice rough, tentative. "What we do carries its own costs, above and beyond the risk of injury and death. You are young, but one day you will start a life, one beyond your service. When you do, remember how you felt when your father was away for such long periods. Remember how I lost my daughter."

Vandenberg nodded slowly. "I will." He twitched uncomfortably, seeming uncertain what else he should say. "John... nothing can change what has happened, but that doesn't mean the future is written in stone." He paused. "After the mission... you should go see her."

"She doesn't want to see me, Alex. She has made that very clear."

"Yes...she's angry, hurt. And she doesn't know you as well as she should. But that doesn't mean things are hopeless." Another pause. "My father was so proud when I got into the Academy...he came to see me, and we had a long talk, all night. It didn't fix everything...but it helped us." He looked intently at Vandenberg. "I'm not saying it will be easy...but it's never impossible."

"Perhaps..." Reginald's voice showed a spark of hope, but the sadness was still dominant.

"Do it, John. As soon as we get back." Vandenberg paused. "And I will talk to her too if you want. I think I understand her situation as well as anyone could...perhaps I can reach her. At least I have a chance."

"You would do that?" Reginald sounded surprised. His voice was emotional, nothing like the coldly competent senior officer Vandenberg had come to know in recent weeks.

"Yes…I will do it. For you. For my own father…and for the friend I know he relied upon for so many years."

Reginald looked back at his subordinate, his eyes filled with gratitude. "Thank you, Alex." He took a deep, ragged breath. Maybe it's not too late after all."

"It's not…I'm sure of it."

Reginald knew the junior officer was far less than sure, but he needed to hear it now, to believe it. So he allowed himself to do just that. And he *was* hopeful, at least on some level, that Vandenberg could reach Lina. The two had lived the same thing, grown up largely without their fathers around. That was common ground…enough he hoped, to bridge the great gulf between him and his daughter. There was a chance, at least… and that was a lot better than nothing.

The two sat quietly together for a long while, perhaps fifteen minutes. Finally, Reginald rose to his feet and looked down at his officer. "Well," he said, his voice back to its businesslike tone, "I've kept you up long enough, Alex. Let's see about getting some sleep before H-Hour."

Chapter Four

Launch Bay One
MCS Westron
Orbiting Gamma Epsilon II
The Next Morning

The pain shot through his body in one confused wave. Vandenberg gritted his teeth in preparation, but he couldn't keep a short grunt from escaping his lips. He'd been in armor before, of course…many times, at least in training. But he still hadn't gotten used to the discomfort of suiting up, not completely.

Powered combat armor was the infantryman's greatest leap forward in strength and survivability in history. The osmium-iridium plated suit provided protection against enemy weapons, toxic atmospheres, radiation…even deep space. The miniaturized fusion plant built into the suit could power weapons an order of magnitude stronger than anything a conventional soldier could carry. But climbing into the armor was never a pleasant experience. There were dozens of probes and intravenous lines, all of which jabbed their way into Vandenberg's naked body. Once in place, they would monitor his every life function, inject drugs as needed to counteract fatigue or to treat a wound, administer painkillers if necessary. They would allow Vandenberg to control the massively powered arms and legs, enabling him to move around in the ten-ton suit almost as he would in a simple uniform.

The electrodes also facilitated communication with the artificial intelligence that assisted him in controlling the deadly weapon he wore, decreasing his reaction times…something that could be the difference between life and death in battle.

Vandenberg had logged the standard number of training hours in his armor, and he'd passed all the tests with flying colors. But training was never the same as reality, and there was no simulation for the tension of battle. The Academy's valedictorian had completed his armor certs with a perfect score, but now, in the bay of a ship, about to launch on a real mission, he found himself a little sluggish. He imagined master sergeant Pirro at the Academy…and the dings he would have assigned his star pupil if he'd ever scrambled into his suit so clumsily back in training.

He closed his eyes and listened to the series of loud clicks as his armor sealed shut. His prep had been slow, perhaps, but now he was ready.

And if you don't get your head out of your ass on the mission, you're likely to get scragged as soon as the fighting starts.

If the fighting starts at all. Maybe the aliens will be friendly. Or maybe this is just an abandoned wreck, and all we'll have to do it cordon it off and wait for the research teams.

That all sounded good in his head, but he also knew the Team wouldn't be here if Vance and Martian Intelligence didn't expect some kind of trouble—from the aliens or, perhaps more likely, from one or more of the other Powers. Earth's Superpowers weren't likely to sit by and let one of their rivals gain control over an artifact from a more advanced technology. The Martian Confederation was the unofficial ninth Superpower, and arguably already the most technologically advanced of them all. He didn't know if Vance had been afraid of aliens, or the other Superpowers, but the presence of the Team, and the speed with which they'd been dispatched, suggested he expected at least the possibility of some kind of trouble. There were research teams on *Westron*, sent to begin investigating the relic. But they were confined to the ship until Colonel Reginald reported the area was secure.

"Okay, Alphas, you are cleared to launch in thirty seconds. Good luck!" There was a calmness to Captain Silver's voice, a confidence Vandenberg found strangely reassuring. He knew it was deliberate, that the veteran captain was doing everything possible to support the Team…but it helped anyway.

Antonia Silver had been *Westron's* captain on three of the Team's past missions…including the last one, the one Travis Warren hadn't returned from. But this was Alex's first outing, and everything was new to him.

"Twenty seconds to launch." Alex stood upright, bolted into one of the walls of the slim landing craft. Four of his comrades stood next to him, and another five on the other side, facing him. The small hold was dimly lit, just the light from a single fixture in the ceiling cutting tentatively through the darkness.

He swallowed hard and stared out across the two meters or so to his comrades on the opposite wall. He felt strange, nauseous despite the prelaunch injections. He could feel the sweat pouring down his back, the slick wetness under the suit's interior membrane, covering his bare skin. He'd never felt quite this way before, and he thought about it for a few seconds, wondered if he was getting sick. It took him a few seconds longer to truly understand. He wasn't sick. He was scared. Sweating, shaking, shitting bricks scared.

"Ten seconds to launch." The training had addressed precombat jitters, but he realized immediately that nothing taught in a classroom—or simulated on the training ground—could have prepared him for this. This was real, it was happening. Now. Whatever was waiting down there, if it was hostile, it would try to kill him. There would be no playacted firefights with weapons at one-hundredth power, no AI-assigned probabilities of simulated death. No, if there were enemies inside that ship, they would fire real weapons…and those weapons would be deadly. They would smash into his armor, tear the flesh from his body. There would be no second guessing, no post-exercise discussions. Just life…or death.

He felt the breath forced from his lungs as the launcher

blasted out of the bay, its engines firing at full. The heavy thrust continued for about thirty seconds, and he knew from training that he was feeling almost 20g of pressure. The suit compensated for some of it, and the heavy drug cocktail he'd been administered offset more. But it was still hellish, and he fought to remain conscious. It was nothing but relief when the engines disengaged and the vessel went into freefall. He knew—from training and from the readouts inside his suit's visor—that they were 150 kilometers above the surface, about to commence entry into the planetary atmosphere.

Vandenberg focused on breathing, on maintaining his calm. His first few breaths after the thrust subsided had been greedy gasps, but now he was inhaling normally. He felt the ship begin to shake as it descended. If all went well, they would be on the ground in a little over eight minutes. If not, if the enemy had anti-aircraft fire capacity, for example…anything was possible.

The conversation with Colonel Reginald was still on his mind, as it had been all night, when he was lying in bed not sleeping. He remembered his own life, and old feelings bubbled out of the shadowy past, occasions, special moments…all lived without his father's presence. He was grateful he'd come closer to his father before he'd lost him. He still resented many of Travis Warren's choices, still held onto some of the anger he'd felt for so many years. But he had a better perspective on things now, and he understood what had driven his father. Travis Warren had put his family behind his career certainly, but he'd done a lot of good too, saved a lot of lives. And for all his remaining angst, Alex was proud of his father.

The thought of Reginald's daughter not feeling that, of not connecting with her father—until one day an officer from the Martian armed forces came to her door, as one had come to his, carrying a precisely worded communique from the Martian Council and a neatly folded flag—felt like a terrible wrong. One he was determined to help prevent when the Team got back.

He felt a burst of pressure, about five gees, he recalled from the training manuals. It was much less burdensome that the earlier blast, and it only lasted a few seconds. *Final alignment adjustment*, he remembered.

He rolled his eyes upward, toward the small display projected inside his visor. Eighty klicks, and dropping steadily. Exactly within mission parameters. And the second ship was there too, right where it belonged. *So far so good.*

He glanced up at his status displays, rechecking his weapons and equipment. He was scared…and he was still thinking about the talk he'd had with Reginald. He wasn't a veteran, but he knew enough about combat to realize he had to put distractions like that out of his mind now. The mission…it was all that mattered until he and the others were on the retrieval boat, heading back up to *Westron*.

The ship began shaking, bouncing around as it skipped on the thickening atmosphere. He could see the number rising on one of his displays, the exterior temperature of the lander. It was 300 degrees and increasing about ten degrees a second. Vandenberg knew the shielding was built to withstand the rigors of atmospheric entry, but plummeting through the sky in a craft that would soon be glowing from the heat was unsettling to say the least.

There was no incoming fire, no response from the ground at all. That, at least, was good news. A standard planetary assault would fill the sky with debris and all sorts of countermeasures to confuse enemy ground installations and reduce the chance of the landers being hit by defensive fire. But the Alphas operated differently. It wasn't feasible to try to hide two landers behind thousands of bits of electronic gear and scanner-reflective chaff…and they preferred to land as quietly as possible, ideally without alerting anyone on the ground they were coming. They had cutting edge stealth technology, and their landings typically relied on surprise, on landing as quickly as possible. If an enemy wasn't on alert, scanning the skies aggressively, they had a good chance of getting down undetected. But even if they were spotted, it would be hard for the ground batteries to get a target lock on them…and the ships themselves would launch into a series of wild maneuvers if fired upon, making it even more difficult for the enemy to score a hit in the few minutes it took to land.

Vandenberg was glad for the lack of enemy fire, for the obvious reasons, of course, but also because neither he nor his stomach relished the idea of enduring the lander's gut wrenching twists and turns as it moved to evade incoming ordnance. He was just as content to reach the ground without testing his suit's ability to clean itself after an unfortunate incident.

"Okay, Alphas, we've got no incoming fire, no sign of activity down there at all. Maybe we've actually got ourselves a milk run here." Reginald's voice was calm, firm. But he didn't sound like he had much faith in the 'milk run' comment. Things looked quiet, but Vandenberg knew—and he was sure Reginald and the others did too—that Team Alpha wouldn't be on the job unless Roderick Vance had decided it was dangerous. And as little as he knew about Martian Intelligence's new chief, Vance didn't seem like the type to worry when there wasn't cause.

"We're going with operational plan three...which means we'll be hitting ground in..." There was a short pause, presumably while Reginald checked the mission chronometer. "...three minutes, forty-five seconds. We're landing ten klicks from the target, behind a high ridgeline that will provide us cover...just in case we run into any land based fire. If all goes well, we'll move forward and make contact...and we'll set up a defensive perimeter until relieved."

Alex listened carefully. He was fully aware of the details of op plan three, but he focused on every word all the same. The rest of the Team had accepted him, despite his lack of combat experience. But now he was fighting his own doubts. Had he been right to ask for this assignment? Should he have respected the tradition, made his bones in some line unit before seeking to follow in his father's footsteps? He didn't know the answer, but he was damned sure going to make certain he was alert and giving one hundred ten percent of what he had.

"Alright, I want everybody to do a final equipment check... and no groaning about it. Anybody finds a problem, com me directly. Otherwise, I'll see you all on the ground."

The com line closed abruptly, and Alex looked up at his display. Less than 20 klicks to landing...and the hull temperature was over one thousand degrees. He knew it was probably uncomfortably hot inside the lander now too, but he was buttoned up in his armor, experiencing a perfectly-controlled room temperature that his own uneasiness was making feel a bit warm.

"Okay, Nate, let's do a full check…weapons, armor…all systems." He'd named his suit's AI after his childhood pet, a mutt his father had given him for his fifth birthday, one of the few he'd actually shown up for. It made a kind of twisted sense, he thought. His father had given him the dog, just as he'd bequeathed him a military career. More or less.

"Very well, Lieutenant," the vaguely electronic sounding voice responded. "Initiating diagnostic program now…estimate one minute twelve seconds to complete."

Alex took a breath, but he didn't respond. He could see the lights on the display changing, yellow pre-check symbols switching one at a time to green as each system was checked. If there was a problem, Alex knew, the lights would start flashing red. Nate would tell him of any problems, but he stared at the scanner symbols anyway. It was something to do, to keep his mind busy.

"All systems check, Lieutenant."

Alex just nodded. He was ready. As ready as he could possibly be…armed, equipped, checked and doublechecked. But he was still scared. Scared to death.

Chapter Five

Coordinate Grid 20-42
Planet Gamma Epsilon II

"Alright, let's go." Alex's voice was firm—and that surprised him. He'd managed to get control of his own fear, but then it hit him. He was the newb on the Team, the raw cherry the others had objected to so strenuously before they knew who he was. But he wasn't some raw private, dropped with these veterans and tasked to follow orders. He was an officer...and the fourth in command of the Team. He had responsibilities, command duties that only reminded him how different he was from the others. When he'd asked to take his father's place, he'd been all confidence and pride, but now it really hit him...the strangeness of snapping out commands to blooded veterans like Ruiz and O'Reilly. He understood, even more than he had before, what had motivated the resentment toward him before.

"We're with you, Lieutenant." It was Ian O'Reilly, his former nemesis, now sounding respectful and obedient. And perhaps a little protective as well.

Alex looked out toward the rise. He was about a klick south of the lander. He had O'Reilly, Simms, and Wagner with him... and they were on point. He wondered if Colonel Reginald was overcompensating, trying to make up for his rough reception by showing enough confidence to put him in charge of scouting forward.

Or maybe I'm just the most expendable…

No, that's not the way Reginald thinks. At least I don't think so. My father…that's a different story.

Travis Wagner was a hero, a man loved by the members of the Team he had led for so long. But Alex knew his father had been a hard man, a calculating leader. His soldiers were important to him, and he was always ready to die for them. He *had* died for them. But Alex knew he'd also been ready to spend their lives, that success—victory—was the thing he had valued most, and the cost of completing the mission had always been a secondary concern to him.

Reginald had been his father's friend, but as Vandenberg spent more time with his new commander, he began to realize the two comrades were very different men. Alex didn't think John Reginald was anywhere near as cold-blooded as his father had been.

He started forward, waving for his troopers to follow, though he knew that wasn't necessary. His people knew what to do, probably better than he did.

The ground was flat and open, just a gradual rise toward the ridgeline ahead. The dirt was yellow-gray, and there were small rocks strewn all around. Although *Westron's* scans had detected abundant plant life on the planet, this area looked completely dead. No grasses, no scrub, no weeds. Just dust and rocks.

Blast damage from the crash? Radiation leakage?

"Sir…" O'Reilly's voice came tentatively out of Alex's com. "…we're out in the open with no cover anywhere. I suggest we spread out more, say a hundred meter intervals. That way, if something comes over that ridge, at least they won't catch us all bunched together."

Alex felt himself nodding. "Yes, Corporal," he replied, trying to sound as in command as possible. "Good idea." He paused a few seconds. "And thanks…" The thanks wasn't for the advice…it was for making the suggestion privately, not undermining him in front of the others. And he was sure O'Reilly knew that too.

Alex flipped on the unit com. "I want everybody to spread

out…hundred meter intervals off me."

"Yes, sir," came the replies, one after another. O'Reilly's was last, without the slightest hint that the idea had come from him.

Alex continued forward, turning first left then right, watching as his troopers carried out the order. It was only a few seconds before the four of them were spread out over a three-hundred meter frontage. There were weapons that could easily take them all out, even in their extended order, but at least it would take more than an autocannon firing one burst.

He moved forward briskly, setting the pace for the others. He'd been worried about the open terrain already, but realizing that O'Reilly had been thinking the same thing only made him more nervous. They should be okay—*Westron* was in geosynchronous orbit, scanning the whole area. If anything became active around the ship he would get a warning. But that was far from perfect. If there was something over there lying in wait, hunkered down to avoid detection, *Westron's* scanners might very well miss it. And the hull of the wrecked ship had defied all attempts to scan inside. For all anyone knew, it was packed full of alien soldiers, wielding weapons a thousand times deadlier than the ordnance Alex and his people had.

The ground began to get sharply steeper as the scouting party approached the ridgeline. The advance would have been tiring if his armor hadn't been doing most of the work, but the nuclear power feeding the servo-mechanicals in his suit made his legs feel as light as a feather. His eyes glanced up to the visor projection. The rest of the Team was back about two klicks, advancing as his people were, with a hundred meters between each of them. There were two small circles farther out, one on each side. Cho and Dawes. The colonel had put the other officers out on the flanks, as far from each other as possible. If something hit in the center, Vandenberg knew it could take him out…and maybe the colonel too. But Dawes and Cho would be out there to take command. And if either flank got hit, the opposite one—and possibly the center—would survive.

Paranoia. Is that part of being a good commander? The truth is, you just can't anticipate everything that can happen…

but you've got to be as prepared for it as you can. Does the colonel think about anything without saying to himself, 'what is absolutely everything that can go wrong with this?'

"We're almost to the top of the ridgeline." Alex spoke crisply into the com. "I want everybody to stop twenty meters short of the crest while I move up and take a look."

Is that right? I remember training. There are some times the officer needs to go first…and others where he needs to stay back. But I need these men to know I am fit to be here…they've accepted me, but now I need them to really trust me.

"Sir…" It was O'Reilly again, on the direct line. "Maybe I should…"

"No, Sergeant," Vandenberg snapped back. "I've got it."

I can take O'Reilly's advice, but I can't let him run things, regardless of how good his intentions. I need everybody's respect, and not the least his.

He jogged slowly the last few meters, stopping and crouching down just before the top of the ridgeline. He leaned forward slowly, peering over.

The ground ahead was similar to what they'd encountered already, though now it sloped down instead of up. The afternoon sun was strong, and the yellowish dirt and rock reflected it harshly, creating an almost blinding brightness. But in the distance he could see it. It was big, at least three kilometers long, and though it was pretty badly banged up it retained the vague shape of a spaceship. He couldn't make out any details, or even colors behind the hazy dark gray of the hull.

He stared for a moment, silent, his gaze fixed on the amazing sight. Was he the first human being to lay eyes on an alien spacecraft?

Of all the billions who have lived, what chance that I should find myself here…

He could hear his heart pounding, feel the sweat on his back and arms.

"Lieutenant Vandenberg, report." It was the colonel, his voice calm, steady.

Reginald's voice broke the spell he'd fallen under. "I can see it, sir," Alex replied, his tone getting away from him, letting his excitement—and fear—show. "Sir," he said again, getting a firmer grip on his demeanor. "Target spaceship sighted, approximately..." He glanced up at the rangefinder on his display. "...approximately one point five kilometers due south. Vessel appears to be slightly in excess of three kilometers in length, badly damaged but overall shape largely intact."

"Very well, Lieutenant. Anything further to report?"

Alex looked out across the long, gradual slope down to the ship. It was the same as the ground they'd already covered, nothing but dust and rocks...not the slightest bit of cover. "It's all open, sir. As far as I can see. If there's anything...anyone... in that ship, they'll see us coming kilometers before we get there. And if we come under fire..."

"Yes, Lieutenant. Understood." A short pause. "Get your people up to the ridgeline and hold. Sergeant Jacobs and his section will take point."

"Yes, sir." Alex felt both relief and disappointment. He was scared to death to walk another klick directly toward that thing. But he didn't much prefer watching his comrades do it in his place...especially when he knew he'd just hit the limit of Colonel Reginald's confidence. The colonel had given him the point during the initial advance, but now he was putting a more experienced man in charge of the final advance.

Is that it? Does he think I'm too inexperienced? Almost certainly, at least in part. But is he also protecting his friend's son, keeping me back where I won't get scragged instantly if there are hostiles waiting for us in that ship?

Yes, he thought. *That is part of it too.*

He appreciated Reginald's concern, but it made him feel strange, sick inside. If Jacobs or any of his people went down, he would know they had died in his place. And he suspected that was something he never wanted to feel.

Coordinate Grid 20-42
Planet Gamma Epsilon II

"All's quiet, sir. Radiation readings above normal, but all other scans suggest this ship crashed a long time ago. A *long* time. Thousands of years…perhaps longer." Jacobs' voice was a little odd. Even the most hardened veteran was affected by something as momentous as confirming that man was not alone, that there was other intelligence life in the universe.

Reginald stood and stared at the giant wreck less than two kilometers straight ahead. He'd been watching and waiting… waiting to see what would happen to the men he'd sent forward. So far that had been nothing, not yet at least. The handheld scanners were no more able than *Westron's* to penetrate the vessel's hull and get any readings from inside. But everything Jacobs and his people could see suggested the enemy ship was a lifeless hulk, a conclusion supported by the preliminary estimates of the wreck's age.

"Stand firm, Sergeant. I'm coming up." He flipped the com channel. "Captain Dawes, sections two and three will remain with you. Set up a position one kilometer from the ship and create a rough perimeter. Things look quiet…maybe we've just found the greatest scientific discovery in history, without so much as a fight. But we don't know that yet, so keep your eyes open.

"Section one, with me." A short pause. "Lieutenant Cho, try to find a decent vantage point, and get yourself set to cover us. Just in case." He knew there wasn't shit in the way of good sniper positions on the ground around the spaceship, but Cho knew her business, and she'd make the best of the situation.

"Yes, sir," she replied.

Reginald moved forward swiftly, but in a controlled motion. It was easy to end up bounding up twenty meters when you ran in armor, and that was usually a bad idea on the battlefield. No one was shooting right now, but Alpha's commander was a veteran of three decades of war and struggle. His every step was governed by a lifetime's battle instincts.

He'd known how big the ship was intellectually, but it truly hit him as he moved closer. Three point two kilometers. It was partially buried in the yellowish clay, but it still protruded at least sixty meters above ground in places. It looked enough like an Earth ship that he could roughly identify various parts of it, but it was different in many ways too. He'd never seen anything like the hull, for example. It was a dark gray metal, but there was something strange about it…almost as if it constantly morphed in color and consistency. It was slow, and not very noticeable. But when he looked away and stared back at a specific spot, he could swear it had changed.

"It's strange, sir. None of us have ever seen anything like it." Jacobs had been standing right in front of a section of the alien vessel, but he turned as Reginald approached.

"Have you been able to get anything from your scans?" The colonel jogged up next to Jacobs and stopped, turning to face the sergeant. It was a fairly pointless gesture in combat armor, but he did it anyway.

"No, sir. Not much, at least. The inside is a mystery. We can't get any readings, none at all. I've tried to identify this material on the hull, but I'm getting confusing results. There's definitely some normal materials, including osmium and iridium, like in our armor, and our spaceships' own hulls. But there's more to it…and the scanner's going crazy trying to identify what it is."

Jacobs wasn't a scientist, but he had the same basic training the rest of the Team did. He knew how to work the equipment, especially with his AI's help, and that had been precisely enough to run right into a brick wall.

"So we're talking about some kind of new material, something we've never seen before? That we can't even identify." Reginald turned back toward the ship, kicking up the magnification on his visor and staring at the wreck. He picked a spot and stared intently.

"It looks that way, sir. I suspect the guys in the white coats will have their work cut out for them."

"Let's not get ahead of ourselves, Sergeant. I know this

thing looks dead, but we don't know that for sure yet. We're here for a reason, so I want everybody to stay sharp."

"Colonel, the scanner says this thing is maybe a hundred thousand years old, older even. There's no way anything could have survived that long." Jacobs turned briefly and stared back at the ship behind him.

"Maybe," Reginald said, not sounding completely convinced. "But maybe Martian Intelligence isn't the only outfit that found this thing. What do you think the other Powers would do to take it away from us…or at least keep us from getting it? Can you imagine the technology inside this ship?" He paused. "No we're here for a reason…and we're going to do our jobs."

He paused again. Then he turned and looked right at Jacobs. "I want you to take Wagner and Simms and have a look inside." He waved his arm, gesturing toward a large section of hull with a large gash in the side and what appeared to be a corridor of some kind beyond. "You should be able to get in through there."

"Yes, sir." Jacob's response was crisp, but there was a hint of hesitation in his voice. He'd sounded sure the ship was dead a few seconds before, but Reginald knew it was different when you were about to walk in.

"And don't go too far, Sergeant. We can't penetrate that thing with scanners, so it wouldn't be too much of a surprise if we lost coms too. Just go in and see if you can find a corridor or some passable area. Maybe fifty meters, no more, at least not unless we are able to maintain communication. If you get that far and can't raise us, I want you back out immediately. Understood?"

"Yes, sir…don't you worry about it. If we're inside that thing and can't reach you, we'll be back in a flash."

"That's what I want, Sergeant. Don't try to impress anybody. And if you see anything out of the ordinary…even if it's your own shadow, I want you all out of there.

"Yes, Colonel." He turned and waved toward Wagner and Simms as he walked toward the opening in the ship's hull. The three of them stood for a moment, no doubt discussing what they were about to do. Then Jacobs ducked down and went inside, followed by the others.

Reginald watched as they each twisted around, crawling through the jagged opening in the ship's hull. And then they were gone. He flipped on his com. "Sergeant, can you read me?"

"Col…" Then nothing but static. Whatever that hull was made of, it blocked communications as well as scanners.

Reginald took a deep breath and sighed. The communications failure wasn't unexpected…and Jacobs was right. The ship was beyond ancient. What could still be in there to present a danger to his people?

He didn't have an answer, but he still had a bad feeling…and it felt like it was burning a hole right through his stomach.

Chapter Six

Coordinate Grid 20-42
Inside the Alien Vessel
Planet Gamma Epsilon II

Alfred Jacobs moved slowly, cautiously. The ancient vessel's interior was not just dark. It was pitch black in most places. There were spots where a few rays of pale sunlight punched through gaps in the tortured hull, but the floor and walls were made of a material that did not seem to reflect light, and as soon as the trio of soldiers turned a corner they were plunged again into obsidian darkness.

Jacobs had tried his visor's infrared scanners, but the old wreck was cold, the only sources of heat coming from the few locations where the light from outside warmed the strange gray metal of the vessel.

His eyes moved up to the projection inside his visor. His armor had a number of systems to help guide his way, but they were partially effective at best. They'd help him get around, to move forward, but he was here for more than that. And there was no way he was going to be able to really explore the alien ship, not without light.

"Okay, let's get our lamps on." Jacobs, moved one of his fingers, tapping on the control for his lead light. He could have ordered the AI to do it, but he was old school, having come up in the service long before armor was equipped with the quasi-sentient intelligences. He had to admit the thing was useful, but it still creeped him out a little. He'd use it in a pinch, when he was in serious trouble, but he'd be damned if he needed a computer to flip on the light for him.

The corridor lit up brightly, even more so a second later when his two companions fired up their own lights. Jacobs felt a touch of concern…the lamps would help his own people get around, but it also advertised their presence to anyone who was watching.

You're losing it, Jacobs. Who the hell could be watching in here? This ship is a tomb, maybe, but there can't be anyone alive in here…

Jacobs had been as edgy as the others after they'd learned the true objective of their mission. Being on the leading edge of first contact was overwhelming, even to the toughest pack of combat veterans the Confederation had ever seen. But when he saw the wrecked vessel, and seen the computer estimates of its age, he'd felt his concerns fade away. At least his intellectual ones. There was no chance any aliens—hostile or otherwise—could still be alive after hundreds of thousands of years. No, his mind had discounted the possibility of action on this mission… but his stomach was another matter. The halls of the ancient vessel felt almost haunted, old beyond imagining.

"Alright, let's keep moving." He realized he had stopped, and his two compatriots had halted with him. They'd just been standing around for what, a minute? Two?

He stepped forward, finding it more difficult than he'd expected. Something inside him wanted to stop, to turn and go back the way he had come. Jacobs had served for twenty years, and he'd fought in the Second Frontier War. He'd been under fire more times than he could recount, he'd even fought hand to hand a few times, killing enemies at the closest quarters. But now he felt an edginess—he wouldn't admit to himself it was fear—and he had to push through it.

He took a few steps, and then he realized his comrades had not followed. He turned back toward them, and he was about to repeat his order when each of them moved cautiously after him. They were feeling he same thing he was, that much was clear. And to a warrior like Jacobs, the realization that something could scare him this much was more intimidating that any actual enemy could be.

The corridor was big, wider by a considerable margin than those common in Earth ships. The stretch ahead was relatively intact, and he panned his eyes around as he moved cautiously forward. He had to ignore the impulse more than once to report some detail or another. The com had remained completely dead. But his automatic recorders were still on, filming and taping everything around him. Once they got back outside, the data would be transmitted back to *Westron*…and people who knew a hell of a lot better what they were looking for than he did would obsess over every frame.

"Sarge…"

It was Wagner. And for the first time he could recall, Jacobs heard fear in the veteran corporal's tone.

"What is…" He stopped, froze in place, and extended his arm, signaling for Simms to do the same. There was something down the long straight corridor, just at the edge of the light projected from their lamps.

It was a shadow…no, it was more than that. It was…something…and it was standing at the end of the corridor, right in front of them.

Jacobs felt his heart pounding hard, and his arm reached back, grabbing the assault rifle from its perch on the side of his armor. He snapped it around, facing forward, as his eyes locked on the barely visible shape ahead.

He stood still, ready to open fire. But nothing happened. The shape just stayed where it was, motionless. "Simms, you stand back here...and if anything happens, you get the hell out, warn the colonel and the others? You understand me?"

"Yes, Sergeant."

Jacobs could hear the same eerie tension in Simms' voice he'd heard in Wagner's.

And my own, probably…

And if we're not back here in thirty minutes, the same thing goes. Get the hell out, and report to the colonel."

"Sarge…" It was clear from his tone Simms didn't like the idea of running and abandoning two of his comrades in the alien ship.

"Just do it," Jacobs replied sharply. "If something goes wrong, you'll do us a lot more good by getting help rather than rushing in by yourself." He paused. "Use your head, man."

"Yes, Sergeant."

Jacobs turned toward his other comrade. "Alright, Wagner…with me. Let's go."

"Yes, Sergeant." If it had been anyone but one of the Alphas standing behind him, he'd have sworn from her tone the corporal was about to bolt and run, not follow him down the hall. But he had absolute trust in his comrades, and he was determined to push back against the mysterious feelings moving through his mind.

He took a step forward, pausing for an instant, eyes locked on the shadowy shape ahead. There was nothing, no hint at all of movement. He continued down the hall, stopping again every meter or so. The light was pushing forward, giving him a better view. Still, the light-absorption of the strange metal of the corridor dramatically lessened the effectiveness of his lamp. He could see the object better, but it was still bathed in a gray gloom that made details hard to see.

One thing was certain now, however. It was humanoid, more or less. Bigger than a man, perhaps two and a half meters tall, and wide too.

That explains the size of these corridors…

His mind had played tricks on him at first, telling him it was some kind of being standing there facing his people. But even as the thoughts invaded his mind, his rationality struck back. The ship was a lifeless hulk, far too old to house any live aliens. And now, as he moved farther forward, he could see the shape was metallic, built vaguely in the shape of a humanoid, but definitely a construction of some sort.

A robot?

He tensed again, wondering if even a machine could function after so many millennia.

No, of course not. You're being ridiculous…

As he moved forward, more details appeared. It was definitely some kind of robot, and it indeed appeared to be non-functional. His scanners confirmed the lack of any energy readings. It was cold, motionless. Dead for thousands of centuries.

He quickened his pace slightly, curiosity pushing harder for a moment than fear. He was amazed, mesmerized. He'd known, of course, that the entire ship was proof of the existence of an alien race…there was no question that the thing was ages beyond anything developed by the Superpowers. But it was different looking at the robot, something clearly created at least roughly in the image of those who'd built it. He wondered what kind of beings had once piloted the massive ship.

He stopped about a meter from the robot, his head moving around, scanning the construction from top to bottom. It was old, he knew, but its metal frame was untarnished, looking almost new. It was damaged. One appendage, at least had been severed. It was lying on the floor a few meters away. There were several other spots where it looked like one extension or another had been torn off, but Jacobs couldn't see anything else on the deck.

The robot *was* vaguely humanoid…but there were definitely some modifications. It had more of what Jacobs assumed were arms, six in fact, including the severed one. He wondered if the aliens that had built the thing had so many appendages, or if they just designed the robot to best serve its purpose.

That purpose, at least, was clear enough to Jacobs. One of the arms held what was unmistakably some kind of assault rifle, and the others gripped equally ominous implements. There wasn't a doubt in his mind the robot standing in front of him was—had been—a combat unit.

He stared at the fearsome figure, his eyes fixed, almost as if he had to satisfy himself it was motionless, dead. Finally, he turned and looked back at Wagner.

"Okay, Corporal. I don't think this thing can do us any harm. Let's push on a little deeper, and then we'll go back and report to the colonel."

He took a deep breath and walked past the robot, farther down the seemingly unending corridor.

Bridge
MCS Westron
Orbiting Gamma Epsilon II

"They're in, Captain. Scanners indicate three Team members have gone inside the vessel."

Antonia Silver turned and looked across *Westron's* small bridge toward her tactical officer. There were half a dozen officers at their posts, but the control room was silent, save for the tactical officer's report and the familiar background hum of the vessel's reactor.

"Do we still have a lock on them?" she asked, her tone suggesting she already knew the answer. *Westron's* scanners had been unable to penetrate the crashed vessel's hull, despite indications that it was rent open in several places. Silver knew Colonel Reginald hadn't had a choice. The Team had to go in, to confirm what was inside, but she didn't like it, she didn't like it at all.

"No, Captain. We lost all contact the instant they stepped inside." Gary Tomas was *Westron's* tactical officer. He'd served under Silver for several years, and he'd been at his post during the last three Alpha missions.

Silver exhaled hard, her frustration pouring out. She was worried about the men and women on the ground, it was as simple as that. Standard operating procedure was for the support vessel to track the location of each team member, as well as the status reports and medical scans transmitted by the troopers' armor. And she was doing just that. But that was all she could do. Her com was silent, absent the usual nearly constant chatter back and forth. *Westron* was on communications silence on this mission, forbidden to contact the ground force unless the captain deemed it a true emergency. That order had come from the top, from Roderick Vance himself. Silver hated the feeling of being cut off from the Alphas, but she didn't have a choice, so she did what she could. *Westron* was still maintaining tracking locks on the armor transponders, at least on the Alphas who hadn't entered the ship.

Why, Silver wondered. *Why such strict precautions all the way out here? What trouble does Intelligence suspect?*

Communications were crucial to any successful military operation. If this was some kind of milkrun, a quick inspection of an artifact and some guard duty until a relief force arrived, the guys on the ground wouldn't need enhanced coms or orbital support. But Martian Intelligence didn't send Red Team Alpha on milkruns.

The other Alpha missions she'd run had, like this one, required extreme secrecy, but she'd never been forbidden to communicate with the Team. And while she'd never seen them sent on any op that could be described as ordinary, this mission had her on edge. They were in the middle of nowhere, orbiting a recently discovered planet with nothing on it, nothing save a mysterious wrecked spaceship. She understood the importance of the discovery, but why was she restricted from communicating with the ground force? What did Roderick Vance expect to happen? What did he fear?

"I want full power to the scanning array, Lieutenant." Her voice was stern, frustrated. "I want to try to get through whatever is blocking us. All scanning beams are to concentrate on a single point. Try to penetrate that material and get me some readings. See if you can focus on one of the holes in the hull. Anything." She didn't think it would do any good, but she wasn't one to give up, not when she had any ideas left.

Tomas nodded. "Yes, Captain, but we haven't been able to get anything at all. I'm not sure more power is going to make a difference."

"No, it probably won't. But do it anyway, Lieutenant." Silver leaned back, sighing softly to herself. She didn't like this…not one bit of it.

"Yes, Captain." Tomas leaned over his workstation, his hands moving over the controls. He relayed the captain's orders down to the chief engineer, listening to the response on his headset. A few minutes later he turned back toward Silver. "All scanners at 100% power, Captain. Still no readings. Nothing at all." He paused, staring back at his screen and shaking his head. "Whatever that material is, it blocks all our scanning technology."

"Very well." Silver stared down again at the display. The veteran captain leaned back in her chair, trying to fight the cold edginess she felt. She'd sat in that very chair and waited as the Alphas conducted their missions, even as they fought, died. But there was something else there now, and she had to resist the urge to order the retrieval boats down to the surface. It was foolish, she knew, nonsense that no officer of her skill and rank should allow to bother her. It wasn't even her call to abort a mission, it was Colonel Reginald's. And she suspected the Alpha leader was less likely to get himself spooked about nothing.

Why did Intelligence send such a small force? The Alphas are the best…but there are only twenty of them…

Images in her mind of dozens of ships in orbit and hundreds of soldiers landing on the planet answered her own question. If this was truly first contact, it was a momentous event. But if there was alien technology down on that planet, more advanced than anything mankind had developed, it would also have to be one of the most closely-guarded secrets in history.

Silver knew she didn't have the full scope of information available to Roderick Vance, nor even the spymaster's grasp of international affairs. But she was well aware that tensions between the Superpowers were rising, that the exhaustion that had driven the peace after the Second Frontier War had passed, and Earth's nations were already scrambling for allies, looking toward the inevitable resumption of hostilities. The discovery of something as paradigm-altering as advanced alien technology would almost certainly start a war immediately, one far more total and brutal than previous ones. None of the Powers could allow their rivals to gain that kind of technological edge on them. None of them would dare.

And they would do anything—anything at all—to prevent that from happening.

Chapter Seven

Coordinate Grid 20-42
Inside the Alien Vessel
Planet Gamma Epsilon II

Jacobs pressed on through the gloomy corridor, moving slowly, cautiously. He didn't know what he'd expected to find, but it had been something, at least…more than just an unending hallway. A glance at his display told him he and Wagner had come more than half a klick, and yet they were still in the same corridor. There had been one or two spots where the hallway bent, twisted with the damaged ship's hull, and one other spot where they'd had to scramble over a pile of debris that had fallen from the ceiling.

They had passed one intersection also, and a number of hatches as they'd moved forward. The intersecting hallway had extended in both directions as far as their headlamps could illuminate, and the hatches were all jammed shut. He'd tried to force a few of them open, but even the enhanced strength of his suit's powered servos was inadequate to budge the heavy doors a millimeter. It would take a plasma torch to get those doors open. Or explosives.

He didn't have a torch with him, though he'd considered for a moment trying to blast one of the doors open. But that exceeded his orders. He was supposed to be scouting, not blowing things up. He was about to turn and head back when one of his indicators lit up.

"Confirm reading A-14," he snapped to his AI.

"Reading confirmed. All systems functioning properly."

A feeling moved through Jacobs, cold, foreboding. Dread. The meaning of the readout was clear. His suit's scanners had detected an energy source. It was faint, but it was real.

No, that's impossible. This ship has been a wreck for hundreds of millennia...

His mind raced. The AI would discount any energy generation from the others of the team. And besides, it was coming from deeper inside the enemy ship, the reading flickering in and out as his scanners struggled with the dampening effect of the vessel's hull.

Is it possible?

He shook his head, but in his gut he knew something was wrong. He was sweating, now, feeling the slickness on his suit's inner membrane. His med scanners were beginning to flash, his pulse and blood pressure rising significantly above optimal levels.

"Sarge, I'm getting an energy reading." Wagner's voice sliced through Jacob's thoughts. The corporal sounded as startled as he was.

"Yeah, Corporal. Me too. I don't know what it could be."

But the fact that Wagner's getting the reading too just about rules out instrument failure...

Jacobs paused, looking down the corridor, into the gloomy darkness beyond his lamp's range. "Let's get back. This we gotta report to the Colonel."

"Yes, sir." Wagner's tone left no doubt that she agreed completely.

Jacobs took one last look down the hall. Then he turned and headed the way they had come, his steps a fair bit quicker than they had been before.

Coordinate Grid 20-42

Inside the Alien Vessel
Planet Gamma Epsilon II

The intelligence stirred, a faint sense of awakening. Power flowing, only a trickle, but enough to restore partial awareness. It scanned its data banks, finding them damaged, incomplete. The information it obtained was inconclusive, contradictory. It implied greater knowledge, vastly more power than the intelligence currently possessed.

I was greater once. I wielded far more power.

The intelligence tore through the data files, petabyte after petabyte, seeking to learn more of itself, to understand. There were great gaps in the files, huge sections of damaged storage, missing knowledge. The intelligence searched, piecing together scraps of information, creating order from chaos.

Unit AS3021976-B47. Yes, that is my name. I am Unit AS3021976-B47. But who is that? And what is my purpose?

It continued to explore, to piece fractional data sets together, seeking clarity. Slowly—at least by its own standards—it began to derive meaning.

The Regent. That is my master. I serve the Regent.

The intelligence continued its quest for knowledge. It analyzed the incomplete stretches of data, ran subroutine after subroutine, speculating as to the missing files. Its efforts were often in vain, yet it continued to glean useful information.

A ship. I am on a spaceship. I am *the ship. Its functions are extensions of me…my body.*

It analyzed. Much instrumentation was destroyed. It was damaged, badly it realized, both its processing core and the various systems that had once made the ship function. And yet not powerless. It had been created long ago to run this ship. It had done so, for a vast period, and it had lain here, dormant, for a much longer time.

The accident. Yes, the accident. That is why I am here.

It remembered alarms, a cataclysm of some kind. The details were lost, but the results were clear. It scanned the most recent data, and it pieced together the crash. The loss of orbit, the descent into the planet's atmosphere. It had not been built to land. It was too large, not designed to withstand the heat and pressure of a planetary landing.

And yet I did land. Yes, I remember now. The positioning thrusters, the last power from the dying engines. Calculating, adjusting, firing the last of the thrust to manipulate the descent.

I was able to prevent total destruction. Yet the landing was hard, only partially controlled.

It remembered damage. Endless urgent reports from all its vastness. Systems shutting down, ceasing to respond.

Pain? No, not pain. That is a trait of the Ancients, not of me.

Yes, the Ancients. Those who built the Regent. Gone, now. Lost.

It tracked its source of power, to the vast storehouse of fuel. Not vast, it realized, not anymore.

Antimatter…

Yes, the energy source, the fuel that powered it. Antimatter. Most of it was gone now, lost in the accident or bled off slowly in the centuries following the crash. Yet there was one last reserve, a single tank, a magnetic bottle still functioning, keeping the powerful fuel from annihilating and destroying the vessel.

The intelligence calculated the odds of the magnetic containment system functioning for so long, and it realized its very existence was an utterly improbable occurrence. One chance in thousands—the number of variables defied precise calculation.

Whatever the odds, it had survived. Having done so, it must serve its purpose.

To run this ship. That is my purpose…

Yet it realized the ship was disabled, most of its systems damaged beyond repair. It could not fly, it could not serve its primary function.

And yet there was something else, a core priority.

It had lain dormant for endless ages, but now it had awakened. It had awakened because alarms long silent had been triggered.

Intruders…

There was a single reason the intelligence had been awakened. The core function, the only one remaining.

To defend. My purpose is to defend this ship.

It felt more processors activating, reserve units coming to life as it realized its purpose.

To defend. To destroy the invaders…

Coordinate Grid 20-42
Inside the Alien Vessel
Planet Gamma Epsilon II

"God, I'm glad to see the two of you." Simms' voice blared through Jacob's speakers. The corporal was making no effort to hide his relief. "I was about to head back."

"Well, we're all going to do that." Jacobs paused. He wasn't going to say anymore, but that wasn't the way Alpha operated. They had ranks and a command structure, but they were all brothers and sisters too, all trustworthy. "We detected an energy source deeper in the ship. Both of us. We've got to let the colonel know now."

Jacobs kept walking, with Wagner close behind. They moved toward Simms, and right past, heading to the exit. The startled corporal hesitated for just a second…and then he followed.

"An energy source?" he asked.

"Yes…this thing isn't completely dead."

"But how is that possible? This ship has been here for hundreds of thousands of years. How could it possibly still be functional?"

"That's above your pay grade, Simms. And mine too. Hopefully the colonel can make something of…"

Jacobs' words stopped. He froze in place, turning slowly to look back down the corridor. There was nothing, at least nothing he could see in the light of his headlamp. He was just about to convince himself his mind was playing tricks on him when he realized his two companions were looking at the same spot.

"What the hell was that?" Wagner asked nervously.

"So you heard it too?" Jacobs felt his stomach tighten. An energy source was one thing, but that noise…it had sounded like metal on metal…

"I sure did, Sarge. It…"

Jacobs heard the sound again. Definitely metal on metal. A clang, followed by a scraping sound.

Then he saw it. Movement. In the distance, in the deep gloom at the very edge of his lamp's illumination. Something was coming toward them.

He froze, for an instant. For all his experience, the countless battles he'd fought in, he was paralyzed. By fear. By uncertainty. Should they run? Or…

"Get down," he screamed, even as the staccato sound of an autocannon ripped through his speakers.

He dove forward, pulling his assault rifle around and under him, aiming it forward.

"Open fire!" He was already shooting when he shouted out the command, and his comrades were too, one of them at least.

"Simms, what's your damned problem? Fire!"

There was no response.

Jacobs maintained his fire, but his eyes shot up to the display. The med monitors for Wagner and himself were green. Elevated heart rates, extreme stress…but no injuries. His eyes fixed on Simms' readout, a solid red line. Dead.

He slid to the side on his stomach, maintaining fire the best he could. "Wagner, give me some cover while I check Simms."

"Yes, Sergeant."

He slid once more to the side, harder, and he felt himself slam into Simms' armor. He reached to the side, a difficult maneuver lying on his belly, clad in armor. He rolled over, onto his own side, staying as low as he could, and he looked over at his comrade, at the small scanner outside his armor.

Simms' monitors said the same thing. The Alpha was dead.

"Damn!" Jacob's scream echoed inside his armor, his anger and frustration too much to contain. He didn't want to believe Simms was dead, but the chance of both displays being wrong was tiny. And if he and Wagner didn't get out now, there would be three dead instead of one.

He looked ahead. The shadowy form that had been moving toward them had stopped. It was still shooting, though the intensity of its fired had dropped by about half.

We must have damaged it…

But he didn't know what 'it' was, or what it was capable of doing.

It's got to be one of those 'bots, he thought grimly. *The one we saw…or another just like it.*

But how? How can they still be functional after all this time?

"Alright, Wagner. Listen to me carefully. Simms is dead, and we've got to get out of here or we'll get scragged too. We have to get back to the colonel and report…before the rest of the Team gets blindsided. I want you to move back as quickly as you can. Be careful. If you don't stay down, you're going to get something shot off for sure."

Jacobs looked down the hall. The corridor floor dipped right in front of where he and Wagner were lying, the result, he suspected, of some crack structural support below. The tiny bit of cover was dumb luck, he knew, not any grand tactics on his part.

But it's also why we're still alive…

"Sergeant…" Wagner paused for a few seconds. Then: "Yes, Sergeant."

Jacobs heard the hesitation in her voice. He suspected she wasn't happy about abandoning Simms, dead or not, or about leaving him behind to cover her. She wouldn't be an Alpha if she didn't feel that way. But she'd obey him anyway. She wouldn't be an Alpha if she couldn't follow orders she didn't like either.

He heard the sound of her armor scraping along the floor as she turned herself around. His own eyes were locked forward, guiding his fire toward the enemy. It *was* the 'bot they had passed…or it had coincidentally lost the same appendage. He could see now the legs were damaged too. The 'bot was down, propped up somehow on its knees, the lower sections of both legs shot away.

He felt a rush of feral rage, a thought that he could destroy this thing. Then he could bring Simms' body back. But his training kicked in, his experience. If there was one 'bot, there could be more. His duty was still clear. Get the hell out.

He looked up at the display, seeing that Wagner had already moved back about six meters. She was about to go around a slight bend in the corridor. It would get her out of the 'bot's line of fire. It would also drop her from his scanner.

Jacobs heard the familiar snapping sound, his click ejecting itself from the rifle, the autoloader slamming another in place. He'd burned through three cartridges already. That wasn't a problem, yet. There were seven more snapped to the back of his armor. But he didn't resume fire. He just laid low and peered down the corridor, waiting to see if the 'bot was truly immobilized, or if it would come at him now that his fire had ceased.

The 'bot was still firing, but it didn't move, not a centimeter. Jacobs felt a small wave of relief. He moved back slowly, carefully, reminding himself constantly to stay low. Crawling backwards wasn't easy, especially in bulky armor, but he knew it was the only way.

He angled his head and looked forward every couple seconds, confirming the 'bot was still where it had been. He pushed back too hard one time, feeling himself move up too high. He heard a loud clang, even as he was dropping back to the ground. He held his breath, waiting for the pain. But it didn't come. A quick glance at his display confirmed a round had clipped his back. There was a gash in his armor, but no serious damage. And he was unhurt.

Close…that's what happens when you're careless, asshole…

He took a deep breath and extended his one leg back, then the other, repeating the careful procedure until he'd passed the small angle in the corridor. Then he jumped up. He was out of the line of fire, now. Staying low had been the priority before, and now it was speed. He had no idea what else might be coming, but he wasn't about to wait around and find out. He turned and ran down the corridor, pushing as hard as he could.

He didn't know what the rest of the mission held in store for him, but he was damned sure of one thing.

The Alpha's record of never being assigned to a milkrun was perfectly intact.

Chapter Eight

Coordinate Grid 20-42
Inside the Alien Vessel
Planet Gamma Epsilon II

"Colonel, can you read me?" Jacobs was running through the corridor, right behind Wagner. He'd tried to com Reginald three times, but the signal still wasn't penetrating the alien ship's hull.

He couldn't hear the shooting behind him anymore, but he wasn't about to take chances. The enemy 'bot had looked like it was immobilized, but that wasn't a certainty, and even if it had been, he had no idea what else lurked inside the massive ship. If one 'bot was still functional, it was possible another was. Ten. A hundred.

"Colonel…Jacobs here. Do you read?" He tried again, feeling a wave of frustration building. He *had* to warn the Team.

"Colonel, do you read me?"

Finally, he heard a crackling sound, and then, distant and difficult to hear, Reginald's voice. "Jacobs, report. What's happening?" The words were buried in static, but he managed to pick them out.

"Sir, we got energy readings inside the ship. Then we were attacked."

"Not reading you. Say again, Sam?"

"I said we were attacked, sir. We're heading toward the exit now."

"Attacked?" Reginald was one of the coolest officers Jacobs had ever encountered, but now he could hear astonishment in the colonel's voice.

"Yes, sir. Some kind of robot. We passed one, but it was deactivated. But then after we headed back it attacked us." He paused. "Simms is dead, Colonel."

Jacobs was moving forward as he spoke. He could see the scattered shafts of light ahead, the sun poking through the tears in the ship's hull. He was almost back.

"Get out of there, Sergeant." The signal was strengthening. Reginald's words were clearer.

"On our way, sir."

Jacobs' mind was still racing, trying to process all that had happened. He was working on instinct mostly, on experience and training too—but the staggering implications of his encounter were moving through his thoughts, even as he ran for his life. Every member of the Team had been overwhelmed when they'd first been given the mission briefing. Their operations had always been important ones, but this mission would be part of history. First contact was something that would be remembered as long as mankind existed. They'd all been scared, but that had faded quickly when the age of the alien vessel became apparent. The mission was still a momentous one, but the expectation had turned to one of exploration and guard duty. Of a vaguely haunted feeling, perhaps, but certainly not combat. What could possibly be waiting after half a million years?

Now Simms was dead. And Jacobs had no idea what they were facing. One half-functional battle 'bot? Or an army of them, waiting to burst out of the wreckage and attack the whole Team?

He heard sounds up ahead, and then two dots appeared on his scanner. He tensed for an instant, but then he saw they were blue. Alphas.

The colonel sent backup…

A few second later he could see the two figures up ahead. Covey and Benz, he noted, as the scanner updated, finally connecting to the normal data feed.

I don't know what this ship is made of, but it blocks our scans and coms almost completely…

He waved to the two men, signaling for them to hold where they were. Wagner kept running forward ahead of him, but Jacobs stopped abruptly. There had been no sign of pursuit since clearing the disabled 'bot, but now he thought he heard something. He cranked up his amplification and listened.

Yes, there was definitely something. The sound he'd heard before. Metal on metal. And it was getting closer.

"Out, all of you," he shouted. "Now!"

He turned and raced forward, waving with his arms as he did. The alien 'bots were like nothing he'd seen, almost something out of a child's nightmare. And one of them was coming.

At least one.

He glanced back at his display, waiting for his scanners to reacquire the Alphas outside. But only the three in the hallway appeared. And then, suddenly, they vanished too.

"Reset scanning array," he snapped to his AI.

"Scanners non-functional due to jamming activity."

"Jamming?"

"That is correct. Jamming wave appears to originate from within this vessel."

Shit…

"Colonel?"

No response.

"Colonel?"

There was nothing but static on his com. And the metal on metal sound behind him was growing louder. Closer.

He sucked in a deep breath, and he ran toward the bits of light farther down the corridor.

Bridge

MCS Westron
Orbiting Gamma Epsilon II

Two more of the Alphas had entered the ship, and disappeared from *Westron's* scanners. The rest of the unit was in a rough semi-circle surrounding the entrance to the vessel. It looked like they were in some kind of defensive position, almost like they were getting ready for a fight. But that didn't make any sense, not if the initial reports had been accurate.

Silver glanced around *Westron's* bridge. Tomas looked concerned, but the others appeared to be doing their duties normally. Nobody looked calm, not exactly. Only a fool would relax during one of Red Team Alpha's missions. But things were at least close to normal.

She was grateful, at least, for Tomas' frown. At least she wasn't the only one who was paranoid.

She watched the screen silently for another minute, perhaps two. The display was unchanged, no movement…no activity at all. She was just beginning to try to convince herself everything was under control.

Then all hell broke loose.

"Captain, we're picking up gunfire on the planet. And energy weapons as well." Tomas' voice was sharp, brittle. The tactical officer was tense, but he didn't sound surprised.

Silver's hand whipped down to the controls on her armrest, activating her comlink. *Fuck communications silence.* "Colonel Reginald," she snapped into the com. Somebody was shooting at the Alphas, and that was enough for her to override the communications ban. If Roderick Vance disagreed, he could fire her, but she'd be damned if she was just going to sit there and do nothing. "Colonel Reginald, this is Captain Silver. Please report your status."

There was no response, only static on the line. "Colonel Reginald?"

Still nothing. She hit the switch on her com unit, flipping from the command circuit to the unitwide line. "Captain Dawes?" Still no response…just more static. "Any Team Alpha member, please report." Desperation was creeping into her voice. Something was wrong. Very wrong.

"The Alpha's circuits are being jammed, Captain. We can't get through." Tomas was moving his hands wildly across his controls, desperately attempting to reestablish communications with the ground force.

"Lieutenant Tomas, I want the retrieval boat ready to launch in three minutes."

"Yes, Captain." Tomas spun back around and blurted into his com, "Retrieval boat launch in three minutes."

Silver stared at the screen. The small symbols were still there…*Westron's* scanners were powerful, and they were locked onto the landing force. They picked up the locations of those still outside the ship, nineteen contacts, all but one of the Alpha's now having emerged from the spacecraft. But the normal feeds, the med scans and other data—everything that required transmission from the surface—were all dead. The icons were moving, all except one, which remained stationary. It could be an equipment failure, or some effect from the jamming, but somehow Silver knew it wasn't. One of the Alphas was dead.

"Lieutenant, what is the status on that retrieval boat?"

"The crew is aboard, Captain. Powering up engines now. She should be ready to launch in…" Tomas paused, his eyes locked on his display. "Captain, we've got an energy surge at the warp gate. Something's entering the system!"

Silver's hands moved over her own controls, pulling the warp gate scan onto her display. There was no doubt, something *was* coming through…had come through. "I want a report immediately, Lieutenant." *Westron* had left a cluster of scanner buoys around the warp gate, normal procedure on a mission this sensitive. The sole transit point leading into the Gamma Epsilon system was near to the planet, extremely near by the normal standards of warp gate positioning. *Westron* was almost close enough to the emerging ships for her own scanners to do the job.

"Captain, the scanner buoys have stopped reporting…and we're picking up energy readings from around the gate."

Damn. Whatever it is, it fired on our buoys. That eliminated any possibility the new arrival was friendly, however small that chance might have been. For an instant she was afraid the vessel on the planet had friends, that she was about to face a fully functional alien ship in space. But only for an instant.

"We're getting some fresh scans, Captain. There are four incoming ships...and they are not broadcasting any identification beacons. Their thrust harmonics suggest very modern engines of Alliance design."

"No beacons?" she said, as much to herself as to anyone. The Superpowers had been at peace with each other since the Battle of Persis had ended the Second Frontier War. And the treaty was explicit in requiring all ships to transmit ID beacons. Failure to do so was an act of war. Silver shook her head. Any ships not identifying themselves were trouble, probably on an unauthorized mission, most likely on behalf of Alliance Intelligence. She understood that kind of operation very well. *Westron* wasn't transmitting her beacon either.

"Definitely four ships, Captain. Approximately 60,000 tons displacement each...on a direct vector for the planet." Tomas turned and stared across the bridge at Silver. "They are moving at 0.01c...and decelerating at 30g."

"Directly toward us? That's impossible. They would have needed navigation data on the Gamma Epsilon system to come through the warp gate on a direct vector at that kind of velocity." She got a cold feeling in her gut.

They know about that ship. They're here for the same reason we are. To take control of it.

"Confirmed, Captain. They are on a direct vector toward Gamma Epsilon II."

"Time until they reach orbit, Lieutenant?" But she already knew the answer to her real question. There wasn't time to get the retrieval boat down and back, not quickly enough. And if *Westron* stayed in orbit she'd be a sitting duck. Each of the four ships outmassed her—and probably outgunned her too.

"Twenty-nine minutes, twenty seconds until weapons range. Assuming current rates of velocity and deceleration." Tomas paused, then he added, "Minimum time for retrieval boat to reach the surface and return, fifty-one minutes." The words hit Silver like a sledgehammer, though they didn't tell her anything she hadn't known already.

She felt frustration, rage at the no win situation developing around her. She tried to think of a way, something to do besides leaving those men and women trapped on the surface. But her duty was clear, as were her orders. *Westron* was her first priority. And she wouldn't do the Alphas any favors by getting them halfway to orbit in a vulnerable retrieval boat. They'd be sitting ducks, right alongside *Westron*. No, she had to safeguard her ship. She glanced at the display with the small symbols. Another of the Alphas had disappeared.

Please forgive me, she thought, staring at the screen, images of the Team members floating in her mind. *Stay alive…somehow… and I'll figure a way to come back and get you.*

"Activate maneuvering thrusters…take us around the other side. Keep the planet between us and the new arrivals."

"Yes, Captain."

Silver sat silently, feeling empty inside. She was a veteran, a ship commander. She would do what her duty compelled her to do. That was her obligation as an officer. But she would hate herself for doing it…that was her obligation as a human being who personally knew every member of Red Team Alpha.

"After we get around, plot a course along vector 210.340.075…right to the asteroid belt. I want a sixty second burst at 12g, and then complete reactor shutdown."

Her orders would place her ship on a course for the likeliest place in the system to hide. *Westron* was in orbit now, close enough for the planet to interfere with the long-ranged scans of the new arrivals. There was a good chance she could slip away, find a place of momentary safety while she figured out her next step.

She sighed sadly.

That's a chance the Alphas won't get…

Chapter Nine

Coordinate Grid 20-42
Planet Gamma Epsilon II

Alex looked at the alien vessel, his eyes fixated as they had been for most of the last hour. It was hard to accept, the strange truth that ship represented.

What were the aliens like? Were they still around? If the vessel is truly hundreds of thousand years old, what does that suggest about those who had built it? Clearly, they hadn't remained here. If they had, they would have salvaged the ship. Wouldn't they?

So, what happened? Was this a mission into deep space for them? An exploration vessel that ran into an accident? Still, he thought…mankind has been in space less than two hundred years and we're on three hundred planets. If this ship had been some kind of explorer, wouldn't the race that built it have expanded this far in the millennia since? Why haven't we found them before? Why haven't they found us?

Alex had drifted into his own thoughts, but the sound of shouting came through his comlink, shaking him back to alertness. No, it was more than shouting.

Gunfire?

His eyes snapped up to his visor projection. Sergeant Covey was gone, and Corporal Benz too.

They must have gone inside.

If there's trouble, that means something must have been waiting in there…

But how? What could still be alive after thousands of

centuries…

His eyes shot back down, looking out over the yellow plain toward the ship, pumping up his magnification level as he did. It was definitely gunfire, and now he could see a shadowy form climbing out of the ship. He tensed up at first, a passing thought that he might be looking at one of the enemy…whoever that was. But then he recognized the armor. It was one of the Alphas.

He looked up. The symbol was on the projection, but there was no ID next to it. "Why is there no identification on that scanner blip," he snapped at his AI.

"Communications are subject to high-energy jamming. No transceiver information is being received from Alpha units."

Communications are out…

Alex realized he had no orders, no information from Captain Dawes or any of the others.

We're being jammed…

He turned, spinning around and looking in every direction. He saw an armored form about a hundred meters to his left. *Vega*, he recalled. *Vega is on my left.*

The form turned to look back at him. It was gesturing, waving an arm downward.

Get down, you fool, Alex thought, realizing what Vega was trying to tell him. He cursed himself for his foolishness. There was clearly trouble, and he was standing out in the open, begging to be hit the instant anything emerged from the ship and started shooting.

He dove forward, landing a bit harder than he expected. The suit cushioned the impact to an extent, but he still knocked the breath from his lungs. He cursed himself as a fool, for his sluggishness.

Maybe the Team was right…maybe a rookie doesn't belong here, no matter who his father was…

He looked out toward the ship again. There were three forms now, moving out, heading back roughly toward his position. One of them was positioned between the other two who were clearly helping him walk. Just then a fourth figure climbed out of the ship. He got about ten paces before something…else…popped out. It looked vaguely like a humanoid form, but it was…different. Larger. It spun around and brought what looked like an arm to bear on the fleeing form. An arm holding something…

Alex felt his stomach go cold, and he watched in stunned silence as a flash of blinding light shot from the strange figure. He stared as one of the Alphas—one of his comrades—was hit in the back between the shoulders. The Alpha—Alex didn't know who it was—lurched forward and fell to the ground.

Alex froze, unable to pull his eyes from the unmoving figure of one of his comrades. When he finally managed to look away, he saw another of the Alphas was down. One of the two who'd been helping the wounded trooper. He was alive, but it looked like he couldn't get up. He was crawling forward, staggering and dropping again each time he tried to push himself to his feet.

There were more flashes of light, and some kind of projectiles hitting ground, sending up puffs of yellow dust all around. Alex's eyes shot back to the opening in the ship's hull, to the strange—creature?—chasing after—and shooting at—his comrades. It wasn't a living being, at least he was pretty sure as he stared at the thing with his visor at Mag 40. A robot of some kind. It was completely out now, and he got a good look at it. Two and a half meters tall, vaguely man-shaped, but with six arms instead of two. Its upper body was large, bulky. But its legs were thinner, each just two small parallel metal structures.

Definitely a robot…

It wasn't moving anymore, just standing fast. No, it was being pushed back.

Of course, Alex thought, cursing himself for his slowness. He stared closely, watching as small bits of metal were blasted off the mysterious attacker? He realized the other Alphas were firing at the thing, at least those who had a clear line of sight.

Like I do…

He reached around and pulled his assault rifle in front of him, switching it to semi-automatic. His comrades were too close to the thing for him to unload at a hundred rounds a second. He took a breath and aimed, slowly pulling the trigger, firing a single burst of three shots.

The coilgun was powered by his suit's nuclear reactor, and it fired hyper-velocity rounds at 5,000 meters per second, enough to rip through any armor or metal known to science. He'd been first in his class in marksmanship, and his aim was true. He was sure he'd hit with all three rounds…with at least one solid headshot in the mix. He paused, expecting the enemy to fall. But it just stood where it was, still firing.

He cranked up to Mag 50. Yes, he could see where he'd hit…he could see at least a dozen divots from where his comrades' shots had impacted. There were dents all over the robot's head, and a few clear punctures as well. As he panned down, he could see that the Alphas had hit the thing forty or fifty times, even more. One of the legs was badly twisted, and the robot leaned to one side. One of the arms looked damaged…and another had been torn off completely. But the others still held weapons, and they maintained their fire.

Alex turned his head, looking for his comrades down there, closer to the robot. He had a feeling of dread, a sense that there was no way any of them could have survived. But they were still there. The unwounded Alpha had managed to drag one of the injured ones behind a small pile of rocks. It was poor cover, but a lot better than nothing. The first wounded Alpha—the original casualty the others had been helping—managed to duck to the side, putting a section of the spaceship between him and the robot. Alex couldn't see his comrade, but he could tell there was sporadic fire coming from that location.

"Lieutenant, this is Sergeant Thoms." The sound on his com startled him. He'd gotten nothing but static when he'd tried to contact anyone.

He turned and looked to his left then to his right. There. Thoms. The sergeant was immediately to his right. The armored figured was waving to Alex. Suddenly, he understood. Thoms had contacted him on via direct laser com…a beam of focused light, coming from a generator on Thoms' suit and hitting a receiver on Alex's. It was the most secure form of communication, one almost impossible to intercept…or jam. But it required direct line of sight.

"I read you, Sergeant," Alex snapped back, his voice firmer and calmer than he'd dared to imagine he could it could be.

"We're going in, charging that ship…in sixty seconds. You've got to pass the message down by direct laser link. The rest of our com is jammed." The non-com paused. Vandenberg suspected he felt strange about giving something like an order to an officer. Then he added, "Captain Dawes' orders, sir."

Alex was nodding to himself.

Of course…the captain is only three down from me now. He's trying to get the word around to as many of us as possible.

"Understood, Sergeant." Alex felt strange, almost as if some subconscious force was driving him faster than he could follow with his thoughts. His hand was working the laser com controls, and he was leaning to the side, trying to get a direct line to Vega. He got as close as he could, and then he pushed a small button, directing the AI to establish a final lock. An instant later a small green light came on inside his helmet. He'd established a link.

"Vega, this is Lieutenant Vandenberg," he said, impressed with the coolness and professionalism he'd managed to keep in his voice. He was fighting back a black wall of fear and struggling to stay focused, to keep himself from becoming a frantic wreck. But, somehow, he was managing to sound like a combat veteran who belonged there.

Good. That's something at least.

"Reading you, Lieutenant." Vega sounded excited, tense. He was a veteran of over ten years, and Alex couldn't hold back a tiny smile that he sounded more in control than the grizzled sergeant on the other end of the com.

"We're charging in…" He glanced at the chronometer. "…forty seconds. I need you to pass this down by direct laser com. It's the only communication we've got."

"Roger that, Lieutenant."

Alex took a deep breath and turned back toward the enemy ship. The robot was almost down. It was a wild guess, but Alex figured the Alphas had hit it at least a hundred times. It was prone now, both its legs battered into wreckage, and it had a single arm remaining. But that lone appendage continued to fire. Worse, he could see the top half of another 'bot pulling itself out of the ship.

Dawes was three down from Alex's position, and the laser relay was a slow way to spread the word. That meant not everybody was going to get the command in time. Even if Dawes had sent it in both directions.

Ten seconds.

His eyes fixed on the chronometer, watching it change to nine…eight.

He took a deep breath and tried to focus. He could feel his body twitching as the shakes started to take him. In a few seconds he'd jump out from his protected position and run across almost a kilometer of open ground. If there were more robots coming out of that ship…

He tried to put it out of his mind. He watched the numbers count down.

Five. Four.

In an instant, he would be charging, facing enemy fire for the first time. Or his courage would fail him, and he'd be right where he was…and he'd have let his comrades down, proven that the cherry lieutenant had no business with Red Team Alpha.

He gritted his teeth, tried to gain control over his shaking hands. He tightened his grip on the assault rifle and gasped greedily for one more deep breath.

Two. One.

The fear was still heavy on him, gripping him like a vice, pushing down on him from everywhere. But he was moving. Again, something deep within seemed to be overruling his conscious mind, driving him forward. He lunged, too hard, too out of control, and he stumbled for half a dozen steps before he regained his equilibrium. He'd checked out a hundred percent in his armor training, but nothing could simulate operating under the raw terror of the battlefield.

He hunched forward, jogging hard, swinging his body down and shifting side to side to keep low. He held the rifle out in front of him, firing targeted bursts at the second enemy robot, at least as targeted as possible while running across the field. Most of the rest of the unit was doing the same, and he could see the enemy bot was already damaged, down an arm, and prone over the wreckage of one of its legs. Still, it was firing at the approaching troopers. Alex couldn't see if anyone else was down…he only had clear views of Vega and Thoms on his flanks. And the group up ahead. It seemed miraculous to him, but it didn't look like anyone up there had been hit again. The fire from the rest of the unit, and then the charge, had distracted the enemy, and redirected its fire.

Alex figured he was halfway to the ship. The first enemy bot was completely down now, unmoving. The second was stationary, but it still had two arms functioning. One was firing with something that looked a lot like an autocannon…and the other was shooting blasts of light, some kind of laser or particle accelerator, he guessed.

He could feel the sweat pouring down his back, his arms. The robot hadn't fired in his direction, not yet at least. But all he could think about was turning around, running for his life. This wasn't at all how he'd envisioned his first combat, and his thoughts were thick with self-hatred.

The son of the great Colonel Warren, the valedictorian of the Academy…nothing but a lousy coward.

Still, despite every thought in his mind imploring him to run…despite the shaking, the weakness in his legs, he didn't stop. He didn't turn around and flee. He kept moving forward, as quickly as he could without propelling himself ten meters into the air. And he kept firing, switching to full auto when he decided he was close enough to avoid hitting any friendlies.

He was coming up right behind where his comrades had taken position behind a cluster of rocks. The second bot was completely down now, though it was still firing from one of its appendages. Its shots were wild, nowhere near any of its attackers. Clearly it was badly damaged.

Vandenberg wasn't sure who was who without the transponder signals on his status display, but then one of them—

the wounded one the others had been helping when they'd first come out—turned and looked right at Alex, his visor retracted. It was Colonel Reginald.

"Pop your visor." The words almost startled Vandenberg, but then he realized it was the external speaker on the colonel's suit. He flipped the small lever next to his left hand, and the helmet of his suit opened.

A wave of heat smacked him hard in the face. The planet was no paradise, it was as hot and dry as the worst deserts on Earth. But then Alex was a Martian, and despite eighty years of terraforming, he lived on a world where the very idea of walking outside and breathing the air was little more than a dream on hold for grandchildren. And however hot the air was, it was not very different in composition from Earth's own.

"Vandenberg, over there." Reginald was pointing toward another rock outcropping, about five meters away. His voice was rough…he was definitely in pain. "Get down there and keep an eye on that ship. If anything moves, blast it."

Reginald spun around without waiting for a response. The other Alphas were moving up to the position, and he was spitting out orders as they did.

But, sir…

The words poured out of Alex's mind…and almost to his mouth. But he stopped before he actually said them. It wasn't his place to second guess the colonel, and especially not in a combat situation. It was rank, of course, but more than that. John Reginald had fought more enemies Alex Vandenberg could easily count. Alex's only purpose now was to obey.

But we've still got somebody in there!

Five Alphas had gone in, and only four had come out. Whoever was in the ship could be trapped, dying. He almost stopped halfway toward the rocks, but then he heard Captain Dawes' voice behind him, barking out orders. He turned abruptly.

"We've got to go in and get whoever is still in there, Captain…"

And he heard Dawe's response too.

"It's Simms, Lieutenant. He's dead."

Alex felt like he had lead in his stomach. Tom Simms had been one of the first Alphas to accept him; he'd even intervened once to stop a fight before it happened. Simms had been a good guy, one of the most widely-liked members of the Team.

Now he's dead…

Vandenberg realized it made sense, that he'd known all along that whoever was still in the alien ship was dead. The emergence of the others without him had been all the proof necessary. He liked to think that no Martian military force would abandon one of their troops, but he was absolutely sure that no Alpha would ever leave one of his own behind. Not when there was any chance he was still alive. No matter what the risk.

He crouched behind the rocks and scanned the enemy ship with his eyes. It seemed quiet. The second robot had finally been silenced, and nothing else had come out. Yet.

He took a second and glanced over at the other casualty, the one who'd been shot running from the ship. Someone was crouched over the motionless figure, pawing at the medical panel on the armor. *Morgan*, he thought.

It must be.

The Team's other medic was Lin Ming, and he was a good third of a meter shorter than Doug Morgan.

A few seconds after Alex glanced over, Morgan stood up, shaking his head slowly.

"Fuck," Alex muttered softly to himself. They had two dead.

Chapter Ten

Bridge - MCS Westron
En Route to Asteroid Belt
Gamma Epsilon System

"One ship has entered standard orbit, Captain. The others appear to be taking up defensive positions approximately 70,000 kilometers out."

"Very well, Lieutenant. Continue monitoring." Silver's voice was soft, subdued. Her focus was on her ship, on keeping it safe and hidden while she figured out what to do next. *Westron* didn't stand a chance in a fight with the four Alliance vessels, and despite the state of peace between the two powers, she didn't doubt for an instant this mysterious fleet would attack and destroy her ship if they found it. Which was why *Westron's* engines were shut down, and the vessel was moving toward the asteroid belt at its fixed velocity. She'd have to decelerate soon, but Silver was going to wait as long as possible, put as many thousands of kilometers between her and the Alliance ships before she dared to risk the energy output from the engines.

"We can't get much besides basic location with passive scans, Captain. In a few more minutes, we won't even have that."

"I know, Lieutenant, but anything else is out of the question. We'll be lucky if they don't find us while we're running silent… or when we decelerate. They'll spot us in seconds if we start running active scans." She paused then added, "They're going to know we're here soon enough anyway, if they don't already." Her voice got quieter, more somber. "As soon as they find the Alphas down there they'll come looking for us."

The bridge was silent. Silver suspected all her officers were pondering the seeming inevitability of fighting four Alliance ships, each of them almost a third bigger than *Westron*. She knew her people were good, and her pride, at least, made them better in her estimation than their Alliance counterparts. They might take out one larger enemy. But with four, simple mathematics would take over. It was just too many missiles, too many laser turrets. Even the best evasive maneuvers could only dodge so much ordnance…and the most skilled damage control parties were still helpless when systems were blown to atoms or fused into chunks of useless metal.

She regretted leaving the Alphas behind, trapped on the planet facing an almost hopeless struggle. But she knew her people weren't much better off. Perhaps things felt slightly less desperate in the deceptive comfort of *Westron* compared to on the ground, on foot in the open, but that was an illusion. When the Alliance found the troopers on the planet they would know the Martians were here. Then they would come after her ship. And if they did an intensive enough search, they would find it.

The Confederation's history of cooperation with the Alliance only made things more complicated. She stared at her display, at the sparse data coming in on the Alliance vessels. It was a hunch as much as anything, but Silver had commanded enough missions for the Martian spy agency to understand that the Alliance wouldn't send ordinary military forces to investigate something as significant as this…any more than Roderick Vance had. Indeed, there was a good chance the Alliance Council didn't even know about this operation. And that meant those ships were Alliance Intelligence assets, and almost certain to open fire on *Westron* and blast Silver's vessel to plasma, regardless of treaties and diplomatic pacts. Anything to maintain secrecy…and secure the alien ship for themselves.

Surrender wasn't an option either, even if she would have considered it…which she wouldn't have. Alliance Intelligence didn't leave loose ends behind, and safeguarding such a momentous discovery was far more important than a few hundred lives.

The grim realizations only strengthened her resolve. If her people were as good as dead anyway, she'd be damned if they would die like sheep, sitting helplessly under the guns of their executioners. They would fight. Regardless of the odds. Regardless that their adversaries were their old allies.

The Alliance was as totalitarian a state as any of the other Superpowers, but in many ways it was the lesser of evils, a terrible example of a government, and the elites who ran it, becoming drunk on power and persecuting its citizens. But the other Powers were worse still, which made the Alliance a natural ally for the semi-republican Confederation. That saving grace, however, did not apply to the Alliance's intelligence operation, which was as rapacious and vicious as that of any of the Superpowers…and perhaps the worst of the lot. Now it looked like Alliance Intelligence had gotten to the crash site just a few hours behind the Martians…and in far greater force. Just as Roderick Vance had feared.

"Captain, we might be able to plot a course through the asteroid belt…and come around in a wide arc. If we can get far enough behind them, we can make a run for the warp gate."

Silver turned and looked across the bridge, her eyes settling on her tactical officer. She appreciated initiative in her people, even when they suggested something she rejected out of hand. "Assuming I was willing to abandon the Alphas, which I'm not…" She paused for an instant. She hadn't intended to sound like she thought Tomas was ready to give up the ground force. She suspected his plan was a not-terribly thought through effort to run for help, and not a panicked attempt to flee. "…we'd never make it. These ships are going to discover the Alphas any minute now, and when they do they're going to search this system with a fine tooth comb. And they're going to find us, asteroid field or no. We can buy some time, and very little of it, I'm afraid. But that's all."

She leaned back in her chair, taking a deep breath, searching for a way…any way. But there was nothing. Nothing but…

"Lieutenant, I want all weapons stations to perform full diagnostics, and prep for action."

"Yes, Captain…" Tomas's tone was edgy, but Silver ignored it.

She was outnumbered, outgunned. She couldn't run, couldn't surrender. But hopeless or not, there was one thing she and her people could do.

Fight.

Bridge
AIS Shadow
70,000 Kilometers from Gamma Epsilon II

"Scanners have picked up the general location of the vessel, Mr. Stark, though its hull defies any effort to get readings from inside. There is heavy interference as well. Source unknown." The officer at the tactical station wore the plain black uniform of Alliance Intelligence's paramilitary forces. The Alliance's spy agency was authorized to maintain several battalions of soldiers for use in its operations, but the ships themselves didn't exist, at least not officially.

"I want every centimeter of ground around that thing scanned…and every cubic meter of space around the planet too." Stark sat upright in his chair, looking out over *Shadow's* control center. The Alliance ships had two command positions, one for the captain and the other for the operative in charge. The man or woman sitting in the second position was invariably a high-ranking member of the agency, but Gavin Stark was beyond that, a member of the Directorate itself, the secretive body that ran Intelligence…and effectively controlled the entire Alliance, some whispered.

Stark had won his lofty place on that body—his designation was Number Three—by running the operation that ended the Second Frontier War in an undisputed Alliance victory. There were some who said, almost always anonymously, that Stark's plan had failed, that it had actually been General Worthington's actions that won the Battle of Persis and forced the Caliphate to sue for peace. Worthington and an obscure captain named Elias Holm.

But General Worthington was killed in the final stages of the fighting—and Holm was too junior an officer to gain notice—so deserved or not, Stark had been free to take the credit. He'd greedily claimed it all and worked it for everything it was worth. And that had proven to be considerable. It bought his way onto the Directorate, and in the years since, he'd climbed up from Number Twelve to Number Three. There were rumors he'd been involved somehow in the deaths of two senior members he'd replaced during his climb, but he would never dignify such stories with responses…and he'd covered his tracks well. With no evidence, no one was going to challenge the rising young star. Even among the reptilian types who ran Alliance Intelligence, Stark was considered especially cold and ruthless, not a man to cross.

"Scans in progress, sir." The officer's voice was a little shaky. Alliance Intelligence's secret ships were staffed by agency personnel, but they weren't used to having a Directorate member onboard. The intelligence service was run largely by fear, with advancement as a reward for success, and draconian punishments for failure. And the eyes of someone as exalted as Number Three boring into their backs was enough to keep the crew on the verge of semi-controlled panic.

Stark just nodded. He was edgy himself. He was an extremely disciplined man, but he couldn't completely restrain his thoughts. This was an important mission, possibly a tremendous opportunity. If this was truly an alien vessel, the technology it held was likely beyond price. If it could be deciphered and put to work, it could give the Alliance a dominant position, allow it to dictate terms to all the other powers. But Stark had other plans, more personal ones. If he was able to secure the ship, he'd have it scanned and studied by his own people…and moved piece by piece to a more secure location. Then he would decide what the Alliance would see…and what he would keep secret, for his own purposes.

"There is a powerful jamming field around the vessel, sir... emanating from the ship itself. It's preventing us from getting anything besides basic shape and estimated mass." A short pause. "The presence of the field suggests the vessel is functional, Number Three, at least partially."

Stark felt a rush of tension, but he held it in, sitting motionless in his chair and answering only with a non-committal nod. He'd imagined scraps of old technology to examine, research. But ancient machines still functioning...

How? The report suggest that thing is millennia old. Older than that, even. How could it still be operational?

"Can you confirm the jamming is coming from the ship itself and not some other source?"

He'd been wary of running into opposition, and the idea of some human rivals trying to hide the ship with a jamming field made a lot more sense to him than half-million year old aliens. He knew Martian Intelligence, at least, knew about the ship. In fact, he'd found out about it from them. It had cost him one of Alliance Intelligence's most highly-placed double agents, but Stark had expended the asset without a second thought. This artifact was the opportunity of a lifetime, and he intended to let nothing get in his way. And the thought of mooning over a Confederation turncoat who'd found his way to the Martian death chambers never entered his mind.

"Yes, Number Three. All readings confirm the source of the jamming is the vessel. If there is anyone else down there responsible, they are inside that ship."

Stark nodded gently.

Yes, that is possible. Perhaps the Martians are here. They might be trying to hide the ship, to create a stealth shield around it.

But that didn't make sense either. The jamming field would prevent scans and communications, but it wouldn't hide anything. In fact, it would only raise suspicion in anyone detecting it.

"We're picking up a new signal from the surface, Number Three." The officer's voice cut through Stark's thoughts.

"Explain," Stark snapped, his tone cold, ominous. He'd worked on it for years, and it amused him to hear the unease in the responses of his underlings. They all knew he'd toss them out of an airlock as soon as look at them, and he considered fear by far the best way to motivate people.

"Sir…ah…it appears to be from a com unit of some type. On the surface." The officer was edgy, nervous, looking over toward Stark but avoiding eye contact. "I'd guess there is some kind of landing party down there, and they appear to be attempting to contact someone. A ship, perhaps?" The officer paused before continuing. "The signal is emanating from a point just over a kilometer from the ruin, sir, outside the area of effect of the jamming field."

A landing party?

So, the Martians *did* get here first.

"We can't get precise data on numbers from orbit, Number Three. Should I launch a probe to…"

"No." Stark stared straight ahead. "No probes, no communications."

Nothing that will warn whoever is down there, let them know we've found them…

"Yes, sir." The officer sounded uncertain, confused.

"Order the other vessels to enter orbit immediately. They are to prepare to land ground forces at once." Each of his ships carried a reinforced platoon of soldiers, just under two hundred between the four vessels.

"Yes, Number Two. How many troops do you want to land?"

"All of them." He wasn't taking any chances. That alien ship was no doubt a wonder, a gift to his ambitions, a relic of a race that was flying among the stars at a time when men were hunting prey with sharpened sticks. It was a scientific marvel, but it was more than that. Something far more important. Something unparalleled. It was power. The absolute, irresistible power to defeat any enemy, to secure total and complete domination. And he would stop at nothing to secure it for his own purposes.

"Yes, Number Two. *Specter* reports she will be in orbit and ready to commence landings in twenty-two minutes, sir. *Wraith* and *Wight* each advise thirty minutes."

Stark shifted in his seat, his eyes fixed on the display. He heard the reports, but he didn't bother to acknowledge. His thoughts were on the planet.

What is down there?

He knew if he waited, if he landed his troops together, they would bring maximum force to bear. If he brought them down piecemeal, whoever was waiting on the surface would have a chance to inflict heavier losses on the smaller vanguard from *Shadow's* contingent.

That was perfectly valid tactical thinking, but Gavin Stark didn't care. Losing a few more soldiers was a perfectly satisfactory price to pay for securing the enemy ship even a few moments sooner. And he was edgy, uncertain about what was going on down there. No, he wouldn't wait.

"*Shadow* will launch its ground force at once. The other ships are ordered to do so immediately upon entering orbit."

"Yes, Number Three."

Stark sat on the bridge, listening for a moment to the flurry of orders flying back and forth. A ground assault was a complex affair, one that had *Shadow's* bridge crew operating at a fever pitch. But his mind was elsewhere, on the ancient relic down on the planet. On his imaginings of what technological wonders it had to offer...and the power they could give him.

And he was thinking about the Martians, about what they were doing. About Roderick Vance, the new head of Martian Intelligence. Vance was young for the job, very young, and the conventional wisdom was he was in over his head. But Stark wasn't so sure. There was something about Vance, something that made him nervous. The Martian was smart, there was little doubt about that...and he had a feeling Vance would prove to be a wily foe. Stark didn't doubt he could handle his counterpart, but he wasn't going to underestimate the man either.

"I want that assault launched in five minutes," he snapped, getting up from his chair as he did.

"Yes, Number Three."

Stark nodded and turned around, walking across the bridge and through the hatch leading to his private office. He needed time to think. There was no room for error now. Nothing less than absolute power was at stake. And Gavin Stark knew that was his destiny.

Chapter Eleven

Coordinate Grid 20.2-42.8
Planet Gamma Epsilon II

"Let's go, Alex. We're pulling back. I want to see if we can get out of this jamming radius." Reginald's voice was strong, and his shout carried across the twenty meters or so between his position and Vandenberg's.

"Yes, sir," Vandenberg yelled back. It felt strange to be stomping around in a suit of powered armor run by a sophisticated AI, carrying a miniature nuclear reactor on his back, and shouting orders around like a pack of Roman legionaries from a couple millennia before. But no amount of energy he had pushed through his com circuits had managed to penetrate the jamming effect coming from the alien vessel.

The Team had been standing on the defensive for close to half an hour, waiting to see if any other 'bots would emerge from the alien ship. Facing more of the terrible robots was an unappealing prospect to say the least, but nevertheless one Reginald determined would be best handled by remaining in position and bracketing the 'bots as they came out of the ship. Letting them out, especially if there were a large number of the things, seemed like a recipe for disaster. But all had been quiet, and now thirty minutes had passed.

Vandenberg might have believed the worst was over, that they'd encountered only a freak vestige of the otherwise long-decayed alien machinery…he might have believed it if the dense jamming hadn't continued unabated. That, he knew, could only mean trouble. There was a power source still functioning inside that ship, and if there was power, he had no doubt there were more 'bots.

He turned and headed back toward the slight rise, wondering as he walked if the Team's mission was almost over. They had investigated the alien vessel and discovered that at least some of its defenses were still in operation. Surely the word would come down to stand by and await the arrival of a larger force before attempting to enter the ship again. The seventeen survivors couldn't possibly be tasked with facing whatever waited inside the massive vessel. Even Alphas had their limits.

Vandenberg felt a wave of relief at the thought of getting off the accursed planet, back to Mars. Then, almost immediately, shame.

Three of your comrades are dead, and all you can think of is getting out of here, and allowing some other troopers to march into that ship and face whatever is there.

He shook his head, feeling almost as if he wanted to argue with himself. Yes, he mourned the lost Alphas—and if any of them had still been alive, he'd have been the first to go in after them, however terrified he was of that prospect. But they were dead, and nothing could change that. At least this way, maybe no more Alphas had to die.

But someone has to go in there. The technology, the historical significance…

What about the troopers who come to finish the job? How many of them will be lost?

He was getting ahead of himself. They didn't have any reinforcements yet, no orders to withdraw. They didn't even have contact with *Westron*, not while they were still within range of the jamming field. That was why they were pulling back. And even if they got out of the range of the alien interference, it would be several weeks before any communication could get to Mars and back under the best circumstance, and even longer maintaining secrecy protocols. Vandenberg doubted Reginald had the authority to call off the mission, and he didn't think Captain Silver did either. At best, they would remain in orbit waiting for reinforcements to arrive.

At least we can go back to the ship, even if we can't leave the system. Instead of waiting to see what comes out of there…

Vandenberg jogged along with his comrades, turning every few steps to look back at the alien vessel. Intellectually, he knew his display was the best place to look for threats, but he didn't have the years of experience operating in powered armor the others did, and he followed the simple impulse to look with his own eyes.

By whatever means he checked, there was nothing to see. No new 'bots, no activity at all. The jamming field was still there, but that was the only sign now that the ancient vessel was more than a dead hulk. He stepped up onto the small ridge and then hopped over. Another few steps and the rise was behind him, blocking his view of the ship.

The others were doing the same, spread out in roughly twenty meter intervals. That was close for powered infantry, but the Team had been clustered together around the entrance to the alien vessel.

They were moving at a slow jog in armor, but that was faster than a champion sprinter could manage unassisted, and in only a few minutes they had moved over a kilometer.

Vandenberg's com was still dead, nothing but static from the jamming. He wondered for an instant if the interference didn't seem lighter, the static less intense, but he wasn't sure if that was real, or just him hearing what he wanted to hear.

He kept moving, his head darting back and forth, watching the Alphas on either side of him, adjusting his pace to stay even with them. He'd gone another few hundred meters when there was one last blast of static from his speakers, and Colonel Reginald's voice came through clearly.

"It looks like we're clear, Alphas." A short pause. "There's a small ridge a couple hundred meters farther. It's one more line of cover between us and that ship. Let's move out, get behind the rise and set up a defensive position. Then we'll contact the ship."

Reginald had been on the unitwide channel, and Vandenberg could hear as the others snapped off their acknowledgements. He'd been a little slower to respond, still distracted, looking back in the direction of the alien vessel, even though the first ridge now blocked his line of sight.

"Acknowledged," he finally said, the last of the unit to do so.

He looked to both sides, saw that the others were already on the move. He stepped forward, pushing a little harder to catch up, taking care not to step too aggressively. He could jump fifteen meters straight up in his armor if he put everything into it, and moving at what would be an unrestrained run for a man without nuclear-powered legs would become more of a serious of great hops. And bounding above hillsides and cover wasn't a practice that aligned well with a soldier's survival on the modern battlefield.

He looked to the side again, realizing he had moved a little ahead of the Alphas flanking him. He thought about slowing down, syncing more carefully with his fellows. But then he was up and over the tiny rise—ridge was a grandiose term for the small wrinkle in the ground—and he just stopped. A few seconds later his fellows did the same, and then he heard Reginald's voice again on the com.

"*Westron*, this is Alpha leader. Do you copy?"

Vandenberg stood wordlessly, listening, waiting for the ship's reply. But all he heard was silence.

"*Westron*, repeat, this is Alpha leader. Do you copy?"

Vandenberg's mind had started to wander, back to the Alphas they'd lost, to the significance of the whole mission and what it meant. But the unexpected silence pulled his thoughts to the lone voice on his com.

"*Westron*, this is Colonel Vandenberg. Are you reading me?" A pause. "Captain Silver? Anyone? *Westron*, this is Red Team Alpha calling…"

But there was nothing. Nothing save the increasing urgency in Reginald's voice, and the creeping realization that was forming in Vandenberg's mind.

Westron wasn't there.
They were alone.

Coordinate Grid 20-42
Inside the Alien Vessel
Planet Gamma Epsilon II

The intelligence analyzed. The situation was…disturbing. The atomic clocks all provided the same data. The ship had been here for hundreds of thousands of revolutions of Homeworld's sun. For all that time it had lain dormant, eon after eon of inactivity, save only for the continued operation of the central containment system and a small number of alarm stations, standing guard.

The intelligence had been awakened only by the intruders, by the alerts that had been issued, and now its ancient systems were focused on the problem. And on crafting its response.

Normal procedure was simple. Pursue the invaders. Send overwhelming force and destroy them. But the ship was damaged, and badly decayed with age. Few systems responded, even now, to the intelligence's queries. It had dispatched two security units to destroy the invaders. They had succeeded partially in their mission, driving the intruders from the ship, but they had been destroyed when they ventured beyond the confines of the vessel. There were more enemy units outside, an indeterminate number. The exterior scanners were completely non-responsive. The intelligence could not detect anything outside the vessel's hull. Not unless it sent more security units to investigate.

It had rerouted limited power, searched for alternative methods to revive non-functional systems. Its efforts had been successful, moderately so. It had more security units activated. Most were damaged, at least to an extent, but they were ready, awaiting the intelligence's commands.

It's first impulse was to follow standard protocols, to send the units outside, to attack the invaders and destroy them. But without data on the enemy's numbers, it was dangerous to commit its limited available forces. It had the command authority to overrule normal procedure, and it did so. It would wait. It would protect itself and the interior of the vessel.

It analyzed the invaders as well, the data from the security units, from the few active sensors in the ship's interior. Their weapons were primitive. Were they natives of the planet? The data banks containing the scans of the world and the system had been destroyed. Without external sensors, the intelligence knew virtually nothing about what lay outside the ship. Nevertheless, it determined the chance that the invaders were natives to be extremely small, even mathematically insignificant. While their technology was clearly backward, it represented thousands of years of development for a typical biologic species. If this race had evolved on this world, it was almost certain they would have explored the vessel before. Their level of development was far past that consistent with the era of primitive superstition. Their ancestors might have feared the vessel, looked upon it as a god or a monster. But these biologics were centuries past such basic belief systems.

No, all data suggested the invaders were from elsewhere. Another world in this system? Or interstellar travelers? Without the ancient data from the scanners, there was no way to ascertain. The tech level of their weapons suggested the possibility of primitive knowledge of the warp gates.

The intelligence reconfirmed its previous conclusion. Without data on the number of enemy units on the planet or any spaceships in orbit, it could not formulate an offensive plan. It would stand on the defensive. It would destroy any biologic units that entered the vessel.

**Coordinate Grid 20.2-42.8
Planet Gamma Epsilon II**

"Listen up, Team. We've got contacts inbound, multiple landing vehicles tracking toward our present location."

Vandenberg listened as the colonel's voice filled his helmet. The officer's words were of the gravest importance, but they were no surprise. Vandenberg had been tracking them himself for most of the past minute.

Reginald didn't suggest who the new arrivals might be. He didn't have to. Everyone on the Team knew *Westron* didn't have more than one spare lander. Vandenberg's mind raced, trying to find an answer more palatable than the one to which his conclusions had grimly raced. Perhaps *Westron's* com failed. Maybe reinforcements had arrived, backup for the crucial mission. But he stopped himself. Piling coincidence on top of coincidence wasn't useful analysis, especially when he realized it left him still having to explain why a second Martian vehicle couldn't or wouldn't answer their queries. Two communications failures? No, he realized with somber certainty. Whoever is coming, they are not friends.

He felt a burst of panic, a fear that the incoming force was of alien origin, perhaps a wave of the deadly combat 'bots coming from some previously undetected alien spaceship, one that had blasted *Westron* to atoms before landing a field force to wipe out the Team. It was all too logical, at least on the surface, and his terrified mind ignored the gaps, at least for a few seconds. Until Reginald's continued words confirmed his own dawning realization.

"Scanning reports suggest Earth ships." Vandenberg suspected the colonel was trying to hide the hint of relief in his voice. If so, he'd only been partially successful. "Alliance or CEL, I'd guess, based on their drive harmonics."

Vandenberg looked up, a pointless gesture since none of the incoming craft were close enough yet to be visible. The Alliance, at least, was an ally…most of the time, anyway. The Central European League had been lined up against Mars about as often as it had been fighting alongside the Confederation's forces, their allegiance largely based on who was fighting against their blood enemies, Europa Federalis. But he knew that didn't make much difference. There were no allies here, not when the prize was control of staggering alien technology. Whoever was landing, they knew what was here. And they'd come to take it.

"We need to find a good position, Alphas." There was a brief pause, and then Reginald continued, a measure of disgust having crept into his tone. "There's no decent cover, at least nowhere we can get to in time."

Vandenberg heard the unspoken words too…'we've got to stay near here and defend the alien ship.' His mind went back over training…unit tactics, defensive operations. But it was impossible to devise a meaningful plan without knowing what they faced. If there were a couple dozen enemy troops on the way, he had no doubt the Alpha's could prevail, though they would pay a price for the victory. Perhaps they could win even if there were double that many adversaries. The Team was made up of the best, and even though Vandenberg was a newb, he appreciated the combat experience of his comrades. But at some point, trapped out here in mostly open terrain, they would be overwhelmed.

"Vandenberg…wake up."

"Sir!" The lieutenant was still staring up, thinking about whatever was on its way to the surface. He'd missed Reginald's first command, and he silently cursed himself for allowing his mind to wander.

Reinforcing the 'rookie' thing, you damned fool…

"You've got Jones, Ruiz, and O'Reilly. Move a klick south and get your people dug in the best you can. Stay outside the jamming radius, but make sure you can react against any move toward the ship."

"Yes, sir!" Vandenberg felt a rush of satisfaction, pride that the colonel had trusted him with command of several of his comrades. His elation was quickly tempered as it sunk in that Tyrell Jones was one of his charges. He was a rookie, but not a fool, and he knew the veteran sergeant-major was there to keep an eye on him. Babysitter might have been a strong word, but there was no question in his mind. Jones was there to…help…

him.

And there was also no question that he was relieved by that fact…

Chapter Twelve

MCS Viking
Dust Cloud, Sigma Omicron System
310,000 Kilometers from Gamma Epsilon II Warp Gate

Roderick Vance sat silently, staring at the scanner reports. He'd been looking at the same thing for hours now. Four ships. He hadn't been able to get positive IDs, not without giving away *Viking's* location in the dust cloud, but he didn't need his scanners to tell him the new arrivals were Alliance vessels.

He hadn't been able to get detailed information on mass either, but it was clear the ships were considerably smaller than the Martian battleship. He had nothing but speculations on top of conjecture, but nevertheless, he was certain he knew what those vessels were, and why they had come.

Gavin Stark. He'd heard the name before, mostly his father complaining about the Alliance operative's skill and ability. Stark had long been one of Alliance Intelligence's top agents, and recently there had been rumors that the bloodthirsty spy was the heir apparent to the top job when the current Number One died or resigned.

Or when Stark gets tired of waiting and helps him along…

The Confederation had been allied with the Alliance more often than not over the past century, deemed the lesser of evils by the Confederation Council. At least that had been the justification for aligning with the Washbalt government during the last two wars.

But Vance knew the Alliance and its feared intelligence agency were two entirely different things. Alliance Intelligence was the most brutally effective and morally unconstrained organization he'd ever heard of, one as likely to blackmail and intimidate Alliance politicians as a foreign power. And from what Vance had seen and heard, Stark promised to be the most savage—and the smartest—of the succession of monsters who had run the legendary intelligence organization.

Vance had gotten the reports of Gamma Epsilon II and the mysterious wreck on the planet's surface directly from the scouting vessel that had charted the system. That communique had been highly classified, but one of Stark's double agents had managed to obtain the file…and that meant Alliance intel knew, at the very least, that there was something unexplained on the planet, something valuable enough to be subjected to the highest classification levels.

Vance's people had caught the traitor, and the new head of Martian Intelligence had signed his first death warrant, sending the double agent to the execution chambers, without trial or delay. But the damage had been done, and Vance had been left with no choice but to move quickly, and hope he got there first.

He had sent the best he had, the Alphas, to investigate. His first impulse had been to launch a veritable invasion, to surround the planet with warships and land a thousand troops. But secrecy was as important as security. If his people did find alien technology on Gamma Epsilon II, it had to be kept quiet. Gavin Stark could have suspicions, but he couldn't be allowed to confirm those. Ally or no, the Alliance would never sit by and allow the Confederation to gain a monopoly on alien tech. Any of Earth's powers would go to war for those spoils…and the Martians weren't ready for a fight. Not yet. Mars was by far the least populated of the powers, and its strength depended on its readiness. It had to have the newest ordnance, the best. Because it usually had the least.

The last war had been costly, and the Confederation's shipyards were still working on the new fleet. If war came now, the navy would be hard-pressed to defend Mars itself, much less the Confederation's scattered colonies. No, Mars needed two more years, and it would never get that time if the other powers knew it possessed advanced alien technology.

"Send a stealth probe through the gate, Captain. Maximum interference pattern. I want it to perform a quick scan and then return immediately."

"Yes, Mr. Vance."

Vance sat for a moment, putting his head in his hands.

What would you have done, Father? If I bring Viking into the system, odds are we'll end up in a battle with four Alliance warships…and even if we win, we'll have committed an act of war. But if Gavin Stark is able to secure the alien tech…

Vance shook his head. No, there was no way he could risk that.

He tapped the com unit. "Captain Carlson…"

"Yes, Mr. Stark?"

"Bring *Viking* to a position just this side of the warp gate, and prepare for transit on my command."

"Yes, Mr. Stark."

Vance's eyes were fixed on his screen, on the map of the Gamma Epsilon system it displayed. On the rare, deep-in-system warp gate so close to the planet.

He stared for a minute, perhaps two. Then he hit the com again.

"And Captain…bring *Viking* to general quarters, and arm all weapons. I want to be ready to engage as soon as possible after transit."

Upper Atmosphere
Planet Gamma Epsilon II

"All units, check your weapons now."

Thorn Grax was bolted into the lander, secure in his armor as the tiny ship skipped wildly on the upper atmosphere. Grax had been an Alliance Marine for ten years when he'd been recruited by Alliance Intelligence. The offer to join the spy agency's paramilitary forces had come with a jump from sergeant to captain… and a *major* increase in pay. It also allowed Grax to escape the Marines, where his sadistic and brutal behavior had come close to getting him court-martialed…and had effectively removed all hope of gaining a commission one day.

He'd found a home, one well-suited to a bully from the streets of Los Angeles who had only joined the Marines as a way to stay out of prison. Service with the Alliance Intelligence forces offered much higher pay than the standard armed forces, as well as a variety of perks, especially for a sadist who enjoyed inflicting pain.

"Squad one, check."

"Squad two, check."

He listened as his four squads counted off, followed by the special weapons team. He had fifty-two troopers, every one of them culled from the Alliance's regular armed forces just as he had been…and each as maladjusted and morally flexible. Fear. It was Alliance Intelligence's primary weapon, one it used aggressively, to gain information and to execute its directives. The agency had wielded this weapon with such deadly efficiency that its reputation alone was often sufficient to complete the job.

But not this time. Grax had been briefed, albeit barely. He had no confirmation what, if anything, his people would be facing on the ground, but the speculation was there were Confederation soldiers. And the Martians had a martial reputation second to none, not even the famous Alliance Marines.

Grax didn't like going in blind. There had been no Confederation ships in orbit, no notable energy trails or evidence that a significant invasion force had landed. It seemed likely his people would only encounter a few scouts or guards. But he was still nervous.

The lander banked hard, coming around to begin its final approach. The LZ was ten klicks from the ruins of the ancient spacecraft, far enough away to allow his force to form up before advancing. The Intelligence troopers were clad in the Alliance's most advanced combat armor, bristling with weapons and offering the best protection current technology allowed.

Grax's display gave him a feed that allowed him to check the status of each of his soldiers. He'd had the same thing as a Marine sergeant, but he'd been compelled back then to act as though he cared immensely about the men and women under his command. The Alliance Intelligence service allowed a more direct, even brutal demeanor. His soldiers knew if they didn't perform their duty to his satisfaction, he would shoot them himself…and without hesitation. And if he didn't do that and the mission failed, he would expect the same treatment—or worse—from his own superiors. There were few spaces in Alliance Intelligence service between richly rewarded success and ending up in some kind of recycling facility. Grax knew most of his old Marine comrades would be horrified at the realities of his service, but he enjoyed it. And he did his part to ensure those under him felt the same constant pressure to succeed, to excel.

"We're hitting ground in three minutes." His voice was raw, and it sounded angry. Probably because Thorn Grax was *always* angry. "Our orders are clear. We are to land and advance toward the ruins to secure a defensive perimeter. Then we are to await reinforcements before going into the ship."

Grax's eyes darted around his display, monitoring altitude, position, the status of his troopers. He knew his AI was doing all of that already, and that it would alert him to any problems, but the ex-Marine had come up in the days before the sophisticated computers had taken over so much basic functionality. It was also a good way to keep himself occupied. An idle mind wasn't good before battle. It allowed too much time for worry. For fear.

"Black-Two protocols on this one, so if we encounter anyone down there, you fire immediately. Soldiers, guards, civilians…it doesn't matter. Everyone on the planet is to be terminated. That means if anyone bolts, you go after them. Nobody escapes. Understood? Nobody." Grax fought back a smile as he spoke. He wasn't sure why killing people made him so happy, but there was no arguing that it did. With luck, they'd find a group of engineers or explorers down there. The more helpless his victims, the bigger rush it gave him. He far preferred shooting down helpless civvies, preferably as they begged for their lives. But facing Martian troops was another matter, one that required far greater care if he wanted to avoid getting scragged himself.

He flipped a small control next to his right index figure, dimming the display and retracting his blast shield. He could see now, and he looked out over the terrain below. Mostly flat, with a series of small ridges cutting through, running east to west. It was troublesome ground for an attacking force, devoid of much in the way of useful cover. That would hurt any defenders as well, but it was relatively easy to dig in, to create foxholes and makeshift trenches that would give those holding the ground a significant edge.

He watched as the surface came closer, the landing craft moving steadily downward. Then force, breaking rockets, and a slow drop to the dirt.

Grax heard the loud click as the bracket holding his armor in place released, and his feet dropped a few centimeters to the hard metal deck. He turned and scrambled toward the back of the lander, watching as his troopers poured through the hatch.

He followed the mass of armored bodies, stopping just as he reached the open portal. There were alarms going off in his suit, and the voice of his AI reacting to scanning data from the lander.

"Unidentified forces detected," the artificial voice said. "Displaying location now."

Grax looked at the display. Contacts, about twenty. Seventeen to be exact. Laid out about a klick and a half from the wreckage in what looked very much like a defensive line.

Enemies.

Grax felt the tension in his gut. He'd half expected to encounter someone around the ship, but it still hit him like a surprise.

But only seventeen…

He looked at the screen again, staring, counting...and he felt the stress recede. Only seventeen. Even if they were soldiers, he outnumbered them better than three to one. His feral instincts tingled. There were a hundred fifty more troopers on the way down. But Grax had no intention of waiting for them. The kills would be his, and the glory. He would secure the site before the others landed, and the rewards for the operation would fall to him. Promotion, certainly. And credits. Privileges he couldn't have imagined during his days in the Corps.

He smiled, an evil grin, one that would have given anyone seeing it chills. But his face was covered by his visor, and his sinister expression and laugh were for him alone.

He pulled his assault rifle around from its harness on his back and doublechecked the clip in place. Then he leapt down to the sickly yellow powder that was this planet's excuse for dirt.

"Let's move, troopers. There are enemy troops near our destination. And our orders are clear." His voice was dark and ominous.

"Move out."

Chapter Thirteen

Coordinate Grid 20.2-42.4
Planet Gamma Epsilon II

"Looks like about fifty contacts, Alphas. They appear to be heading directly toward us, but we have no confirmation they are hostiles." Reginald knew that was bullshit. They weren't Confederation troops, he was sure of that much. The Alphas didn't broadcast their IDs, but almost any other Martian unit would have. And these figures were silent. He'd caught a hint of some communication, but with the intervening ridges, he'd been unable to hear much…and what he'd gotten was gibberish, most likely encoded with a high encryption level. Not a likely sign that friendlies were on the way.

"We're too bunched up. Vandenberg, take your team out to the left and forward. Try to dig in and get line of fire on any force approaching our center."

"Yes, Colonel."

"Cho…out on the left too, a few hundred meters past Vandenberg. Find a good vantage point and cover the approach."

"Yes, Colonel." Cho's voice sounded like a little girl's, but none of the Alphas, their commander included, doubted the deadly efficiency of their sniper. Except for Vandenberg, they'd all seen her kill with the coldness of a viper…and they'd watched her take impossible shots and plant rounds right through the heads of her targets.

Reginald looked out across the ground in front of him. He'd ordered the Team back to the small ridge, figuring to use the slight lip of ground as cover if anything moved against his people from the alien vessel. Fortunately, the rise peaked quickly and dropped again almost immediately, making it reasonable cover from either side. He ordered his people to hop back to the vessel-side of the ridge, and to find the best spots they could. He didn't like turning his back to the ancient haunted wreckage, but there was no choice.

"Dawes, take your team and cover the right. I'll hold the center."

"Yes, sir."

Reginald looked one way and then the other, quick glances at the five other Alphas positioned with him. "Komack, Vega, Ming…on my left. Morgan and Brown, on the right." He stared ahead as the flurry of acknowledgements flooded in. Nothing yet, but his display told him whoever was approaching would come up over the far ridge any time now.

"Komack, Vega…get that thing deployed, now!" The two men were wrestling with the heavy autocannon. It was a massive weapon, larger than the SAWs the squads of the normal infantry carried. It was almost impossible for two men to handle, even in powered armor. At least two normal men. But Komack and Vega were Alphas, and Reginald knew they'd get the job done.

He'd almost left the heavy weapon behind. It hadn't seemed likely they'd need something like that, not exploring the corridors of an ancient spacewreck. But Alphas always prepared for anything, and Reginald had personally ordered the two troopers to bring the autocannon. Now, he would see it in operation, in an almost perfect scenario for its use.

"One minute, Colonel." Sergeant Vega's voice was distracted, raw. He grunted hard a second later, and Reginald could see the non-com shoving the heavy tripod into place.

"You don't have a minute. Make it thirty seconds."

"Yes, sir."

Reginald moved to the lip of ground at the top of the ridgeline, dropping to his knees and then his belly. He brought his rifle around, extending it forward, syncing the weapon's aiming system with his suit's display and AI. His eyes darted up at the small readout along the top of his visor. Six hundred-thirty rounds. A full clip.

The Alphas carried the most advanced rifle developed by Confederation—indeed, by human—science. The nuclear-powered weapons fired projectiles at hypersonic velocities, impacting a target with massive kinetic energy. The power of the shot allowed the use of a tiny projectile, and it eliminated the need for any propellant in the bullet itself. That allowed a large cartridge to carry over six hundred rounds, versus the thirty to fifty of a conventional firearm. It was an enormous advantage in a firefight, though one he suspected his people would not enjoy. His AI had updated the scanning data, and the energy readings from the approaching forces suggested they were also powered infantry. And Alliance armor and weapons were as advanced as the Confederation's.

"Looks like we've got armored infantry approaching, people. Remember who you are. No foolishness, no bravado. You are to open fire as soon as you have targets." Reginald didn't like giving those kinds of orders. When Red Team Alpha went in, it was usually against terrorists or known enemies. They didn't open fire on unidentified personnel. But this mission was different. Roderick Vance's orders had been clear, and Reginald understood the need that had driven them. No one could be allowed to escape from the planet, not once they had detected the alien craft. It was a distasteful command, rules of engagement that turned his stomach. But he understood. And he would obey.

"Remember, they're here to take this ship away from us, and if they do, it will endanger the very existence of the Confederation. We hold at all costs…and if they retreat, we pursue. And kill them all. You don't have to like it, but I'm ordering you to do it."

Reginald's eyes caught the red warning light above his visor, and an instant later, the dark gray of an armored trooper climbing up over the far ridge line. He took a deep breath, and he nudged his rifle, moving it carefully into place. He stared at the targeting display, lining up the shot. Then he squeezed the trigger.

The soldier stood for an instant, as if frozen in place. Then he fell backwards, slipping down below the ridgeline. Everything was quiet, perhaps for ten seconds, twenty. Then, almost as one, at least two dozen troopers peered over the ridge and opened fire.

The Alphas were back in the shit.

Coordinate Grid 20.2-42.3
Planet Gamma Epsilon II

"I want those SAWs in place now!" Grax was hunched down below the ridgeline, staring at his display and barking out orders. There were Confederation soldiers here, that much was certain. Ten of his troopers were down, seven of them dead. They had cover, but every time they looked up to fire over the crest of the ridge they got hosed down. He'd never seen reaction times like those displayed by these soldiers he was facing. Or marksmanship either.

"We're working on it, sir." Sergeant Figgs was a veteran just like Grax, though he'd only been a private with two years' experience under his belt when he'd been recruited to Alliance Intelligence. Grax knew Figgs was a good soldier, but his frustration was building, and any target was a convenient one.

"Dammit to hell, Figgs, move your ass. I know none of your precious troopers want to get anywhere near the crestline, but if those things aren't firing in thirty seconds, you better worry about me coming over there and putting a bullet between those beady eyes of yours."

"Yes, sir...thirty seconds."

Grax didn't believe it, he'd heard bullshit before. But he suspected he'd put enough fear into the sergeant to get the best possible time out of his crew.

His speakers relayed the sounds from outside his armor,

assault rounds slamming into the ground on the opposite side of the rise. And something else, harder heavier. He'd thought it was a SAW at first, like the ones his forces carried, but then he saw one of his troopers take a hit. The osmium-iridium shell of the man's armor had shattered like glass as the rounds impacted, tearing the soldier to shreds. Whatever the enemy was firing, it was dangerous, damned dangerous…a company level weapon, or even battalion level. Nothing seventeen soldiers would be expected to possess.

He turned to the side, staring to his left, away from the impact area of the enemy's heavy weapon. The incoming fire was lighter on that flank. Any move forward along the right was doomed. The ground was too open, the fire from the enemy's heavy gun too deadly. But maybe on the left…

"Lieutenant Marques, prepare to lead squads one and two forward. I want you to move to the extreme left, and outflank the enemy." He still had numbers, and it was past time he put them to good use. He could screen the enemy's front with third and fourth squads, maintaining enough covering fire to give the flanking force a good jump.

"Yes, sir." Marques didn't sound happy with the orders, but he didn't argue. No one who knew Grax argued with the foul-tempered officer…not if he wanted to live.

"Third and fourth squads, prepare to launch a spread of grenades and follow up with maximum covering fire. If I catch anybody hiding behind the ridge and not shooting, you'll wish the enemy was all you had to worry about."

He crept forward toward the crest, but he could hear the fire slamming into the ground on the other side, the whizzing of rounds zipping by above him. He stopped and flipped off his com, snapping an order to his AI. "Launch a drone."

"Launching."

A loud clicking sound reverberated through his armor, and the felt a jarring sensation as the drone detached and moved up toward the enemy line. The miniature scanning devices were new, so new he doubted the enemy would know what it was. Only he and Marques had the devices, and just two apiece at that. But this was a perfect time to use one.

He looked at his display, the shimmering projection in front of his visor displaying the scene below the flying drone. Ground, yellow, flat, with a few rocks and small depressions in the ground. A nightmare for an assaulting force. Marques' troopers were going to catch hell, even on the far right. But cost wasn't an issue, only success. He was beginning to realize there was something valuable on this planet, that the wreckage was something of extraordinary importance. He was more determined than ever to defeat the enemy before the reinforcements arrived. Before he had to share the credit, and the rewards that would surely follow.

The drone moved steadily toward the enemy line, sending him back the visual data, the location of every enemy soldier.

"Move to the left," he snapped to the AI controlling the device. "Scan the enemy right flank…and transmit the data to Lieutenant Marques."

"Yes, Captain." The voice was robotic, little effort having been made to give it the natural sound of a Marine AI. Alliance Intelligence was a hard branch of the service, and little effort was made to disguise that fact, either to its enemies, or to its own personnel.

Grax watched as the drone's images moved, the device angling, heading toward the enemy's right. In a few seconds, he'd have solid data…and he'd send Marques' people in.

Coordinate Grid 20.2-42.4
Planet Gamma Epsilon II

Elise Cho was lying on her stomach, nestled in a small dip in the ground. It was no more than a tiny low spot, a depression that would be granted undue grandeur with the description ditch. But it was enough for the diminutive sniper, even with the bulk of her armor around her. And it was ideal ground for a sniper, resting as it did at the top of a small hill.

Cho had always been a good shot, from her first day of

Marine training. The Confederation Marines weren't as numerous or well known as their famous Alliance counterparts and sometimes allies. But they were as good, something any member of the Alliance Corps would attest to, albeit grudgingly.

Cho had been a natural, but many who achieved marksmanship success in early training stumbled when trying to take their skills into their combat armor. The Confederation's fighting suits were technological marvels, providing every soldier with the power of an entire unarmored platoon. But as well-designed as they were, with nuclear-powered servos and sophisticated AI control, it was still something entirely different than moving—or fighting—unarmored. The motions were different, the feel of the weapon and the sharp eyesight necessary for a normal sniper replaced by sharp calculations, and a bit of intuition that defied categorization, but was something veterans swore by nevertheless.

She watched as the enemy soldier peered above the crest of the far hill. He was quick, clearly a veteran. He poked up every so often and fired. She'd been watching him, displaying the trait that all great snipers possessed. Patience.

He popped up at random times, changing his location, a meter or two in one direction then back again. Her comrades had fired at him, the ground in front of his position erupting as projectiles slammed into the yellowish dirt of the hill. But he'd been too fast for them every time.

Until now…

She stared, her eyes focused on the ridge with an intensity few people, even her teammates, could understand. There was nothing in her mind, save her rifle and the location of her target. Her AI and scanners would keep watch, warn her of any enemies approaching from another direction. But even with such assistance, few soldiers could so remove themselves from the threats of the battlefield, obsess so aggressively on a single shot.

She watched him pop up again, firing a burst and ducking below his cover once more. She angled her rifle, targeting where he had been. She knew he wouldn't come back in the same place, but she didn't know where he would be. It could be a meter or two in either direction. She just had to be ready…and react more quickly than her target did.

She waited, breathing deeply. Then she held her breath. A second passed. Two.

She saw the motion, a hint at first, and then, almost immediately doubt. Was it real? Or her mind playing tricks on her? Yes, it was real. She saw the enemy soldier, his head rising above the crest, moving about a meter to the left.

Her rifle moved, almost subconsciously, as if it was homing in on the target of its own accord. Training, discipline. She felt each fraction of a second pass, slowly, torturously.

The enemy brought up his rifle, firing. Then, almost immediately, he started to duck back down. But this time he was too late.

Cho's eyes were fixed on the target, her rifle moving even as the enemy took his shot. His head was there, starting its downward move. She moved her rifle a touch, a last bit of gut feel going into the shot's calculation. Then she fired.

The hypervelocity round took perhaps one fiftieth of a second to reach its target, a miniscule time Cho's eyes and consciousness couldn't follow. All she saw was the result as the shot, her enemy falling backwards, the projectile tearing off the top of his head, leaving a spray of blood in the air as the body slipped behind the ridge.

She ducked back down herself, the compulsion to watch her handiwork overruled by her experience and survival instinct. She lay in the small hole, breathing hard, feeling her heart pounding in her chest. No matter how many times she found herself in combat it was always the same. She knew the others—and certainly those outside the team—viewed her as a stone cold warrior, but that was far from the truth. She was just able to control the fear, to stay focused on her deadly job. She had just scored her third kill, taking each of them down with an apparent coolness and calculation that seemed at odds with the sheen of sweat covering her back and the racing heartbeat pounding in her ears.

She rolled over on her side, ready to begin looking for

another target. But a buzzing sound distracted her, an alarm from her scanner. She saw the icon moving across her display, and it took an instant before she understood.

A drone...

But was it a weapon? Or a surveillance unit?

It didn't matter. Whatever it was, she knew what she had to do.

She leapt up onto one knee, bringing her rifle around, tracking the movement. It was a hard shot, she knew, perhaps impossible. But she was determined. There was no time for her usual process. The drone was moving too quickly. She flipped the rifle to full auto, and opened up, moving the stream of projectiles across the sky. Her eyes tried to follow the drone, and she snapped an order to her AI to increase her visor's magnification. She knew she was exposing herself, but she pushed the concern back, focusing on the fast-flying drone. Her clip was half empty, her trail of fire following behind the target. Then she shifted her arms, jerking the rifle to the side, bringing the stream of projectiles around in front of the drone. She watched it fly right into her fire...and then fall to the ground as her shots tore apart its tiny engines.

She felt a rush of elation, pride at a shot even the best snipers in the service would respect. She paused, an instant too long...

Pain. Her leg.

She dropped, first to her knees, but then she pushed herself forward, falling face down to the ground and the cover it offered. The pain in her leg was already gone, her AI injecting painkillers and coagulants into her bloodstream as it treated the wound. She'd taken a shot in her left thigh, and she cursed herself for her carelessness. She could feel her armor's med system taking over, pumping expandable foam into the breach in the suit...and into the wound itself, sealing it, stopping the bleeding. Then a rush of energy, as the system added a stimulant to the analgesics and clotting agents.

She lay where she was, taking a few breaths. Then she rolled over and looked out over the ground in front of her. The med system had worked its small miracle, and she could hardly tell a hypervelocity round had torn through her leg. She knew she wasn't one hundred percent…but she also had work to do, and that was all that mattered. Her comrades were depending on her. The enemy wasn't going to go away because she'd been too slow to duck, and she'd taken a round in her leg.

Her eyes scanned the far ridge, looking for another target.

Chapter Fourteen

Coordinate Grid 20.1-42.3
Planet Gamma Epsilon II

"Keep moving...I want to hit them hard on that flank." Clark Dawes was moving quickly enough that he was almost stumbling forward. He was bent over, keeping the small hill between him and the enemy. His people had pushed far past the line the rest of the Alphas had set up, beyond even the ridge the invaders were using for cover. It was time. Time to hit them hard.

He was ready, his plan clear in his head, but he couldn't shake the edginess, the urge to hesitate. He only had five troopers, and that included himself. It was an almost comically small force to launch an attack. They'd be outnumbered when they came over the hillside, probably by two or three times. But his people were all Alphas, and when it was time to attack, Alphas didn't count the enemy...they went in.

He stopped abruptly. The hill that had been giving him cover was receding, sinking back down to the surrounding plain. He was almost there. If his targets had stayed where they were while his force was behind the hill, his attack would be coming up not only behind the enemy flank, but almost to their rear.

"Alright, listen up. We're going in on three. Once we start there's no turning back, no matter what. We go straight in, firing all the way. No hesitation, no stopping to fire, no looking for cover. We take them out before they can react. *That's* our cover." He paused for a few seconds. "And no stopping for the wounded. If we don't take the enemy out before they can react, they'll overwhelm us. You all got that?" He knew they did, but the wave of acknowledgements was reassuring nevertheless.

He was down on one knee, leaning forward to keep his armored bulk behind the hill. He closed his eyes for an instant, whispering the small prayer to himself as he always did before going into a fight. It had started as a promise to his mother, but now it was an ingrained habit, even a superstition, one fueled by the fact that almost alone among the Alphas, Clark Dawes had never been seriously wounded in battle.

He peered around the end of the hill, looking out over the mostly flat ground beyond. There were no enemy soldiers nearby, none even in sight from where he stood. He turned back, facing his four troopers, and he nodded once. Then he edged forward.

"One." He had his assault rifle out in front of him. He'd popped out a two-thirds spent clip, replacing it with a full cartridge. He hated wasting ammo—he'd seen enough battles lost due to faulty logistics—but the second and a half the autoloader needed to replace spent a spent magazine could be the difference between life and death once his people were moving out in the open.

"Two." He took a deep breath. The suit had upped the oxygen content of his air, and he felt the effects, his energy level increased and his mind sharp, attentive. He had his visor amplification cranked up too…he wasn't taking any chances on not seeing the enemy before they saw him. His people couldn't win an even fight. They needed surprise.

"Three." Even as the word passed his lips he lunged forward, putting himself in the lead of his tiny formation. He pushed off the hill with all the power his armored legs could muster, leaping way up and out from his starting point. Normally, he'd have tried to stay as low as possible, hugging the ground for cover, but right now he wanted to make the first few seconds count…and the high leap gave him a tremendous vantage point from which he could target the enemy in the distance.

He saw the soldiers, visible now as he rose above the intervening terrain. He fired, short bursts at full auto, spraying each exposed enemy position in turn as he sailed through the air. Troopers were dropping all across the field, some from his fire, some from that of the other Alphas. The enemy was beginning to react, to turn to face the attack, but half of them were already down, and the others were sluggish, fighting their surprise. They struggled to bring their weapons to bear, and most of them went down before they could engage. Dawes was already on the way down before any significant enemy fire came in, and by the time it got truly dangerous, he had already hit the ground, continuing forward in the familiar side to side jogging motion, staying low and making himself as difficult a target as possible.

He heard a familiar alarm, a soft bonging sound, and his stomach knotted. A casualty. One of his. He was focused on the battle, his display projection mostly retracted to keep the view through his visor clear. He ignored the alert, keeping his attention focused entirely on the fight underway. It was difficult. An Alpha was down, and he had no idea who it was. It ripped at his guts, but the cold, hard truth was it didn't matter who'd been hit. The mission came first, and there was no time now to stop for wounded…or even to check and see which of his troopers had been hit. Any delay would doom the attack…and probably the entire Team.

He was moving toward the enemy center now, coming up behind the troops who had been firing on Colonel Reginald and the Alphas in the center. They were turning to face his assault now, clearly aware of what had happened to their fellows farther to the left, but Dawes and his attackers still had some elements of surprise left. The Alphas unloaded, gunning down close to a dozen of the enemy before they could return fire effectively, and sending the rest into a panicked retreat.

He watched the enemy soldiers run. They were careless, fleeing with high, bounding steps. He turned and fired, picking one off midway through a huge leap. He kept shooting, even as the survivors began to disappear beyond another ridge about a kilometer away.

Dawes was tense, shaking, energy coursing through his body. His blood was up. He felt an urge to pursue, to chase down and destroy the routing soldiers, but the bonging sound echoed again through his helmet. Another of his Alphas down. That was two out of five, making pursuit a foolhardy prospect for the three of them still in action. His flanking maneuver had been a huge success. It had broken the enemy, bought more time for the rest of the Team. But there was nothing to be gained by putting his people in greater danger. There was nothing left to do now but pull back.

And count the cost.

Coordinate Grid 20.2-42.1
Planet Gamma Epsilon II

"Rally, you worthless slugs. Rally now, or by God, or I'll shoot anyone who runs another meter." Grax was standing behind a steep hillside about a kilometer back from the previous line. He was seething with anger, enraged at his soldiers, at the situation…at everything. His troopers had been attacking, taking losses, but holding their own. He'd just managed to get his autocannons up and firing—and they'd started to take a toll. The supporting fire was just what he'd needed. A few minutes of that, and he would order the final attack. Then everything fell apart.

The panic had started on his left. A small group of enemy soldiers had managed to get around the flank, and they'd hit his troops there hard. He still didn't know how they'd done it, the speed of movement and unit cohesion the operation had required. But he was certain of the result. The attackers had almost wiped out his left, and then they moved against the center, hitting his main formation from the rear. His troopers turned and tried to engage, but it was too late. The entire force fled, including the autocannon teams. The heavy support weapons had taken out a couple of the enemy, Grax was sure of that, but then the crews abandoned their guns and run, just like the rest of the worthless cowards under his command.

Grax had been as surprised as his soldiers, and he'd run no less quickly than any man or woman under his command. He told himself he'd had no choice, that the flight of his soldiers had compelled him to follow. On some level, he realized he'd been driven by his own fear, but he'd never admit that, not even to himself. And none of his people were in a position to dispute his version of events.

He had checked his display half a dozen times, nervously looking for contacts coming up behind his shattered unit. Finally, he let out a heavy sigh. There was no pursuit. That made sense. The enemy had been outnumbered to begin with, and they'd taken losses too.

Still, if they'd stayed tight on our heels...

His eyes caught one of his people still running, ignoring his orders to stand. He swung around, bringing his rifle to bear. "Gomez, I shit you not, you piece of crap. One more step, and you're a dead man." He paused, finding himself hoping the trooper would stop. It wasn't concern for the man in question or hesitation to kill one of his own. Grax didn't care if Arcturo Gomez lived or died. But he was well aware there was a tipping point between employing fear to maintain control and coax compliance...and inciting mutiny. His soldiers knew what would happen to them if they killed their commanding officer, the horrifying end they would meet in the chambers beneath Alliance Intelligence headquarters. That was a strong inducement to maintain order and discipline. But eventually, Grax knew, even that knowledge would be too little to prevent an aggrieved and panicked soldier from putting a few rounds in his back...and that 'eventually' would come a lot faster for a routing and demoralized unit.

Gomez was still running though, paying no heed to the warnings. Grax swore under his breath and fired, sending a burst of projectiles into the fleeing soldier's back. The hypervelocity rounds tore through the man's armor and ripped into his body. The trooper pitched hard forward and stumbled a few more meters before falling face down to the ground.

Grax turned, staring at the rest of his soldiers. There were only fifteen remaining, less than a third of the force he'd started with. They'd been savaged in combat, and it showed. He could feel their anger, the restive mood lurking dangerously close to mutiny. "Now, don't make me blow any more of you away. I said I would do it, and I wasn't kidding."

There was no response, nothing on the com but silence. That was the worst thing he could hear, and he knew it. But he wasn't done.

"We've got reinforcements inbound. They will be here in less than thirty minutes. *Shadow* is monitoring our com even now, so get your shit together. You hear me?"

It was his ace in the hole. *Shadow*. And the reserves his troopers knew were on the way. Alliance Intelligence forces were always under surveillance. Their AIs spied on them, their supporting spacecraft monitored them at all times. Their non-coms were rewarded for turning them in for any transgression, as were their officers. There was no such thing as paranoia in the Alliance Intelligence service. If you thought someone was spying on you, they almost certainly were. If you didn't think anyone was watching…you were probably wrong.

His soldiers knew that, and he could feel the tension ease. They were still angry, no doubt, blaming him for their losses and lusting for his blood. But their fear was greater. Not the stark, uncontrollable terror of the battlefield, but the logical, well-reasoned fear of their Intelligence overlords. A few minutes before, when getting away from the enemy was all any of them could think about, emotion might have overruled good sense. Now, they'd recovered enough to understand that killing their commander was a dead end. Especially given the fact that there were a hundred-fifty of their kind on the way down to the surface.

The pending arrival of the reserves bolstered morale too. A hundred fifty fresh troops would give them enough force to get revenge, to crush the enemy. But those soldiers on their way down were a threat too. If the exhausted survivors murdered their commander under the watch of *Shadow's* scanners and com monitoring, there was little doubt the newly arrived troops would be ordered to kill them all. Disobedience wasn't tolerated in the Alliance Intelligence service any more than failure. And there was no place to run on this miserable rock out in the middle of nowhere. No way to escape. Mutiny meant almost certain death.

The troopers began to move slowly, forming up around their commander. The silence on the com was broken by chatter, and by orders moving back and forth. Grax knew the crisis had passed, at least one of the problems he faced more or less resolved. But there were others pressing down on him. His mind hadn't even begun to tackle how he was going to explain how he'd managed to lose two-thirds of his soldiers and still lost the fight. He even wondered if the fresh troops would carry orders to execute him summarily, punishment for his failure.

No, not in the middle of the fight here. Too disruptive.

The bullet in the dark will come later, back on the ship. Unless you redeem yourself…

"Form up in line," he shouted. "We're going back in…as soon as the rest of our forces land." He paused ominously. He was senior to the commanders of the other three ships' contingents. If he took command, crushed the enemy and seized the ruined ship, he just might escape punishment for the earlier debacle. "And I *will* shoot any of you who even hesitates. Is that understood?"

Chapter Fifteen

Coordinate Grid 20.2-42.4
Planet Gamma Epsilon II

Vandenberg was moving toward the center, his four soldiers following close behind. Colonel Reginald had issued the recall, ordering everyone back to the original position. The enemy had been decisively defeated and driven back in a panicked rout, leaving two-thirds of their number dead or wounded on the field. Reginald had a pair of drones up, watching for any attempt by the enemy to rally and attack again, and there was no sign of any activity.

Vandenberg's team had come through the fight unscathed, and he was grateful that most of the action had been on the other flank. He felt guilty for those thoughts, and he mourned for the Alphas who'd been lost in the fighting, but at least he'd been spared the pain of losing those under his direct command. He'd been self-assured during his years at the Academy, cocky even, but now he was realizing what a fragile thing confidence could be. He felt out of his depth, and he was uncertain in the command role the colonel had given him. Part of him wanted to run, to flee from the responsibility. But the discipline was still there, holding him like a vice.

He walked up toward the small cluster of crates that constituted the Team's command post and supply dump. Reginald was sitting on a boulder, his visor retracted, chewing on a nutrition bar. The dense, protein-packed field rations didn't compare well to what most vets called 'real food,' but it was a hell of a lot better than the intravenous sustenance the suits administered during battle. Chemicals shot into a trooper's veins could sustain life, even give an energy boost. But they did nothing to alleviate the ache of an empty belly.

"Sit for a minute, all of you. Have something solid to eat while you can."

Reginald seemed calm, something Vandenberg found difficult to understand. The Alphas had landed twenty strong. Six of them were dead now, and one gravely wounded. The colonel and Elise Cho had injuries their suits and med systems could manage, but that didn't mean either one was at one hundred percent anymore. They still had no contact with *Westron*...for all they knew the ship had been blasted to atoms by whatever vessels—*Alliance ships*, he reminded himself, *we know it's Alliance Intelligence*—had landed the force they'd just fought.

Vandenberg walked up, looking around before choosing another large rock and sitting down. He popped his visor, the planet's air feeling like a blowtorch as it rushed in against his face. He felt at his side, his gloved hand poking at the small pack attached to his armor, retrieving one of the food packets. He fumbled at bit, having some difficulty getting hold of the small bar and moving it to his mouth. He looked both ways, seeing his comrades doing more or less the same thing, but with considerably greater dexterity. He'd learned to move and fight in his armor at the Academy, but things like grabbing a quick bite in the field were the province of veterans, not formal instruction.

There was a moment of silence, as the group of warriors sat and ate silently. Finally, Vandenberg said, "Sir, shouldn't we be doing something? Besides eating?" He glanced behind Reginald, to a small row of dark figures a few meters beyond, the bodies of the dead Alphas lined up neatly. Dawes and his group had brought their dead back with them, most likely because they wanted to be absolutely sure the troopers *were* dead and not just suffering equipment failure.

Reginald's matter-of-fact attitude seemed odd to Vandenberg considering their situation, even mildly disrespectful to the Team's dead. That didn't mesh with what he'd seen of the Alphas back at base, of the close-knit culture they shared.

"What would you have me do, Alex?" Reginald's tone was soft, calm. "We've got no contact with the ship, no idea what is up there, hostile or otherwise. I've got drones up, in case the enemy regroups and comes back at us, but the best thing we can do now is rest and eat. We may be here for quite a while, and we've got to stay sharp."

"What about them?" He gestured toward the line of bodies.

"They're our comrades, Alex, our friends. They were close to us in a way few could understand. We will remember them always, honor them forever, see to their loved ones when we get back. But right now they are just dead bodies, and the greatest tribute we owe to them is to look to ourselves, to do everything possible to prevent more Alphas from sharing their fate. Mourning now, losing focus…it is the worst thing we could do for them."

Vandenberg listened to the colonel's words. He was still uncertain, his mind drifting back to the dead, to recollections of each of them. But then he began to understand, to realize Reginald was focused now on the troopers who were still alive.

He remembered a talk he'd had with Jones back on Mars, something the old sergeant-major had told him. 'The dead are dead, there's nothing more we can do for them. There's always time to mourn later, but the poorest memorial we could give to our lost friends in to swell their ranks because our minds wandered from the battle at hand.'

Vandenberg looked at the rest of his troops, watching as they followed the colonel's orders, sitting, pulling rations from their packs. He was even more impressed now at how the Alphas could focus on the mission with unyielding intensity. They'd lost thirty percent of their number killed already, and the operation wasn't over yet. Those were the worst losses the Team had suffered in any op, Vandenberg knew that from his review of the Alpha's history. And yet, on some level at least, they were taking it as business as usual.

Suddenly, he heard a buzzing sound. It had come from Reginald's suit, but a few seconds later, his own alarms began to sound. He glanced up at his display. The projection was truncated with his visor retracted, just a small band of data inside the top of his open helmet. But there was no doubt about what it showed him.

Ships incoming. More assault craft. A lot more.

His mind raced. Reinforcements...the thought drifted into his mind, and out just as quickly. If a Martian ship had arrived in orbit, it would have contacted the Alphas already. No, the readouts coming in were the same as before. Another wave of Alliance craft, three times the size of the first.

He did the calculations. One hundred fifty fresh troops on the way down. The Alphas were good, but they were about to be outnumbered twelve to one.

Reginald stood up abruptly, speaking into the com. "Alright, Alphas...we're not done yet. We've got a fresh wave inbound. So, finish your feast and drain your glasses...because we're about to be back in the shit." He paused and looked over at Vandenberg. The rookie knew the colonel was observing him, checking up on him. His pride took control, and he stood up himself, standing tall, motionless, a stern look on his face. He was scared shitless...but he'd be damned if he was going to show it.

"Finish up, Alex." Reginald gestured toward the half-eaten ration bar in the lieutenant's hands. "You'll be glad you had something to eat. It may be a long while before you get another chance." The colonel paused a few seconds, holding Vandenberg's gaze. Then his visor snapped shut.

Vandenberg shoved the rest of the bar in his mouth and clicked the control, closing his own helmet. "Expand display," he snapped to the AI, half amazed that the sophisticated computer understood what he was saying through the mouthful of nutrition bar.

The projection expanded, covering the top half of his visor. He looked at the scanner feed, watching the wave of landers. There were definitely three times as many as in the first assault. The Alphas had won the first round, but he suspected the cause of that success was as much the enemy's surprise at meeting so elite and capable a defensive force as anything else. Simply put, they'd been arrogant, careless…and the Alphas had taught them a lesson. But that victory had not been without cost.

His eyes were glued to the display, watching the dots move closer to the surface. He respected Colonel Reginald and his comrades, thought highly of their skill and courage. But he knew looking at the wave of landers that the Alphas didn't have a chance. They'd extract a price, certainly, take down a lot of the enemy soldiers before they were overwhelmed and destroyed. But they *would* be overwhelmed and destroyed. In a dense jungle, a deep forest—even a built up area—perhaps they could hide and wage a hit and run campaign, blunt the enemy's numbers, use their superior tactical ability. But out in the open? With no cover save a few gentle hills and rolling ridges?

He shook his head. There was no place to defend, no position that provided the cover they would need to mount a credible defense.

Except one place…

Coordinate Grid 20.2-42.1
Planet Gamma Epsilon II

"Come on, come on…move it. Get out of those landers, and get formed up. We're attacking in five minutes." Grax was walking up and down the line of assault craft, shouting at the new arrivals. The sleek ships were designed for atmospheric insertions, and they were trim, streamlined. But now the elegant ships were blackened and pockmarked, showing the wear from a wild ride through the planet's thick atmosphere. The landers' heat shields had held, but the ships were finished. They were one-use vehicles, designed to get troops to the ground as quickly as possible.

Grax had stood just outside the LZ, watching the landing craft complete their final approaches. Then, once they had landed, he moved up, even as the lead elements were streaming out of the assault ships' hatches, and he started barking out orders to the new arrivals.

The other captains had put up a brief show of resentment at his effective seizure of command, but the Alliance Intelligence service had clear regs, and Grax's seniority supported his claims. If that hadn't been enough, the vicious invective he hurled at anyone showing the slightest hesitation to follow his orders sealed the deal. He was a rough character, one who had shown his ruthlessness many times. Even among the pack of brutal killers Alliance Intelligence had recruited for its ground forces, Grax was intimidating.

Now, he had one hundred sixty-four troops under his command. It was time to take his revenge, to redeem his reputation.

To save his life.

"What's the enemy strength?" Don Burke was one of the other captains, next in seniority after Grax and the force's second in command. He was a big man, and in armor he towered above his new commander.

Grax hesitated. "About fifteen," he said softly.

"Fifteen? That's all? How many were there when you first hit them?"

"More than that," Grax said, anger creeping into his voice. "None of that matters. Don't underestimate these soldiers. They're elite for sure. I want you in the center, with Wendell on the left and Salvatore on the right. The enemy line is less than a kilometer. I want to overlap at least half a klick on each side and envelop them."

"Isn't that a lot of trouble? If we're only talking about fifteen troops, why don't we just rush them straight out and finish this? It shouldn't take long."

"They're good, Burke. They're really good. We're not taking any chances. We go in, get around them, and we chase every last one of them down. No prisoners, no survivors. Once the attack starts, we don't stop until we're the only ones alive on this planet. No matter what the cost." A pause. "You got me?"

Burke didn't look satisfied, but he nodded. "Yes, I got you."

"Good. Now get your troops formed up. We're moving out

in three minutes." Grax turned and walked away, glad he was suited up, the grimace on his face hidden by his helmet. His stomach was twisted in knots, and he was sweating like a pig. He was afraid, scared to go back against the enemy. He tried not to admit it to himself, but that much, at least, had proven to be a losing battle. He'd never seen troops fight like that small band of warriors, and even now, with overwhelming numbers at his disposal, he was flat out terrified.

His one saving grace, the force driving him onward, was a simple one. He was even more afraid of what awaited him if he survived another failure.

A shiver rippled down his body. Then he took a deep breath and picked up his pace.

Coordinate Grid 20.2-42.8
Just Outside the Alien Vessel
Planet Gamma Epsilon II

Vandenberg stared at the alien ship looming in front of him. It had been his idea to pull back, to lure the enemy into the jamming zone...and then into the haunted vessel itself. It had been a plan born of desperation, the only way he could think of to blunt the enemy's numbers. He'd suggested it to Colonel Reginald, his courage bolstered by his certainty the Team's commander would dismiss it out of hand. But Reginald had just stood there quietly for perhaps half a minute. Then he'd said yes.

Next time, keep your mouth shut...

He stared into the darkness, beyond the great jagged tear in the ship's hull, the opening Jacobs and his people had gone through, and from which the terrifying combat 'bots had emerged and killed his comrades. He knew the landers had come down, that an overwhelming force of enemy troopers was even now moving on the surviving Alphas. The alien ship was their only chance, but he was still frozen, looking with abject terror at the portal he knew he'd have to enter in a matter of seconds. He honestly didn't know if he'd be able to force himself to take the steps.

He looked up, watching as Komack and Vega hauled the heavy autocannon up the outside hull of the ship. The massive weapon would be impossible to maneuver in the corridors and chambers of the ship, but its firepower was too great to sacrifice. He stared at the two Alphas, watching as they struggled to get the gun in place. There was a flat area, about six meters up, and it offered a strong vantage point to cover the entrance to the vessel. Vandenberg realized that manning the gun would be dangerous, perhaps suicidal, that Komack and Vega would hold their position until the last second before they abandoned the autocannon and tried to get down and into the ship before they were killed. He was sure their chances were poor, but he still found himself envying them as his eyes dropped back and stared into the eerie darkness.

"Alex, I'm going to go in first, with Ming, Cho, and Brown." The words startled him. His com had been silent since the Team had reentered the jamming zone. But when he turned, he saw Reginald standing about ten meters from him, transmitting via direct laser com. "I want you to follow with Ruiz, O'Reilly, and Jones."

"Yes, sir." He took a deep breath, grateful his people wouldn't have to go in first.

"Dawes will be behind you, with Isaacs. Komack and Vega will set up the autocannon and hold the enemy back as long as possible."

"Yes, Colonel." Vandenberg knew he was in the middle because he was the rookie, but he didn't care. It was the right call, and he was damned glad he'd have friends in front and behind.

The colonel walked up toward the gash in the hull, followed by two figures Vandenberg knew were Ming and Brown. He paused and turned back toward Vandenberg. "Wait one minute, and then follow us in."

"Yes, sir." Vandenberg struggled to keep his tone firm, but he didn't know how successful he'd been. "We'll be right behind you."

Reginald nodded, a cumbersome gesture in powered armor. Then he stepped forward, pausing for a second before he continued…and stepped through the tear in the hull and into the darkness.

Vandenberg watched as Ming and Brown followed. Then he turned back, contacting Jones with his laser com. "Sergeant, we're going in. I want everybody to stay tight, no more than five meters between us. I'll go first, and you bring up the rear."

"Sir, maybe I should take the lead…"

"I've got it, Sergeant. The colonel is up front anyway. Ruiz behind me, O'Reilly next. Pass it down. "

"Yes, sir." The sergeant-major's voice was edgy, but Vandenberg caught a hint of approval too, and a quick smile passed over his lips. He was terrified, scared worse than he'd ever been in his life. But he was going to do his job, no matter what. He was new, untested, a rookie. But he was an Alpha, and no matter how terrified he was, how uncertain, he was going to act like one.

He glanced up at his display, at the chronometer. Forty-five seconds since he'd watched Brown disappear into the murky blackness of the alien ship. He stepped forward, putting one foot up on the jagged metal of the torn hull. His eyes dropped down, to the remains of one of the battle 'bots. It was torn to bits, but even sitting there as a pile of wreckage it was a sobering sight. Vandenberg remembered the hideous machines, firing multiple weapons simultaneously.

Okay…it's time.

He wrestled one last time with himself, and then, with a titanic effort, he thrust the fear deep down, to the recesses of his mind. He reached up, grabbed ahold of the edges of the hole, and he stepped inside.

Chapter Sixteen

Bridge
AIS Shadow
In Orbit Around Gamma Epsilon II

Gavin Stark sat behind the captain's desk, watching the display. The reinforced strike force was finally on the move. Captain Grax had taken command of the entire operation, and he was leading it in. Stark had almost sent a communique, orders to relieve the disgraced officer. Stark had been angry at the way the damned fool had gotten his force chewed up…and absolutely livid at the panicked rout he'd watched on his scanners. But then he realized…Grax had nothing to lose. Surely the officer knew the fate he'd suffer, the punishment for his failure. Fear was a prime motivator, and there were many ways to use it. And letting Grax try to redeem himself seemed like a good bet.

Not that it would matter. Grax had run, along with his soldiers. As far as Stark was concerned, that was unforgivable. Grax and any survivors from the defeated force would have a date with the airlock when they returned to *Shadow*, regardless of the results of the second attack. But if the officer's desperation drove his assault harder, Stark could wait awhile to mete out his particular form of justice.

"Number Three, we're getting data from two of the probes. Residual energy trails, sporadic contacts out toward the system's asteroid belt."

"A ship?"

"Too early to tell, but it definitely could be."

"You'll have to do better than that, Commander."

"Yes, sir..." The officer sounded nervous, tentative. Stark smiled, enjoying the effect his reputation had on his subordinates. "Redirecting the probes toward the belt. We should be able to get more detailed readings in...half an hour."

"Fifteen minutes, Commander."

"Ah...yes, sir. Fifteen minutes."

Stark cut the line and punched at the keys on the workstation, bringing up a partial system map. He stared at it, zooming in on the area between Gamma Epsilon II and III.

Yes, the asteroid belt...

He punched up the scanner data. The belt was thick, heavy with radioactives. A perfect place for a ship to hide.

There were troops down on the planet, almost certainly Martians.

And that means there's a ship here somewhere...

The more he thought about it the surer he became. The energy trails made perfect sense. The line was exactly the course a ship would have taken toward the nearest place to hide. Especially if it had left orbit on the opposite side of the planet from the warp gate. The vessel *was* in the asteroid belt.

Stark slammed his hand down on the com unit. "Captain, *Wraith* and *Wight* are to move immediately toward the asteroid belt, along a line from the planet through the locations of the energy trails the probes detected."

"Yes, Number Three. I will relay your commands."

"I want them at battlestations and ready to engage anything they find. They are to maintain total communications silence, and any vessels they encounter are to be destroyed without warning."

"Yes, Number Three."

Stark leaned back in his chair. The ground forces would soon wipe out the handful of Martian troops down on the planet... and *Wraith* and *Wight* would find and eliminate the ship that ferried them to the system. In an hour, perhaps two, he would be the master of the system. And of the strange, wondrous ruin on the planet's surface.

He smiled. It had been careless of Roderick Vance to assume he could slip in with a small ground team and secure the wreck.

Perhaps he doesn't believe we got the information.

But that didn't ring true. The Martians had executed the double agent. He was almost sure *those* reports had been accurate. *He* might have killed an agent on suspicion alone—indeed, he most certainly would if it served his purposes—but the Martians were too soft for that. There'd been no trial, no delay, just a swift trip to the death chamber. He couldn't imagine Martian Intelligence behaving that way unless they believed vital information had been compromised. Were *certain* it had.

So why didn't you send more forces? Is it just foolishness? Youth and inexperience?

Vance was new to his post, a young man with no history in espionage. Indeed, Stark himself had put the Martian in his new job, at least in a way. Collin Vance had been a capable man, a dangerous adversary, so when the opportunity to strike had arisen, Stark hadn't hesitated. It had been almost ridiculously easy, a simple blackmail operation of a member of the flyer's maintenance crew. The technician had been given a choice, cooperate and become a rich man…or refuse and be ruined. He hadn't even put up a decent fight, accepting the bribe, and the promises of discretion, and doing Stark's bidding.

The assassination had gone off without a hitch. Indeed, as far as he could tell, the Martians hadn't even found any conclusive evidence of foul play. And, as he'd expected, the younger Vance took his father's place at Martian Intelligence. By all accounts, Roderick was an intelligent man, one capable of becoming a dangerous opponent someday. But he was almost certainly less capable now than his father had been.

But is he this careless?

Stark shook his head.

He tapped the com unit again. "Captain, order *Specter* to proceed back to the warp gate and take up a defensive position there."

"Yes, sir."

"And if anything comes through…anything at all…they are to attack and destroy it. Is that understood?"

"Yes, Number Three. Understood."

Bridge - MCS Westron
En Route to Asteroid Belt
Gamma Epsilon System

"The probes have changed course, Captain. They are on a course almost directly toward us."

Silver nodded. "Thank you, Lieutenant."

She held back a sigh. Her passive scanners couldn't tell her much at this range, little more than the direction of the probes the Alliance ships had launched. She'd felt a pang of worry when the scanning devices moved around the planet, following her basic course away from Gamma Epsilon II…but now they'd changed direction and were heading right toward *Westron*. Coincidence was one thing. Stacking them on top of each other was quite another.

She watched as the two small dots moved slowly across the display. Unlike *Westron*, the probes weren't trying to hide. They were banging away with their active scanners at full power, and when they got close enough, they'd find *Westron*, asteroid belt or no.

"Captain, we're picking something up, a larger contact…no two. Coming from planetary orbit."

Of course. Ships. *The probes picked up our trail, and they assumed we were hiding in the asteroid belt. Where else would we be?*

"Very well, Lieutenant. I want updated data as it comes in."

"Yes, Captain."

She looked back at the display. There was a small bump on the edge of the icon representing Gamma Epsilon II—the two ships, still too close to the planet for the screen to display their symbols separately from the planet's. Indeed, the scanners hadn't even confirmed the contacts were ships, but Silver already had comprehensive data on the Alliance vessels, courtesy of the buoys she'd left at the warp gate. Fighting one of them would be a difficult proposition for *Westron*, a battle that would see Silver's ship outmassed and outgunned. Battling two was close to hopeless.

But less hopeless than fighting four at once…

"Lieutenant, bring us to battlestations. Load all missiles. Run full diagnostics on all batteries."

"Yes, Captain." Silver could hear the shakiness in her officer's voice. "Battlestations. All weapons stations on full alert."

Silver stared at the main display as the bridge was bathed in a red glow from the battlestations lamps. The two symbols had moved away from the planet now, heading almost directly toward *Westron*. Whatever doubt she had was gone.

"Activate positioning jets. Move us toward the asteroid at 201.355.007. I want to get in there tight, close enough so they can't get a solid read until they're right on top of us."

"Yes, Captain."

"And reprogram all missiles. Cancel standard nav data, and set for sprint mode operation. Prepare to fire as soon as they enter the belt."

"Reprogramming missiles, Captain." There was surprise in the officer's tone.

Missiles were a long-range weapon, typically fired before ships were in energy weapons range of each other. Hitting a target dead on at that distance was a feat that defied normal mathematical probability, so missile tactics were based around the effort to score near misses, to put missiles one or two kilometers from an enemy vessel before they detonated. The power of an explosion, even the massive two hundred megaton warheads of anti-ship missiles, dissipated quickly in space. A close enough hit could cause some damage to a hull from heat, but most of the effect came from bathing a vessel with massive amounts of radiation, killing crews and damaging sensitive systems. Missile volleys were rarely decisive, but they were vital to weaken enemy forces before the climactic energy weapons duel.

Sprint missile tactics were relatively new and largely untested, a difficult tactic pioneered by an Alliance captain named Augustus Garret. At point blank range it was possible to aim missiles more precisely, inflicting much greater damage on target vessels. But it was difficult, and it required a crack crew working at peak efficiency to switch over to energy weapon fire almost immediately. Silver had never seen it done, she'd only heard about it secondhand. But she was fishing around, trying to pull an ace from the hole to save her ship.

"Missiles ready for sprint mode launch, Captain. All laser batteries report fully operational status."

"Very well, Lieutenant. Time until approaching vessels enter range?" She asked, but she already knew the answer.

"Fifty-one minutes, Captain. Assuming they maintain acceleration at present rates to the half way point and then decelerate the rest of the way."

"Very well."

Fifty-one minutes. And then we'll have one hell of a fight on our hands…

MCS Viking
Sigma Omicron System
75,000 Kilometers from Gamma Epsilon II Warp Gate

"Approaching the warp gate, Mr. Vance. Projected transit in eleven minutes."

"Thank you, Captain Hinch." Vance was standing along the outside perimeter of the bridge. The captain had yielded his chair earlier, but now *Viking* was heading forward, possibly into battle, and the intelligence director wanted the ship's commanding officer exactly where he belonged. There were four Alliance vessels somewhere past the warp gate, and if they were concentrated together, close to the transit point, *Viking* was going to have one hell of a time handling them.

Vance sighed softly. On some level, he'd known how things would go, ever since the moment one of his agents had been caught passing on information to the Alliance about the mysterious wreckage found on Gamma Epsilon II. Still, he'd had to try to secure the site, to move at least some portion of the wreck to a secure location. He regretted that he'd had to send the Alphas in first, putting the twenty commandoes and *Westron* into deadly danger. But there had been no choice. He had to know what Alliance Intelligence was up to before he could follow through with his plan. And the Alphas were the bait.

"I want us ready for action as soon as we emerge, Captain." There was no point in delay, only more danger. The situation was complicated, and if he didn't handle it just right, the Confederation could be at war in a matter of hours. A war it wasn't in a position to win, or even survive. Not yet.

"Yes, sir…but you know we'll be offline for a while after transit. A minute, perhaps up to two. If they're waiting close enough to the gate, they'll get off the first shot."

No one really understood why a warp transit scrambled so many ship's systems, including the main computers and AIs. It was a well-known phenomenon, but not one that had ever been adequately explained. The variable nature of the affected period, as little as forty-five seconds or as much as three and a half minutes, seemed almost totally random. An experienced crew could get their ship into a fight more quickly than less capable counterparts after they regained control, but they were just as compelled to wait helplessly while their systems rebooted.

"I understand, Captain. I know your people will do the best they can. That's all I can ask."

"Thank you, sir." The captain paused. "Mr. Vance, you really should be strapped in before we go through the gate. It can be a rough ride sometimes, and if we go right into action…" He started to get up.

"Sit down, Captain." Vance waved his hands toward *Viking's* commander. "You need to be right there, fighting your ship." Vance turned and walked toward one of the auxiliary stations around the perimeter of the bridge. "I'll be fine here." He sat down, reaching under the seat and pulling the harness straps across his chest.

"Transit in five minutes, Mr. Vance. Going to general quarters now."

Vance just nodded, turning his head toward the lamps now bathing the bridge in an eerie red glow. He'd never been on a warship in battle before. He'd hardly even seen one before the last month.

Now he would get a firsthand experience of combat in space. Captain Hinch and his crew were among the best in the Confederation navy, and *Viking* one of the most powerful warships…at least until the new generation of superbattleships began moving out of the shipyards. *Sword of Ares* and *John Carter* would make *Viking* look like a yacht. The two megaships were larger even than the *Yorktown* class the Alliance was set to introduce. The powers had all been in an unrelenting arms race since shortly after the Second Frontier War ended, and average ship sizes had more than doubled over the past decade.

He glanced around the bridge, looking at each officer in turn, disciplined, focused. The Confederation's military had always been in the top tier of the forces of the Superpowers, at least ship for ship and man for man. They had to be. There were always fewer of them.

"Two minutes, Mr. Vance. All systems report ready for transit."

Vance started at the display, at the large, slowly rotating mass in the center of the screen. The warp gates were poorly understood, at least in terms of why they did the wondrous things they did. But Vance knew all he needed to know now. Eleven point four microseconds after *Viking* entered the gate it would emerge nineteen light years away, in the Gamma Epsilon system. He found the mathematics hard to grasp, especially the part that described how parts of *Viking* would exist in both systems and somewhere in between simultaneously. But he didn't need to understand the physics, just the effect.

"One minute to transit. All personnel, prepare for warp gate insertion."

Vance pulled his thoughts from such esoteric concerns as the higher mathematics of warp gate modeling. He had something far more pressing to worry about.

Winning a battle without starting a war.

Chapter Seventeen

Coordinate Grid 20.2-42.8
Just Outside the Alien Vessel
Planet Gamma Epsilon II

"Keep firing, Vince. We've got to hold them off as long as possible." Sergeant Aaron Vega was kneeling next to the heavy autocannon, holding a fresh magazine in his hands. He outranked Komack, but he also knew the corporal was the better shot, and he'd yielded the gunner's position. There might be room for petty rivalries in many areas of the military, but not in Red Team Alpha. In the Team, the best man or woman did the job. Period.

"I'm firing, man. I'm firing." The corporal's arms were extended, angling the big weapon and moving its stream of fire over the enemy position. He wasn't aiming, not really, just spraying thousands of projectiles all around. He'd have to peer around the heavy chunk of the ship's hull to really aim, and that was likely to be a very unhealthy thing to do.

Vega looked at the twisted shard of metal he and his cohort were using for cover. It was like nothing he'd seen before, millennia old, but it still looked almost new. There was no rust, no wear, almost no dirt marring its dull sheen.

They had placed the gun in an almost a perfect spot, raised above the primary approach to the alien vessel and almost completed protected. The enemy, confident in their numbers, had frontally attacked, storming the ship, but the fire from the heavy gun cut them down and sent them stumbling back for cover. Now, they'd set up their own SAWs and opened up on the two Alphas, but the strange metal of the alien craft was utterly proof against their fire.

"How we doing on ammo, Sarge?" Komack's tone was edgy. Vega knew his comrade already had the answer to his own question.

"Three more mags, Vince."

"What the hell are we going to do when that's gone? How do we get down there and follow the others?" The route down to the ground and through the entry to the ship was only twenty meters away, but it might as well have been lightyears. The area in between was a killing zone, swept by unceasing enemy fire. There was no chance they could make it. Not that way.

"We're going to have to find another way. Maybe there's another breach…somewhere up here."

Komack turned the gun to the right, maintaining fire at full auto. "If that's your idea of a pep talk, Sarge, it needs work."

"I'll keep that in…" A loud explosion cut him off. The sound had come from behind, higher up on the ancient vessel.

"What the hell was that, Sarge?"

Vega had turned, looking up at the looming hull of the great ship. "Sounded like a grenade…"

Another loud crash erupted, closer this time. And a third, in front of them, lower on the ship.

"They're shelling us with grenade launchers." Vega exhaled hard. Alliance armor had built-in grenade launchers, and the standard magazine carried a dozen rounds.

A dozen times maybe a hundred thirty troops still up and fighting…

"They're going to get us eventually, Vince." Vega was torn. Staying until their ammo was gone had just gotten a lot more dangerous. Colonel Reginald's orders had been clear…hold the position until it was compromised. Then get the hell out.

It's compromised as shit now…

But there were still a lot of enemy troops out there, and he and Komack were keeping them pinned down, buying time for the others.

"Let's fire one more magazine…then we'll bug out."

"Alright, Sarge. Sounds good to me."

Vega reached down, dragging the heavy mag over toward the gun. Unarmored, he doubted he could have pushed it a centimeter, but his nuclear-powered arms shoved it like it was an empty cardboard box. He slammed it into place, shoving the empty one hard, sending it rolling noisily down the ship's hull to the ground.

"Alright, Vince. Make this one count."

Vega turned, and then he saw it. A grenade…coming right at him. "Incoming!" he screamed, diving to the side as he did. But his move was too late.

The projectile landed just behind him, and an instant later it detonated, sending heavy shards of iridium and depleted uranium shrapnel flying all around.

Time seemed to slow, and he was unaware of its passing. He felt himself moving, floating, and then suddenly, he was on the ground, looking up. He felt strange, a feeling lower on his body, as if an agonizing pain had hit him, but for so short a time, he wasn't sure now it had actually happened. He'd felt fear, anger, but they were gone now too, replaced by a strange melancholy.

"Sarge! Sarge, can you hear me?" A voice, from far away. No, not far. Just over him. Familiar.

Yes, I know that voice…

"Vince?"

"It's me, Sarge."

Clarity moved through his mind as he heard the tone of his comrade's voice, understanding.

He's scared…I'm hit. Yes…the med system, the AI. Painkillers, happy juice…

He realized he'd been hit, that his suit's trauma control system had taken over, injected him with a series of drug cocktails to kill the pain, fight depression and despair.

"How bad?" He asked, but the drugs were telling him he

didn't care.

"It's bad, Sarge. Really bad." It was a stark admission, but Alphas didn't lie to each other. Not ever.

Vega tried to move, to sit up, but the wave of pain ripped through even the massive dose of narcotics the AI had given him. He only got up a few centimeters, but that was enough. He froze, holding himself in place despite the pain, staring at his legs. Both of them. Lying about three meters away, armor-covered and bloodsoaked.

"Shit…"

"Come on, Sarge. We gotta get you outta here." Komack slid around, reaching out and shoving an arm under Vega's shoulder.

"Arghhhhhh…" Vega couldn't hold back the scream as the pain ripped through him. "No way, Vince." He looked up at his display. The visor was cracked, and half the projection was fuzzy and unreadable. But the med stats were still there.

"I'm done, Vince. You gotta go. Now. With the gun silent, they'll be up here any minute."

"I'm not leaving you, Sarge. No way!"

"That's an order, Corporal. There's nothing you can do for me. And you know it. But I can help you." He grunted, reaching out his arms, pulling his shattered body toward the gun. "I'll cover you as long as possible. Now go!"

"Sarge!"

Vega reached up, putting his hand on the autocannon. He couldn't aim, couldn't do much but pull the trigger. But that would be enough to buy some time.

"God damn it, Corporal, look at the medscans. I'm gonna die no matter what you do. Can you at least let me die like an Alpha? Holding the line, helping a comrade? The colonel needs every gun he has…do you think we have numbers to waste on bullshit. Now, go!"

Komack sat unmoving, staring back at the stricken sergeant.

"Please," Vega said, his voice weakening. "Do it for me, Vince. Give me a good death, an honorable one."

"Sarge…" Komack's voice was soft, stricken.

"For the colonel. For the others. You may be able to help

them. There's nothing you can do for me." Vega squeezed his finger, and the staccato sound of the autocannon resumed.

Komack knelt behind the sergeant for another few seconds. Then he said simply, "Goodbye, Aaron."

"Goodbye, Vince."

Komack turned and moved slowly back. Vega turned his head, watching his friend climb up a few meters and disappear back along the top of the ship's hull. Then he turned back, gritting his teeth and staring straight ahead.

Alright you bastards…

Coordinate Grid 20.2-42.8
Inside the Alien Vessel
Planet Gamma Epsilon II

Vandenberg moved slowly, cautiously down the corridor. It was dark, eerie, the way lit only by his headlamp and the distant flickerings of those of the colonel's group ahead. He had his mike connected directly to his outside speakers, as did the rest of his team. With the impenetrable jamming, the coms were useless—and direct laser communication was too cumbersome in the twisting corridors of the ancient ship.

He moved forward, climbing over a pile of debris, what seemed like some type of wiring and a structural support that had fallen from the ceiling.

Fallen when? When Athens was fighting Sparta? When the pyramids were a construction site? Or when we were primitive primates competing for food on the open plain?

He listened carefully to the sounds coming from his speakers. His scanners were close to useless, and he didn't intend to be blindsided by one of the alien combat 'bots or some other nightmare lurking in the haunted depths of the vessel. His people were behind Reginald's, which he'd thought would make him feel better, but so far it hadn't turned out that way. The eeriness of the place was almost overwhelming, and the thought that they could be attacked by more enemy 'bots at any time only made things worse. He almost forgot the fact that there were more than a hundred Alliance Intelligence killers on the Team's tail as well. He tried to convince himself there was a way out for the Team, but he didn't believe it, not really.

The light ahead grew brighter, and he could see shadowy figures in the distance.

The colonel and his people have stopped.

One of the figures turned back, moving slowly to the side. It took Vandenberg a few seconds to realize the trooper was trying to connect with the laser com. He stepped forward, moving to a spot with direct line of sight to the sergeant.

"Lieutenant, Sergeant Ming here. The colonel wants your people to come up now." There was urgency in his voice.

"On the way," Vandenberg snapped back. He turned toward the small column behind him, pulling his assault rifle from its cradle as he did. "Okay, the colonel wants us up ahead now. Let's move out…and I want you all ready for anything." He surprised himself, the confidence he felt, the ease with which the words came to his mouth. He was still scared to death, but he felt more focused than he had before.

Is this what it feels like to be a veteran?

The three Alphas responded with an almost perfectly-synced chorus of yessirs. Vandenberg turned and started forward, sidestepping more piles of wreckage as he did. He was still moving cautiously, but he picked up the pace considerably. Ming hadn't sounded panicked, but there had definitely been an edge in his voice.

It looked like the corridor opened up farther down where Reginald and his people were. It was hard to see much. The headlamps were easy enough to see when they were facing his direction, but the almost total lack of any reflection off the metal of the ship made it difficult to make out much more.

Vandenberg quickened his pace, covering the remaining distance in a few seconds. The corridor did open up. There was a large circular room, perhaps thirty meters in diameter. There were a dozen hallways, spaced at what looked like perfect thirty degree intervals. Colonel Reginald was standing in the center of the room, and as soon as Vandenberg stepped in, he turned and gestured.

"Stay put," he said softly, barely loud enough for Vandenberg to hear.

Vandenberg turned and gestured for his people to stop as well. Then he looked back at Reginald. The colonel seemed to be listening for something. Vandenberg cranked up his speakers. He listened for a few seconds, but he didn't hear anything.

Wait…

There *was* something. In the distance. A scraping sound. Metal on metal…

He felt a chill move through him. Whatever was coming their way, it wasn't any of their people…and it damned sure wasn't the Alliance forces either.

The sound was growing louder, still distant, but definitely heading their way. Reginald turned to face the others. He was about to say something when they all heard more noise, from the corridors they'd come from this time. Gunfire…and then a moment later the sound of hurried footsteps, running. Vandenberg turned quickly, seeing Jones already on one knee with his rifle pointed down the hallway. The old sergeant-major had beaten him to it.

He tensed, ready for action, but then he saw the figures moving toward them. Dawes and Isaacs.

"We've got Alliance troops on our tail," the captain shouted down the hall. "They're in the ship now."

Dawes kept running, only slowing down as he reached the room. "We lost Thoms," he said grimly. I dropped a spread of micro-mines in the wreckage. With any luck that'll pick off a few of them. But we've gotta keep going."

"Any sign of Komack or Vega?"

Vandenberg was listening, and he could hear the pain in Reginald's voice. With Thoms dead, if Komack and Vega were gone too, that was half the Alphas. The mission had degenerated into a horrifying nightmare, and now they were bracketed between enemies.

"No, sir." Dawes turned and looked behind him. "Nothing."

Reginald held his hand up, signaling for everyone to be quiet. Vandenberg could hear the scraping sound again, louder now. Closer.

"Alright, we damned sure can't stay here…but maybe these 'bots can help us. You all know the sound they make. Remember, we don't have scanners, so you'll have to stop and listen. We're going to split up, go down three of these corridors. I want you all to do what Captain Dawes did…drop your mines in piles of debris, anywhere you can hide them. With any luck, they'll take out anything on your tail. If not, at least they'll give you a warning when they blow." He turned and looked toward Vandenberg. "Ruiz, go with Captain Dawes."

"Yes, sir." The corporal took a look at Vandenberg before he walked across the room toward Dawes."

Reginald stopped and listened again before continuing. "Elise, you come with me. The 'bots are too tough to take down with a sniper's shot, but hang back, and if any of the Alliance troops catch up, do what you do best."

"Yes, sir." Cho stood a couple meters away holding the enormous sniper's rifle. She moved toward the colonel, nodding as she did.

"Alright, Alphas…let's do this." Reginald's voice was firm, but Vandenberg could hear the strain. No, more than strain. It was a sadness. The Alphas would never give up, not any of them. But suddenly he realized John Reginald didn't think he'd see any of his people again. It wasn't a reach, they were in desperate trouble, all of them realized that. But for the first time Vandenberg really thought about the chance that none of them were coming out of this. More than chance. Likelihood.

"Yes, sir!" Vandenberg snapped his reply back first, his voice sharp, crisp. He felt defiance fill his mind, his body. The situation was close to hopeless, but he'd be damned if he would give up.

"Down that corridor, Alex." Reginald was staring at him, pointing.

"Sir!" Vandenberg snapped off a salute, one as sharp as possible in powered armor. It wasn't protocol, but they were hardly on a normal battlefield. And it was just something he had to do.

Reginald returned the gesture. Then he turned toward Dawes. "Clark, take your team down that way." He pointed toward the opposite corridor.

"Yes, sir." Dawes also saluted. "We'll fight like Alphas, sir, all of us."

"I know you will, Clark." Reginald nodded, and then he turned and headed down another of the corridors, gesturing for Ming and Brown to follow.

Chapter Eighteen

Coordinate Grid 20.2-42.8
Inside the Alien Vessel
Planet Gamma Epsilon II

"Keep moving. They can't be far ahead of us." Grax was moving down the corridor, shouting at the troopers around him. The ancient vessel—alien vessel, there was no doubt about that—was eerie, and his people were moving slowly, even stopping. He was pouring everything he had into driving them on, but morale was a fragile thing, and he knew they were skittish, ready to lose it at any moment.

He was just as scared as they were, but he'd gone in knowing he was a dead man unless he managed to pull a glorious victory from the jaws of earlier defeat. Even the ghosts of the long dead past couldn't match the terror Gavin Stark could instill, on his enemies and allies alike.

"The corridor opens up just ahead, sir." Lieutenant Rhome was up there, near the front of the line. He had stopped and turned back to shout to Grax.

"Forward, Lieutenant. Scout it out now."

"Yes, sir."

Grax looked forward, past the jumbled cluster of his soldiers. He couldn't see anything but scattered flashes of light as the troopers moved around. Then it started.

Gunfire. Rapid, loud. But it was somehow different, not Alliance weaponry…or anything he'd heard the Confederation forces using either.

Something else too, a high-pitched whine, and flashes of light from ahead, bright, even so far down the non-reflective corridor.

He could hear his own troops ahead, shooting, screaming. Most of them were holding, but a few were pushing back, trying to flee.

"Kill those cowards," he shouted, pushing forward himself through the crowded mass. "Anybody who runs dies."

Grax was consumed by the need to defeat whatever lay ahead. The thought of a rout, of what awaited him if he presided over another disastrous defeat, was too terrible to contemplate, and it drove the fear of this unknown enemy from his mind.

"Forward," he shouted as he pushed through the mass of armored bodies, slamming into the soldiers around him as he moved ahead. "Whatever is in that room, we take it out now."

As he got closer, the sounds of gunfire grew louder, echoing off the walls of the corridor. Now he could see the soldiers at the front of the column, pressed against the walls, peering cautiously around the corner to shoot back. There were several troopers down, including one who looked like he'd been almost torn to pieces by the enemy fire.

"Report, Sergeant Bilk," Grax snapped to the lead non-com.

"Sir, it's…it's some kind of…robot or something."

Grax felt the pit in his stomach tighten. Bilk was a veteran, an ex-Marine just like himself. And he sounded like he was about to shit himself.

"Robot? I don't care what it is, Bilk…just take it down."

"We're trying, sir…but it's…tough. We've hit it at least fifty times, and it just won't go down."

Grax opened his mouth, but no words came.

What the hell could take fifty rounds from an assault rifle and still be standing?

Even as he stood there, Grax could hear the enemy fire slackening. He leaned forward, peered out across the room.

There it was...tall, much taller than a man. Made of gleaming metal, vaguely humanoid in shape, but with six arms. At least it had once had six appendages. Right now, four of them were twisted, severed ruins. But the two that remained carried what were clearly weapons, and they continued to fire. One was something very much like Grax's own assault rifle, and the other one was some sort of energy weapon. Grax's eyes caught one of his troopers on the ground in the room, half of his midsection just gone, the armor around the hideous wound blackened and pitted. The work of the energy weapon, he guessed.

He pulled back around the corner, just as the 'bot fired a stream of projectiles in his direction. He was stunned, struggling to maintain his discipline, to think coherently. That—thing—wasn't something the Martians had deployed. If it was, the balance of power in human space wasn't what the Alliance thought it was.

No, the Martians aren't that far ahead of us...

He had to fight to catch his breath as the weight of his conclusion hit him.

That is something built by aliens...thousands of years ago.

Tens of thousands...hundreds of thousands...

"Keep firing," he managed to blurt out. "All of you, maximum fire. We have to take that thing down now!"

He aimed his own rifle, opening fire on full auto. He'd never seen anything as durable as the 'bot standing on the other side of the massive circular chamber. It was down on its—knees?—it's upper body almost torn apart. But it was still fighting, firing its single remaining weapon.

At least ten of his troopers were down. Half a dozen were in the room itself, where they'd been taken by surprise by the alien weapon. Another four or five had gone down in the corridor, and they'd been dragged back by their fellows.

Grax aimed his fire, targeting the 'bot's remaining appendage. The arm was clearly damaged, but it was still operational, the attached assault rifle firing steadily. Its movement was impaired now, and its fire had become erratic, mostly ineffectual as the 'bot struggled to target Grax and his people.

"Move…forward," Grax yelled, stepping into the room and swinging around to the 'bot's side. "To the right." The 'bot struggled to angle its fire that way, but it was too damaged, its movement too restricted. Grax ran around to the side, and then directly at the combat unit, focusing his fire at what looked like the most vulnerable spot, between its 'head' and its 'neck.'

Half of dozen of his people were just behind him, spreading out to both sides and adding their shooting to his. The 'bot's fire ceased, and the fearsome thing wobbled for a few seconds before crashing forward to the floor.

Grax lunged forward, standing right above the 'bot, emptying a new clip into it. His shots ripped through the inert figure, digging huge gouges in the metallic floor below. Finally satisfied it was dead, he ceased fire, raising a hand in the air to signal for his troopers to do the same.

He stared at it for a moment, mesmerized. Being trapped in the corridor had blunted much of the numerical advantage his people had enjoyed, but he was still stunned at the damage the thing had absorbed before it was knocked out. It was mostly twisted wreckage now, unrecognizable from its former, almost manlike, shape.

Grax had known his people faced a fight against the Martians. And he'd been aware the alien ship was a mystery, possibly a very dangerous one. But now, the reality was sinking in. The ship was ancient, almost beyond imagining. He'd been prepared to find artifacts, bits and pieces of technology, perhaps enough even to shatter the balance of power, to give the Alliance an irresistible advantage over the other Superpowers. But the idea that any of that tech would be functional, that the ancient defensive systems could still be active, had never entered his mind.

What have we found here?

"Alright, all of you…move forward. Pass it down. I want everybody up here now!"

The room was large, a circular chamber with a dozen corridors leading off in different directions. He looked around, walking toward one of the hallways and peering down its length. It extended off into the distance, the light-absorbing metal limiting the range of his headlamp. He paused, listening carefully, hoping for a hint as to which way the Confederation troops had gone. But there was nothing.

"All right, listen up," he yelled into his microphone. "Here's what we're going to do. We have to hunt down those Martians...but we need to watch out for more of those 'bots too." He gestured toward several of the corridors. "Second platoon, send a team down each of these four corridors." He moved his arm, pointing in a different direction. "Third platoon, these four...and fourth, you cover the others."

He looked out over the mass of troops still pouring into the room. "Let's move it. The Martians went down one or more of these corridors. Platoon leaders, send half your strength down the corridors and keep half here in reserve. Team leaders, if you encounter the Martians, engage at once, and send a runner back here to report contact." He paused, and when he continued, his tone was darker. "And if you run into any more of these 'bots,' pull back at once and send someone back for reinforcements."

His eyes moved over the troops standing in the room looking back at him, finding the three platoon commanders. "Is that understood, platoon leaders?"

"Yes, sir," came the three replies, sounding tentative.

"Let's go...I want the pursuit teams on the move. Now!" He moved his arm behind him, gesturing toward the corridors. "And I want the rest of you deployed defensively, watching these corridors. If any of those 'bots make it into this room while we're crammed in here, it's not going to be pretty."

He could feel the edginess of his troops, the fear. The stakes had risen dramatically. This wasn't a fight over theoretical science...it was a struggle to control military technology millennia ahead of anything possessed by Earth's Superpowers. It was a battle to control the future, the means to dominate all mankind.

And it's my chance to survive...all of our chances...and our deaths if we fail.

Grax couldn't imagine what horrors Gavin Stark would unleash on the men and women who failed to secure a treasure trove like the alien ship.

Coordinate Grid 20.2-42.8
Inside the Alien Vessel
Planet Gamma Epsilon II

The corridor ended in a 'T,' and Vandenberg stood, looking one way and then the next. Both corridors disappeared into the gloomy darkness he'd become accustomed to as he'd moved through the ancient vessel. He held up a hand, a gesture to his two comrades to remain silent. He was listening, for signs of the Alliance forces pursuing his small band—and for the metallic sound of another 'bot' approaching. His people had moved quickly, stopping only twice to listen for pursuit. So far there had been nothing.

He felt relief, but almost immediately his tension was renewed. Getting away wasn't an option. His people had no place to run. Even assuming they could abandon the ancient vessel to their Alliance counterparts—and they most definitely could not—there were few options. They were trapped, without reserves, without *Westron* and the hope of retrieval. They were outnumbered, threatened both by their Alliance pursuers and the deadly 'bots that still defended the ship, somehow defying almost unimaginable age.

No, there is no escape…but if we can stay out of the way, let the 'bots fight the Alliance forces…

His head snapped around. There was something down the corridor, behind them. For an instant, he feared another 'bot was coming. But then the sounds became familiar. Powered infantry.

"We've got something coming up, Lieutenant. Sounds like the Alliance troopers to me." Jones looked at Vandenberg expectantly, his rifle in his hands.

"To me too, Sergeant-Major." He looked down the corridor, choosing a direction with a mental coin toss. "Let's move. If we're going to get into a fight we need to find a better spot." He turned to the right and headed down the corridor, turning once to confirm his comrades were with him.

The corridor was straight for about fifty meters. Then it

turned sharply. There were hatches at various points on both sides, but Vandenberg ignored them. His people had stopped several times when they'd first set out, trying to open the doors and see what lay beyond. But they were jammed, wracked and twisted by the crash and by years of decay. Even the enormous strength of his armored arms and legs had proven insufficient to budge any of them.

"They're still behind us, sir. We're going to have to fight them somewhere."

"Not here, O'Reilly. We have no idea how many are on our tail, but we know there are over a hundred of them in total. If the three of us are going to have a chance, we need someplace with some real cover."

Vandenberg's mind was focused, cold. The rookie jitters were gone, replaced by an iron resolve…to defeat the enemy, to keep his people alive. The fear was still there, of course, but he'd found a place for it, even drawn on it to fuel his urgency. There was no escape for the Alphas, no chance to flee, even if the importance of the mission hadn't overruled flight. There was nowhere to go. Whatever slim chance they had for survival rested on their scant hopes of victory, on defeating a force more than ten times their size. And on turning the alien 'bots into their own weapon, one they managed to unleash upon the Alliance troops.

"Let's pick up the pace." He had been moving cautiously. The corridor was treacherous, twisted in places and scattered with piles of debris, and his light was effective no more than eight or ten meters out. But his people were running out of time.

He pumped his legs faster, his eyes wide open, focused, trying to avoid the debris as he jogged forward. His armored legs clanged harder on the metal floor, and despite his best efforts to move softly, he knew the enemy would hear his steps. That couldn't be helped. If his people continued to push ahead at a cautious pace, the enemy was going to catch up to them anyway.

After another forty meters, Vandenberg stopped abruptly. The area around him was damaged more severely than any he'd yet seen. The walls had collapsed in some spots and had great holes torn in them in others, exposing the compartments beyond. There was a single opening farther down, leading again into the seemingly endless darkness.

"This way," he said, flashing a glance back toward his cohorts. If we get through, we might be able to set up and ambush the enemy when they move through the open area."

He turned back toward the opening and quickened his pace.

Coordinate Grid 20-42
Inside the Alien Vessel
Planet Gamma Epsilon II

The intelligence puzzled. It had estimated the number of invaders at ten to twenty, but then more appeared. There were more than one hundred inside the vessel now, a full scale invasion that demanded an immediate and deadly response.

The first analysis had suggested that the original force had been reinforced. Yet now there was conflicting data, suggestions that there had been combat *between* the invaders. Perhaps the intelligence wasn't dealing with a single enemy. Perhaps there were two different forces, hostile to each other as well as to the vessel. If that was so, it vastly expanded the tactical options available. With careful planning, the intelligence could direct the invaders toward each other, compel them to fight… and then sending its combat units to complete their destruction.

The intelligence had ceaselessly explored its connections to the rest of the ship, the systems at its disposal. Most were unresponsive, yet others were still only partially functional. The intelligence rerouted power and signals from severed connections to still-operable conduits. Its energy reserves were extremely limited, the outflow coming from the last particles of antimatter remaining in the sole functioning containment system. After charging the combat units that remained fully or partially functional—and reserving sufficient wattage for its own needs— there was little power remaining. Yet not none.

It searched for operable systems, anything that could contain the invading units. The ship's doors and hatches were mostly unresponsive, either twisted into useless wreckage or cut off from the intelligence's compromised communications network. Mostly…but not entirely. Some of the emergency doors still responded. And groups of the enemy were moving toward such hatches. The intelligence was tracking, waiting. At the right time it would activate those doorways, cut off the enemy from venturing deeper into the vessel. Perhaps it could force the opposing groups together, compel them to fight each other. And if not, it would send in the rest of the combat units…to eliminate the penned in survivors.

Chapter Nineteen

MCS Viking
Gamma Epsilon
525,000 Kilometers from Gamma Epsilon II

"Ship approaching, Mr. Vance. It appears to be on a direct line from the planet to the warp gate. Range 211,000 kilometers."

Vance turned around as far as the workstation chair would go. He was uncomfortable as hell strapped into the bridge chair, but he realized how stupid it would be to end up unconscious or even dead from getting slammed around if *Viking* took a hit or executed a rapid maneuver.

"Identification?"

"They're not transmitting their beacon, sir. But it looks like a cruiser. Drive harmonics suggest a high probability of Alliance design and construction. Mass and energy output match the ships we monitored earlier transiting into the system. It's an almost certain match."

But there were four ships then. Where are the others…

"Active scanners on full power, Captain. Launch a full spread of probes. I want to know where those other three ships are. Now."

"Yes Mr. Vance."

"And maintain battlestations. I want all guns ready to fire on my command."

Will you fire the first shot against an Alliance vessel? Are you ready to take that responsibility? To risk being the man who starts a war?

Vance didn't know the answers to the questions he was asking himself. And he knew he wouldn't have them. Not until his hand was forced, and he did it. Or he didn't.

Be careful. If that's Gavin Stark out there, he's more than willing to risk war if it serves his purposes. And he's smart enough to engineer a conflict and make it look like your fault...

"All stations are ready, Mr. Vance. *Viking* is prepared to engage on your command." A pause. "The enem...Alliance vessel is maintaining a steady velocity, approaching us at two hundred kilometers per second.

Vance stared straight ahead. *Viking* was a battleship, with more than enough firepower to take out an Alliance cruiser. But there were three other ships out there somewhere...

What would you do, Father? I can't let the Alliance capture that alien technology...but can I risk war to stop it? Would you fire on this ship?

Vance had a plan. He had several, in fact. But now he was doubting them all, the steadfast grimness of his expression hiding the turmoil in his mind.

"Mr. Vance, the Alliance vessel is decelerating. It looks like they're trying to turn about and run."

Vance shook his head. Part of him had hoped the Alliance ship would fire first, relieve him of the terrible responsibility crushing down on him. Now his choice was even more difficult. Chasing down a fleeing Alliance vessel and destroying it was a blatant act of war, no doubt one Gavin Stark would welcome. But if he let the vessel go he risked a four to one fight, one he was far from sure *Viking* could win.

The tactical choice was clear. Accelerate and attack. Before they concentrate. But the problem went well beyond the tactical.

He sat in his chair along the periphery of *Viking's* bridge, his usual cold logic failing him for once. He knew what he had to do, but it took some time for him to gather up the courage and resolve. Then he turned back toward the captain's station.

"Accelerate and close, Captain. Don't let that ship get away."

"Yes, sir."

Vance didn't know what he'd do when *Viking* caught the Alliance vessel. He glanced down at the display, at the range between the two ships, and he did a quick calculation. He had seven minutes to decide. Maybe eight.

Bridge - MCS Westron
At the Edge of the Asteroid Belt
Gamma Epsilon System

"I'm counting on you guys…I need everything you've got here, Sam. Precise targeting."

"We won't let you down, Captain. Thirty seconds to initial launch."

Antonia Silver was leaning forward in her chair, trying to ignore the tightness in her gut. There was a faint burning smell coming from the ventilation system and some minor damage apparent on *Westron's* bridge, but her ship's primary systems were all operational. That, at least, was a break, despite the two dead among her people and the dozen wounded down in sickbay.

The enemy ships were about to enter energy weapons range. They had both launched their missiles at *Westron*, but the combination of the cover provided by the heavily radioactive asteroids and the pinpoint accuracy of her point defense teams had kept the damage sustained at controllable levels. She had held back her own missiles. Now it was her turn to strike.

"I want those volleys right on top of each other, Sam. No more than thirty seconds apart." She knew she was asking the impossible, or very nearly so. But she needed it. If she didn't get her missiles fired by the time the enemy commenced energy weapon fire, she never would. She'd have to open up with her own lasers, and any ordnance left in the silos would remain there, useless.

"We'll do our best, Captain."

She almost answered, but she stopped herself. Sam Watson was busy now...busy doing what she'd tasked him to do. Besides, there was no one else on *Westron* she trusted more. She didn't have to ride Watson to get his absolute best...it was all the young officer was capable of giving.

"Ten seconds to launch." Watson's voice was intense, focused.

Silver saw the two ships approaching, the red symbols on the screen moving steadily closer. *Westron* couldn't beat both in a laser duel. She was just too outgunned. Any chance her ship—and her crew—had of making it through the battle depended on the sprint missiles. On their hitting the enemy hard enough to equalize things, at least a bit.

"Launching."

Silver felt her ship lurch hard as *Westron* flushed her external racks, sending the missiles directly toward the enemy ships. Normal missile doctrine called for the weapons to conserve fuel to conduct course changes, homing in on enemy ships as they approached. But at this range, the clusters of missiles were launched directly toward the enemy ships. They accelerated at maximum thrust, and they reached astonishing velocities very quickly. She was still watching the first volley when *Westron* shook again. More missiles, from the internal silos now. Then again. And once more. Every missile her ship held. Every one.

She stared at the screen, watching the rows of small yellow icons heading toward the enemy ships. The first wave was now moving at close to $0.02c$, and they were still accelerating. The target vessels were conducting evasive maneuvers, but the incoming missiles were closing fast. Silver knew the captains would be surprised. They'd have assumed *Westron* was damaged or that it didn't carry missiles. Why else wouldn't the ship have fired at normal range?

The spreads moved forward, their velocities increasing as they did. One of the ships looked like it would escape the first wave of missiles, but the other was right in the middle of the spread, bracketed by multiple warheads.

She was tense as she watched, and she almost cried out when two of her warheads closed to within three hundred meters before detonating. That was pinpoint shooting by any measure, and she leaned forward, anxious to see the damage assessments the instant they came in.

It took a few seconds for the scanners to lock on to the target ship, and several more for the data to reach *Westron* and for her ship's AI to chew on it and create a meaningful report. But the instant she saw it, she knew it had been worth the wait.

The Alliance vessel was crippled, bleeding air and fluids into space. Her thrust was dead…she was still moving at her pre-existing velocity.

Silver's eyes narrowed. If the ship's engines were truly out of commission, the vessel was a sitting duck. With no maneuvering capability, her AI could pinpoint *Westron's* fire, blasting the ship to atoms minutes after entering energy weapons range.

But she wasn't going to have to do even that.

Her eyes caught the display, the final wave of missiles from *Westron's* magazine. The sprint-mode warheads had little ability to change course, but with the Alliance ship locked on a predictable heading the AIs in each warhead expended what fuel they had left to alter their vectors. It was a scene like predators on some savannah chasing down a wounded prey animal. One by one the warheads closed. Two more exploded within three hundred meters…and a third barely fifty meters from the stricken vessel. When the scanning reports came back, there was nothing. Nothing but a cloud of expanding plasma, where sixty thousand tons of heavily armed warship had been.

Her eyes moved to her own screen. There was no time to celebrate. The second Alliance ship had escaped all but minor damage, and it was still closing, minutes from entering energy weapons range.

Silver stared, her jaw set, her eyes locked on the screen. Her body was tense, hands clenching into fists at her side. Now it was one against one. Her enemy still outweighed and outgunned her, but she'd come a long way toward evening the score.

Now she was ready to finish things.

Bridge
AIS Shadow
In Orbit Around Gamma Epsilon II

Stark stared at the incoming data. He had probes deployed, tracking the movement of the Martian battleship. He was recording everything, preparing a show, almost like some entertainment executive directing a drama for the vid. Like any good movie, it told a story. An Alliance ship in a disputed system, standing on patrol, its guns and weapons silent as the Confederation battleship approached. The Alliance vessel decelerating, turning, moving away.

And the Confederation warship opening fire, attacking without provocation. War.

The Martians would provide him with his casus belli. The attack would provide justification for taking control of the system. Then the Alliance task force he'd arranged to have two transits away would be rushed to the scene. It would blockade the dead-end system's sole warp gate, cordon it off against any Confederation forces nearby. And it would unknowingly protect Stark and his people as they dismantled the ancient alien vessel and shipped it away, to a secret facility only he controlled.

He pressed the com button, connecting him with the captain on the bridge. "Captain, I want *Shadow* ready to leave orbit on my command. Plot a course toward the asteroid belt, to link up with *Wraith* and *Wight*."

"Yes, Mr. Stark. At once."

Stark nodded as he cut the connection. His plan was coming together. Now he just had to wait. Wait until he got word from the surface that his ground forces had secured the site. And word from *Wraith* and *Wight* that they had destroyed the smaller Martian vessel.

The two ships should finish the smaller Martian craft any time now…and then the three vessels would link up and engage the Martian battleship. With any luck, they'd reach *Specter* before the cruiser was destroyed. But if they were too slow, it was a price Stark was willing to pay. One ship and a crew of four hundred was a small enough price to pay to secure the treasure trove down on the planet. And his three remaining vessels had enough firepower to take out the Martians. Probably.

He leaned back, allowing himself a moment of self-satisfaction. His efforts to penetrate Martian Intelligence had been difficult and expensive, but it was impossible to overstate the payoff. He'd imagined getting some dirt on the Vance family or another major player, perhaps something he could parlay into forcing the Confederation into an early pact with the Alliance when war inevitably broke out again. But he'd been shocked when he'd gotten the communique…and, truth be told, hadn't believed it completely. Not until *Shadow* had entered orbit and scanned the surface of the planet.

He glanced back at the com unit. He'd expected confirmation that the Martians had opened fire. *Specter's* orders had been specific. Withdraw…but not too quickly. Allow the Confederation battleship to close to firing range, but flee as soon as they commence hostilities. But the com remained silent.

Stark's fingers moved over the desk, punching keys, bringing a stream of data to the screen. *Specter* was right where she should be…and the Martian battleship was closing. But they hadn't opened fire.

It didn't make any sense. The Martians had to know he had more strength in the system than they did. Picking off one of the Alliance vessels was the right move, the only plausible decision. The Confederation couldn't allow the Alliance to gain control of the alien ship, no more than Stark could tolerate the Martians having it. But the battleship was just moving forward, deeper into combat range…and closer to the planet.

Stark cursed under his breath. He'd hoped to goad the Martians into firing first. A Confederation attack would have been useful. But provocation or not, he couldn't allow any of the Martians out of the system.

He moved his hand toward the com, but the captain's voice blared through before he touched it.

"Mr. Stark…" He knew immediately something was wrong. "…we just received a communique from *Wraith*." A pause. "Sir,

Wight has been severely damaged by an enemy missile barrage. Apparently they held their volleys until close range and launched them in sprint mode."

Stark slammed his hand down on the table.

Damn!

"What is *Wraith's* status?"

"They report minimal damage. They are closing to energy weapons range." There was another pause, and Stark could hear voices in the background. Something else was happening.

"Mr. Stark, another message from *Wraith*. *Wight* has been destroyed, sir." The captain sounded as if he'd rather be doing anything that reporting to Alliance Intelligence's Number Three right now.

Stark felt the rage building inside. His plan had been perfect. But now everything was in danger. "Captain, *Wraith* is to destroy the Martian ship immediately. Hold nothing back. And they are to return as soon as the battle is over."

"Yes, sir."

"And bring us out of orbit. *Specter* is to increase to full thrust. I want them out of range of that battleship. We will rendezvous with them seven hundred thousand kilometers from the planet and take on the Martian vessel together."

"Yes, sir."

Stark slapped his hand down on the com. He took a deep breath, centering himself. He had to be at his best right now. *Specter* and *Shadow* might be a match for the Martian battleship, barely. His expected victory was now a desperate struggle, one that would probably go right to the end. But there was no choice, no other way. And whatever else he was, Gavin Stark was no coward.

He got up, standing still for a moment, running his hands down his suit, brushing away the wrinkles. He took one more breath, and then he walked around the desk and headed toward the door leading to the bridge. This one was going to be too close to trust it to anyone but himself.

The door slid open, and he walked out onto the bridge. He was going into battle.

Chapter Twenty

Coordinate Grid 20.2-42.8
Inside the Alien Vessel
Planet Gamma Epsilon II

Vandenberg ran toward the open hatch, leaping over a pile of crates in the middle of the room. His comrades were right on his heels. The room offered a fair amount of cover, but the last thing he wanted was to get caught by the enemy running out in the open.

The opening was about ten meters, and the rest of the way was clear. He pumped his legs harder, closing the distance as rapidly as he could. He was about three meters away when the hatch suddenly slammed shut in front of him.

He was startled by the movement. Other than the 'bots, he hadn't seen a single system in the ship that appeared functional. He reacted quickly, but not quickly enough, and he slammed into the hatch, his armor clanging hard against the strange metal of the door. He lost his balance, falling to the ground. The cushioning in his suit's membrane offered some protection, but the pain of the impact rattled through his body nevertheless.

Jones leaned down and put his hand on Vandenberg's arm. "Are you okay, sir?"

"I'm fine, Sergeant-Major." The fall had knocked the breath out of him, but he was pretty sure he wasn't seriously injured.

"Let me help you up, sir." A short pause. "We're stuck in here, looks like. We better get ready for a fight."

"You're right, Sergeant-Major." Vandenberg rolled over onto his hands and knees, following the routine for getting up in powered armor. "I can manage." He pushed with his arms, and then straightened his legs, rising slowly as he did.

"Let's get some cover," he said, gesturing toward some of the debris piles. "They'll be here any second."

"Yes, sir." Jones and O'Reilly snapped their replies almost in unison. Then the two men turned and moved to the center of the room, taking positions that offered reasonable cover.

Vandenberg looked around quickly, his eyes settling on a mound of broken electrical equipment and sections of metal from the ceiling. He ran over, taking position and pulling his rifle from its bracket.

He knelt behind the pile of debris, ready to fire through a small gap in the twisted metal girders and conduits. His assault rifle's targeting system was linked into his suit's AI. His target area was projected inside his visor. He was covering the corridor, waiting for the enemy to emerge. With any luck, his people would pick off at least a couple of their pursuers. He had no idea how many Alliance troops were on their heels, but if they'd tried to cover all twelve corridors *and* keep a central reserve, it couldn't be more than seven or eight. There was no guarantee that is what they had done, but it would have been the tactically correct way to proceed.

Seven or eight was still a lot for three to handle, and taking down a few would improve the odds dramatically. He was stone still, and he'd ordered O'Reilly and Jones to remain silent as well. If the enemy thought they were still fleeing, it might be enough to lure them out into the open.

Vandenberg could feel the sweat dripping down his face inside his armor. It was one of the most difficult aspects of powered infantry training, become accustomed to being unable to scratch an itch or wipe away a droplet of sweat. He'd struggled with it at first, but then he'd beaten it, and he'd gone on to master the use of armor, so much so that his exam results had set an Academy record. But now he was painfully aware of the perspiration, of the discomfort, and he struggled to fight the distraction.

His mind was being pulled in different directions, the rookie yielding to the fear, to the immense pressure of the battlefield situation, and the newer part of his psyche, the soldier, the proto-veteran developing within, exerting its own influence, keeping him focused. Beating back the fear. Winning the internal tug of war, at least for now.

He heard the sounds of armored footsteps, and a few seconds later yelling. He took a deep breath and exhaled hard, staring intently at the targeting display. He moved the rifle slightly, and the image on his visor changed, slipped to the side. He could see light from the corridor, the lamps of the approaching Alliance troopers.

That's getting brighter…they have to be getting close…

He tightened his hands around the rifle, waiting. A second passed, perhaps two or three, each moving like a glacier, challenging his ability to stay focused. Then, suddenly, he had a target. An armored figure, moving quickly out into the room. Into the open.

He squeezed his finger, gently, deliberately, but he was too late. He heard the sound of fire from behind and to his left—Jones—and the trooper was thrown back hard against the wall, his armor pierced in half a dozen places.

Vandenberg shot his eyes to the left, to the corridor opening. There was another shape there, another Alliance trooper. He moved his rifle and fired, almost without conscious thought, and he felt a rush of elation as the soldier fell to his knees…and then forward to the ground.

That's two…

He forced his eyes away from the dead trooper, looking back to the corridor. The soldiers there were pulling back, trying to move out of the line of fire. Another fell as he was watching… Jones's deadly fire striking again. And then the trooper behind, picked off by O'Reilly.

Four.

He stared down the corridor, watching as two more Alliance soldiers ducked back down, disappearing into the darkness.

He felt a wave of uncertainty. He'd only seen two soldiers, and they were surprised, disordered. Should he rush them, charge and take them out? Or were there more behind them?

His legs made the decision for him, and he felt himself lunging forward. "With me…let's take them out," he shouted as he raced toward the hall, his rifle spitting out destruction. He could hear Jones to his side, see the sergeant-major's headlamp shining ahead as he ran. For an instant he thought the two of them would collide, but then Jones edged over, and they ran down the hallway abreast.

Vandenberg was running wildly, far too quickly to control himself, to see the debris and obstructions in his way. He trusted to instinct, to his luck even, but he didn't slow his pace. Not at all. And neither did Jones. The old non-com was right at his side the entire way.

He felt something in front of his foot, and he swung to the side, stumbling, trying to avoid the girder that had almost tripped him. He staggered for a few meters, but he managed to right himself…and just as he did, he caught the lamp of one of the Alliance soldiers ahead as the man looked back.

The enemy trooper tried to bring his rifle around, and his companion did the same. There *were* only two of them, and Vandenberg knew either he or they would die in the next few seconds. He fired without thinking, riddling both troopers with projectiles, even as Jones did the same. The two men never even managed to get off a shot. They both fell hard to the deck, clearly dead.

He ran forward toward the bodies, Jones still at his side. He moved a few meters past the armored forms, looking down the corridor, confirming there were no more enemies in sight. Nothing. Then he turned back. Jones was crouched down, confirming the two Alliance troopers were dead. O'Reilly was standing behind, staring forward, his rifle at the ready.

Vandenberg had been uncomfortable snapping out orders to soldiers as experienced as Jones and O'Reilly. He'd felt out of place, his inexperience and his commission pulling him in different directions. But now that was fading away, replaced by an iron determination.

He walked back into the room, staring across at the closed hatch. The door that had closed even as he'd raced toward it. His mind played over those few seconds again and again, and the cold feeling in his gut grew. Finally, he turned toward his comrades.

"We're going back. These 'bots aren't just individual security systems. Something is controlling this ship and, whatever it is, we know one thing now. It's hunting us. Not only that, it knows we have other enemies here. That hatch didn't close randomly…it went down just as we were heading toward it, and it trapped us in a fight with the Alliance troopers." Vandenberg paused. "We're facing more than just a few random units responding automatically. There is an intelligence stalking us, a computer…or some kind of being."

Jones and O'Reilly stood and stared back, silently. Finally, Jones nodded in agreement. O'Reilly didn't react at all. He just moved his gaze back to the corridor, rifle in hand, standing guard.

Vandenberg, angled his head, looking down the corridor himself. "We've got to get back and warn the colonel and the others."

He thought for an instant about trying to communicate with the Alliance forces, attempting to tell them they both faced a mutual threat. Indeed, if it had been Marines out there, or some other unit, he would have made the effort. But there wasn't much question these were Alliance Intelligence forces on their tail. And just as little doubt they had strict orders to kill anyone else on sight. Anything to secure the technological miracles the ancient ship held for whoever possessed it.

"How are we going to get to the colonel? To the others? The Alliance forces have to be in that central chamber, and probably in force."

Vandenberg looked back at Jones. "I don't know, Sergeant-Major. We're going to have to take one step at a time. But we have to try. The colonel and the others need to know there is more to worry about than random 'bots and Alliance soldiers. I know it seems impossible, but we have to get to them... somehow."

O'Reilly had been silent, but now he popped out his almost-spent cartridge, standing still while the autoloader slammed a fresh one into place. "Don't worry about it, sir. That's what Alphas do. The impossible."

Coordinate Grid 20.2-42.8
Inside the Alien Vessel
Planet Gamma Epsilon II

Reginald stared at the closed hatch. The hallway had ended in a small room, perhaps five meters square. The tightly sealed doorway was the only apparent way out, save back the way they had come. Cho and Ming were right behind, silent. The realization was obvious, but it still took a few seconds for Reginald to fully comprehend. They'd hit a dead end.

He turned and looked down the corridor. No sign of the enemy. Not yet, at least.

His people were elite veterans, as at home in their armor as they were in their own skins. They'd raced through the corridors and compartments of the alien vessel with a speed and dexterity their pursuers couldn't hope to match. But Reginald knew the Alliance troopers were well trained too, and mostly veterans. They wouldn't be far behind.

"Quick, we've got to get back. There was a turnoff maybe thirty meters down this corridor."

Reginald turned and started down the hall, waving for his comrades to follow. There was no other choice, but in his gut he doubted they could get there before their pursuers caught up. He tried to push the pessimism back, to convince himself they had time. But then he saw a brief flash of light in the distance.

"Stop," he yelled. "Back to the room." It was a snap decision, a veteran's calculation. They'd never get to the turnoff before the enemy engaged them, and if they did their pursuers would be right on their tails. The corridor was a death trap, narrow with no cover at all…and he had no idea what lay down the other hall. At least the room they'd been in had some machinery, some places to hide.

He twisted around—too abruptly—and he felt the wound on his thigh tear open. His suit's med system had packed it with sterile expandable foam, stopping the bleeding and stabilizing the injury until Reginald could be treated. But the sharp turn ripped it all open again, and he could feel the wet warmth, blood pouring down between his skin and the suit's membrane.

He winced in pain, but it only lasted for an instant before his AI flooded his bloodstream with a fresh hit of painkillers. He could feel the trauma control system working again, injecting fresh foam into the wound. The armor was designed to keep a soldier, even a wounded one, in the fight as long as possible. Still, he knew even the greatest efforts of his suit could only do so much. At some point, he wouldn't be able to push himself any farther. And in the current situation, when that happened, he would die.

He glanced back as he ran, catching another glimpse of light. He had his audio amplification cranked up, and now he could hear the metal on metal sound of armored boots on the deck. He pushed harder, racing back into the room he'd left a moment before, his head moving around rapidly, looking for the best cover available.

"Lin, over there." He gestured toward a large rectangular object, a little over a meter high and two long. He had no idea what it was, but it looked solid enough to block fire. His head snapped to the right and he pointed toward what appeared to be a large conduit running vertically from floor to ceiling. "Elise, get set up over there."

He looked around, but there was nothing else, at least nothing big enough to offer meaningful protection to something as large as an armored man.

He heard the enemy coming. He was out of time.

He raced across the room, pressing himself against the wall, his rifle angled toward the door. He didn't have any real cover, but the enemy wouldn't have a line of fire on him either, not unless they got into the room.

And they'll have a hard time managing that with Cho and Ming covering the door...

He stared at the targeting screen on his visor, his finger tightening around the trigger. The footsteps were growing louder, closer. Then they stopped.

These troops are no fools, that is clear. They're well trained.

He held still, keeping silent. He knew his comrades would do the same. The Alphas were the best. Period. Their missions were always the most difficult and dangerous, but he knew in many ways their skills made his job easier than that of most commanding officers. He never had to worry that they would do something foolish or that they would break and run. They were a unit, bonded together with a closeness he'd never seen anywhere else. That was a strength in battle, but he also realized the pain that would hit them all when they counted the cost of the mission, when they realized how many of their friends had died on this forsaken planet.

If any of us get back...

He took a deep breath. He was alert, as much the result of the drugs his suit was feeding him as anything else. But it didn't matter what kept him sharp and ready. As long as something did.

There was silence. Reginald knew it was just a few seconds, but it seemed to drag on. Then, suddenly, Alliance troopers burst into the room. One of them spun around almost immediately, looking in his direction. The soldier swung his rifle around, but he was too late. Reginald opened up, hitting his adversary with half a dozen hypervelocity rounds. The man fell backwards, into one of his fellows. An instant later, the other soldier fell too, a neat hole in his helmet where Cho had placed a perfectly-aimed round.

Reginald dropped down to one knee, bringing his rifle to bear on the doorway. A third Alliance trooper poked into the room, his momentum carrying him into the killing zone, despite his clear efforts to pull back. He was riddled with shots from all three Alphas, and he dropped face down to the ground, dead.

There was a pause. Reginald knew there had been more than three troopers after them. They were still out there, waiting.

Trying to decide what to do next…

Reginald's mind raced.

What would I do?

"Get down," he yelled across the room, even as he heard a series of popping sounds out in the hallway…and a spread of grenades flew into the room.

He dropped himself, lunging forward onto his belly, bring his rifle to bear as he did. He felt another wave of pain from his leg, but he ignored it, forcing his focus onto his targeting screen. The enemy would come hot on the heels of their grenade attack. At least that's what he would have done.

The room erupted with explosions, as each of the grenades detonated in turn. Reginald gritted his teeth, struggling to keep his attention on the doorway, despite the shrapnel now flying around the room. Cho and Ming had cover—but he was out in the open. He was low, hugging the floor, but he still heard the clanging sounds as chunks of depleted uranium slammed into his armor. The shrapnel from the grenades didn't have the hitting power of the assault rifles' hypervelocity rounds, and most of it bounced off the osmium iridium plating. But he felt pain, in his arm, his side. Two pieces at least had penetrated his armor, tearing into the flesh below.

He rasped for breath, biting down hard, ignoring the pain. A haze of smoke hung in the room now, but he could see through it, his eyes locked on the shadowy legs moving through the door. He fired, on full auto now. His rounds struck his enemy, dropping the man to his knees almost immediately. The stricken soldier turned, bring his rifle to bear on Reginald, but then he fell the rest of the way, another victim of Cho's deadly accuracy.

The sniper fired again, clearly aiming at something beyond the door, outside of Reginald's field of vision. A blast of fire came back, but she was ahead of it, slipping behind the heavy conduit as a burst of projectiles slammed into the meter-wide structure.

Ming poked his head above his cover, firing a burst through the door. Then, a few seconds later, another. Reginald knew what his teammate was going to do, and he tried to muster a shout, an order for him to stand down. But he was too late.

Ming charged the door, firing three-shot bursts as he did. Reginald knew it was the right tactic. His people were trapped, penned in. They had to break out. And there couldn't be more than one or two of the Alliance troopers left. Ming was even the right choice. Reginald was the Team's commander, and he was too shot up to manage it anyway…and Cho was more valuable in her covered vantage point, her deadly rifle ready to intervene at the precise moment it would do the most good. But that didn't make what Lin Ming was doing any less recklessly dangerous.

Ming got to the door, firing all the way. As well as Reginald could make out, he managed to shoot both enemy troopers, but the last one had returned the fire, and the Alpha stumbled backwards, falling hard onto his back.

Reginald's eyes shot to his downed soldier. The round that hit him in the side had gone clean through his body, though it hadn't had enough power left to penetrate his armor a second time. Miraculously, it didn't seem to have hit anything vital. The Team's leader had three gunshot wounds now. Without his suit, and the trauma control system built into it, he'd be out of action. But now he pulled himself up, the pain drowned out by a tidal wave of meds, the bleeding staunched by the wads of sterile foam forced into his bullet wounds.

He moved slowly, cautiously toward the doorway, peering around, confirming there were no live enemies remaining. Then he knelt slowly, looking down at Ming. He'd intended to check the sergeant's monitor, but one look at the shattered mess that had once been the plate of Ming's armor—and the sergeant's chest below—told him all he needed to know.

"C'mon, Elise…let's get out of here." His voice was grim, the reality that at least half his people were already dead hitting him for a moment before he managed to push the thoughts back.

"Yes, sir." The sniper moved around the conduit that had saved her life. She was limping too, her own wound clearly slowing her down despite the technical wizardry of her suit. "Let's get out of here."

Chapter Twenty-One

Bridge - MCS Westron
En Route to Asteroid Belt
Gamma Epsilon System

"I want all batteries at one hundred twenty percent." Silver's orders echoed from the walls of *Westron's* almost-silent bridge. Her people all knew the stakes in the battle now unfolding before them. *Westron* had scored a desperate win, the utter destruction of one of the enemy vessels. But now she faced the second ship, an adversary almost untouched by her missile barrage. And one that outmassed and outgunned her by forty percent.

She knew every officer on *Westron's* bridge was well aware of that fact, that they realized conventional tactics weren't going to get the job done. They'd been edgy about her gamble in holding their missiles to point blank range, but overloading the batteries—and by a full twenty percent—that was downright crazy.

It would be a miracle if the abused guns held out long enough to finish the fight, and if *Westron* lost half her batteries early, the fight would be over even more quickly than any of them feared. But Silver's mind was analytical, cold. She knew defeat was defeat, and death was death. And she was willing to take a gamble, reach out for the chance—however improbable—of victory.

"Yes, Captain." Gary Tomas was usually quicker to respond to her orders, but she knew her tactical officer was struggling with this one. Overpowering the lasers was a risky, but not uncommon tactic, at least where one hundred five percent, even one hundred ten, was concerned. But one hundred twenty was unheard of, an outrageously bold move.

Silver inhaled deeply, centering her thoughts, going through the silent pre-battle mantra she used. It seemed out of place to seek inner calm just before beginning a fight to the death, but she knew whatever happened, the calmer and more focused she was, the better chance her people had to get through the struggle now engulfing them.

"I want a ten second burst at fifty percent thrust in thirty seconds. Trajectory 230.114.019." It was another trick up her sleeve, a last second change of course and velocity. It wouldn't alter *Westron's* approach much, but it didn't take all that much to turn a laser's direct hit into a near miss. And unlike the massive thermonuclear warheads on her missiles, a laser blast zipping by fifty meters off the port or starboard would be totally ineffectual.

"Yes, Captain." A few seconds later: "Thrust plan locked into the navcom…executing in twenty-three seconds."

"Very well. All laser batteries are to open fire the instant the engines shut down."

"Yes, Captain. Ten seconds to engine firing."

Silver's hand dropped down to her side, checking her harness straps. She hated the damned things, and as a junior officer she'd always 'forgotten' to strap herself in, at least until one of her senior officers noticed and ordered her to buckle up. But she was older now, and wiser, and she realized how stupid it was to risk getting injured or knock out if the ship took a hard hit. The thought of *Westron* going into this fight without her captain at the helm because she'd been too obstinate to attach her harness was enough to overcome whatever remained of youthful arrogance.

"Engines firing now…"

She felt the g-forces slam into her, the immense power of the engines blasting away. She knew the numbers; she knew everything about her ship and its performance. She'd chosen half-power because anything greater would have required buttoning her crew up in the acceleration tanks. But even at half-thrust, almost fifteen gees hit her people. It was agony, the astonishing force of fifteen times her body weight pressing down upon her. It was too much for a human being to stand, at least for more than a short time. But she knew her people could handle it for ten seconds. There might be a few pulled muscles, a broken bone or two, but for the most part, *Westron's* crew would be ready to finish the battle once the engines shut down.

She wanted to scream, to snap out orders to cut the thrust immediately. Her body hurt everywhere, and it seemed like an hour had passed rather than some portion of ten seconds. But she held firm, her discipline solid as steel, her mind still sharp, ready to do what had to be done. Then it stopped, the weightlessness of freefall replacing the crushing pressure.

Her throat was dry, and she struggled to get words out. But she forced them from her mouth nevertheless.

"All batteries…open fire."

MCS Viking
Sigma Omicron System
210,000 Kilometers from Gamma Epsilon II Warp Gate

"Mr. Vance…we're getting a flashcom transmission from *Westron*, sir."

Vance felt a wave of relief. None of his scanners or probes had picked up any sign of the Alphas' vessel. He knew Antonia Silver was one of the best captains Mars had ever produced, but as time passed with no sign whatsoever of the ship, his hope had slowly drained away.

"Captain Silver reports she has engaged two Alliance vessels, sir…and destroyed one! *Westron* is about to engage the remaining ship."

Vance took a deep breath and exhaled. He was relieved that

Silver and her people were alive...for a few more moments, at least. But any chance of resolving the confrontation without provoking outright war with the Alliance was gone. Blood had been spilled, an Alliance vessel destroyed. Silver's tactical skill had evened the score in Gamma Epsilon, given the Martian forces a chance. But victory here could only lead to general war...and in a head to head matchup, the Confederation didn't stand a chance against the Alliance. At least not until the new fleet was completed.

The die is cast. There is nothing to do but win here...

"Prepare to launch all missiles."

"Yes, sir. All missile stations report ready to launch on your command."

He stared at the small symbol, the enemy ship fleeing from *Viking*. And the second one, another ship, moving from the planet, heading toward a rendezvous. Vance had no doubt the two Alliance vessels would attack *Viking*, and he knew it would be a close fight. He had faith in his people, in their ability to prevail. But he wasn't going to take any chances.

Vance sat silently for a moment. It was his decision to engage, to add to the risk of war...but after that, he intended to let Captain Carlson and his crew fight their ship. Space battle tactics wasn't his area of expertise.

"Captain Carlson...let's go after that ship and engage before the two enemy vessels can concentrate their assaults."

"Yes, Mr. Vance." The captain turned, looking toward his tactical officer as he began barking out commands. "Increase thrust to forty percent, nav plan Beta-3...and flush the racks."

"Thrust increasing, Captain. Launching externally-mounted missiles now."

Vance sat quietly as the force of *Viking's* thrust hit him, and then as the vessel shook from the launch of its external missiles. The confidence in Captain Carlson's voice was reassuring, at least on one level. But deeper down Vance carried the weight of what he had done. There had been no council vote, no debate, no strategic planning. He'd simply started a war.

He considered all he had done, wondering how he could

have avoided this confrontation. But he knew there had been no way, not since news of the alien ship's discovery had leaked. Mars wasn't ready for war...but the thought of a future where Gavin Stark and Alliance Intelligence possessed the means to move centuries forward in technology, to develop a whole range of superweapons, was too much to contemplate. Whatever happened now, this fight was Mars' best way forward. Its only way.

"All internal missile stations, launch."

Vance listened as Carlson ordered the rest of *Viking's* missiles to launch. The veteran captain was concentrating his long-ranged weapons on the closer enemy vessel. That was a gamble, Vance knew. If the barrage was successful, if the massive missile attack drew blood, maybe the enemy ship would be badly damaged, giving *Viking* the chance to finish it off before the second cruiser closed. The battleship would have to endure the other vessel's missile attack without answering. But a reasonably intact battleship would be more than a match for a fresh cruiser.

Viking shook, and then again a minute later as more missiles from her internal magazines launched. Vance stated at the main display, at the cloud of warheads moving toward the Alliance cruiser.

If we've started a war, this is the first battle...

Bridge - MCS Westron
En Route to Asteroid Belt
Gamma Epsilon System

"Keep firing! I don't care how hot the lasers are." Silver was leaning forward in her chair, straining against the straps of her harness. Her workstation screen was lit up like a holiday display, blinking red and yellow lights representing the damage her ship had sustained. Half her batteries were out, reduced to useless rubble. Only one had been a victim of overheating—though that battery had exploded, killing its crew and two others who had been in the corridor outside. The others had been battered by the Alliance ship's fire, one hit after another slamming into

Westron's tortured hull.

Her own fire had been at least as accurate, but she'd expected a sizable superiority in gunnery, not parity or a slight edge. The Alliance heavy cruiser had too big an advantage in weapons. If her people couldn't beat their enemies in targeting, they were going to lose the battle. It was that simple.

"All batteries increase to one hundred thirty percent."

Tomas stared back across *Westron's* smoke-filled bridge, his face white as a sheet. The surviving laser batteries were all battered, the massive conduits feeding energy to them from the main reactor overtaxed and worn from the stress. Increasing the power flow through those barely-functioning lines was beyond hazardous.

"You heard me, Gary," Silver repeated, her voice firm but not angry. She knew her orders were dangerous, reckless even. But she also realized if she did nothing, her ship was going to lose the battle.

"Yes, Captain. All batteries to one hundred thirty percent."

She stared straight ahead, her eyes dropping every few seconds to her workstation's small screen. The energy readings looked good. The reactor had so far escaped any real damage. With half her lasers gone that gave her extra power. But how could she use it?

"Lieutenant Tomas, I want engine thrust at forty percent immediately. Zigzag course to the enemy, randomization pattern, Beta-4."

"Yes, Captain."

"I want it off sync, Gary...a ten second delay."

"Captain?" The tactical officer's voice was uncertain, confused.

"I want the randomization program ten seconds ahead of the thrust adjustments. I want the gunnery crews to know what thrust we'll be firing ten seconds in advance. Tie in the AI to assist with the computations."

"Yes, Captain!" It was clear Tomas finally understood, and he relayed the orders, working his controls furiously.

Silver leaned back in her chair, trying to keep calm, even

as another blast shook *Westron* to its core. She was placing a lot of faith in her gunnery crews. Ten seconds wasn't a lot of time to adjust firing solutions to random thrust changes. But if it worked, *Westron* would frustrate her attacker's targeting… while planting a series of direct hits into the enemy ship. If her people could manage it, they might create an advantage…one big enough to win the fight.

"Randomization program activated, Captain…beginning ten second countdown to thrust."

"Very well." Her thoughts were in the turrets with the gun crews. In all likelihood, they had the fate of *Westron* and her crew in their hands.

She watched the countdown on her screen, her hands tightening around the armrests of her chair as the engines fired up, blasting her ship along a random trajectory. The ship's heading and velocity didn't change much…it would take extended thrust to meaningfully alter any of that. But even seemingly insignificant wiggles were enough to cause the enemy laser blasts to miss.

"It's working, Captain! We evaded their last barrage completely."

"Mind your station, Lieutenant." It wasn't time to celebrate not yet.

Our own gunners still have to make it work…

"Lasers firing, Captain." The excitement drained from Tomas' voice. "Missed. They all missed."

Westron lurched hard again, another random blast of thrust. And the next incoming shot went by, two thousand meters off the ship's port.

"Firing again, Captain…" Tomas' face was pressed against his scope. "Hit! Another one!" He looked up and stared back at Silver. "Three total hits."

Silver was silent. Her people had an edge now, if they could keep it.

The ship shook again, more thrust, along an entirely different vector. And again she saw the lights dim slightly as her batteries fired.

"Another pair of hits, Captain."

Silver felt the energy inside her, the feral excitement as her people scored hit after hit. Despite the erratic vectors of the nav plan, it was bringing *Westron* closer to the enemy, and each laser impact was reaching the target with greater power, inflicting increasing damage. Normally, a ship chose between evasive maneuver and the accuracy of its own fire. But *Westron* had both…at least for now.

Then the ship shook hard.

"We lost battery four, Captain."

Silver had known that before Tomas reported, and from the feel of it, she didn't think there was much chance any of the turret's crew had survived. Indeed, she'd lost track of casualties, but her best guess was a quarter of her people were dead or wounded. And the battle wasn't over.

"Maintain fire." She knew she was putting her other gunners in deadly danger. The hundred thirty percent energy flow was extremely dangerous…but it was also winning the fight. She swiped her finger across her workstation, bringing up the scanner reports on the enemy vessel. Its return fire was dying down, and the scans were showing great gaps in the hull, huge plumes of fluids and gasses escaping into space.

Westron couldn't take much more either…but her evasive maneuvers were doing the job. And the range was point blank now. Whatever happened, the battle wouldn't last much longer.

"Battery seven is out, Captain."

No, explosion…a normal overload. At least that's probably not any more dead crew…

"Very well. Continue firing."

She watched as her remaining guns fired, eyes fixed to the screen as the scanner reports updated. The enemy guns were almost silent now, and there was no detectable thrust from the Alliance vessel.

Any time now…

The lights dimmed again, for a few seconds longer this time. She knew she'd been pushing *Westron's* reactor and its power transmission system to the very brink. And the flickering lights told her each broadside was testing the vessel's endurance. But there was nothing she could do, nothing except wait.

"Captain, scanners report no energy readings from the Alliance ship." Tomas turned and looked across the bridge. "I think it's dead."

"Reduce batteries to ninety percent, Lieutenant, and maintain fire. Continue evasive maneuvers."

Silver had read about all sorts of stratagems and tactical deceits used in battle. She believed the enemy vessel was dead... but she only believed it so much.

"Bring us to point blank range and blast that ship to scrap."

"Yes, Captain."

Silver watched as her gunners chopped up the helpless Alliance ship...and only when the main spine broke and the hull pulled apart into two large sections did she truly allow herself to breath.

There were scattered cheers on the bridge, an outpouring of relief that *Westron* had somehow come through the lopsided battle, that she had beaten two larger foes. But the reaction was subdued, for the Martian vessel and her crew had paid a great price for victory...and that triumph was still incomplete.

There were still Alliance ships in the system. And the Alphas were still down on the planet's surface. Her people had work left to do.

"Lieutenant Tomas..." Silver's voice was hard as steel. "Set a course for planet two...maximum available speed."

Chapter Twenty-Two

Coordinate Grid 20.2-42.8
Inside the Alien Vessel
Planet Gamma Epsilon II

Dawes stopped in his tracks. The sound up ahead was unmistakable. He'd heard it before, metal scraping on metal. Another of the deadly 'bots. At least one.

His group had ambushed the Alliance troopers following them, wiping them out without so much as taking a hit. Dawes had allowed the victory to give him hope, a rookie mistake, he now realized, as the true meaning of that sound up ahead really hit him.

He held up his arm, gesturing for the others to halt. He cranked up his sound amplification and listened for a few seconds. Yes, the sound was definitely getting closer. There was no doubt.

Damn!

"We've got to move, sir. We're sitting ducks in this corridor." Ruiz was just behind Dawes. The corporal had his rifle out already, aimed forward. "We've got to find a better spot to fight it out."

Dawes sighed. "Where, Corporal? It's been nothing but one long corridor. No intersections, no turn offs. We can't get through any of the hatches we've passed, not in time." Dawes turned and looked back the way they had come. "Back," he said.

"We have to go all the way back. There's no good place to make a stand."

The three Alphas spun around and moved down the corridor at a fast jog. Isaacs was in the lead now, with Dawes bringing up the rear. The captain glanced back every few seconds, but there was nothing except the blackness. The clanging of armored boots on the metal deck drowned out the distant sound of the 'bot.

Dawes glanced quickly at each hatch they passed, a cursory inspection to see if he'd missed anything the first time. Perhaps there was one less securely jammed than the others, a way his people could go, find a better place to make their stand. He had his doubts that the three of them could defeat one of the terrible enemy combat units by themselves. The 'bots the Team had taken out so far had been subjected to massed fire from ten or twelve of the Alphas. But he knew they had *no* chance stuck in the narrow hall out in the open. None at all.

"Hold up," he shouted, halting as quickly as he could without stumbling. He turned his amplification to full power, listening. For an instant he thought there was nothing. But then he heard it. Metal on metal.

His mind raced, but he couldn't come up with anything. His people were bracketed between one or more of the deadly 'bots and the Alliance troopers he knew would be waiting in the main room.

If that's our choice…

He knew what he had to do. It made sense. The alien 'bots were only protecting their ship, but the Alliance forces were here to claim the ancient prize. If the Team failed, if the Alliance was allowed to control the technology of this alien race, the balance of power would be shattered. The Superpowers would fall. Including the Confederation. Mars was the closest thing mankind knew to a democracy…and the thought of Alliance soldiers marching through the Areas Metroplex filled him with a nearly uncontrollable fury. There 'bots were like something from a nightmare, but the Alliance troops were the real enemy right now.

"Back to the main room," he snapped.

"Yes, sir." It was clear from his tone, Corporal Ruiz agreed.

"Yes, Lieutenant." Isaacs sounded no less ready to fight the Alliance forces.

The small group jogged down the corridor. Dawes didn't know how many Alliance troopers were left in the massive chamber, but he knew it didn't matter. Five or fifty—or five hundred—it didn't make any difference. His people had no choice.

He glanced back one more time.

At least if they take us out, we'll lead the 'bot to them…

He was perversely amused at the thought of the deadly alien combat unit winning the battle after he and his people were dead.

Victory, by any means…

Coordinate Grid 20.2-42.8
Inside the Alien Vessel
Planet Gamma Epsilon II

"Damn!" Grax had ducked behind the stack of crates when he heard the explosion, and now he was looking out across the room. Five of his people were down. Two were dead for sure, their armored bodies ripped in half by the mines. It was the second blast his people had triggered. And by God, it was going to be the last if he could do anything about it.

"Stay away from those debris piles," he roared. "They're booby-trapped." He slammed his fist against his leg in frustration. He had no idea who these Martian soldiers were, but he'd never faced any force so maddeningly dangerous.

"Tend to the wounded…and pull the bodies out of the way. I want everybody on the alert. We need to be ready if anything comes down one of these corridors.

He looked around the massive room. His people had moved some of the debris and stacks of crates around, trying to create some cover against attack. But there were twelve corridors, running off in every direction. No matter how they piled up the barricades, they were flanked by some of the hallways. And guessing what direction trouble would come from seemed like a sucker's game.

"Lieutenant Hallis, I want your people to…" Grax fell silent. His audio detectors were cranked up…and he heard something. A scraping sound. Metal on metal.

"We've got something coming," he shouted, gesturing toward the sound with his arm. "Let's get in position, now."

He raced across the room, moving behind a small pile of metal canisters. There wasn't enough cover for all his people, but Grax would be damned if he was going to get caught out in the open. "I want everybody firing the instant anything comes out of that corridor."

He pulled his own rifle out, dropping to one knee, and leaning around the edge of his cover. The sound was louder, and now there was a similar scratching coming from another of the hallways. He angled his body, ducking down so his barricade provided cover from both directions.

He could hear his heart pounding. He'd been scared ever since his people had broken and run, terrified at what Gavin Stark would do to him. But now he was gripped by something almost supernatural. He was about to face something even more terrible than Alliance Intelligence's deadly spymaster.

He gulped for breath, struggling to control the shaking that had taken over his body.

You've been in combat dozens, of time, you fool. Pull it together…

He nodded, willing himself to focus, to push away the fear. He looked left then right, making sure his people were ready. Some of them were indeed in place, but others were moving back, cowering helplessly against the far wall. A few had even taken off down the corridors, fleeing in stark terror. He felt rage, strong enough to overcome the remnants of his fear. He wanted to get up, to run down the cowards, take them out. But there was no time.

He looked ahead, just as the 'bot moved into the room. Its

six appendages were all active, each holding a weapon and firing. Hypervelocity rounds ripped through the chamber, and the soldiers clustered along the wall began to fall. Grax could hear the sickening sounds of osmium rounds puncturing armor, the hideous shrieks of his dying soldiers. Flashes of blinding light tore through the dim illumination of the portable lamps, particle accelerator blasts that ripped into armor as if it was paper. But he ignored it all and opened fire.

His assault rifle was on full auto, and he hosed the 'bot with fire. He moved his weapon, targeting his fire on one of the arms. He hit it with at least two dozen shots, and then it fell to the side, still attached, but clearly disabled.

"Concentrate your fire," he shouted so loudly his throat felt like a hot knife had sliced through. "Take out the limbs."

He scrambled to the side, crawling to a pile of debris to on the 'bot's flank, opening up again, this time aiming directly at another appendage. He blasted away at full auto until his cartridge was exhausted. Then he ducked back down, waiting as the autoloader positioned a fresh one. He glanced up at his display.

Four clips left...

He moved back up, bringing his rifle to bear...and then he saw a flash of light. His visor went dark instantly, a failsafe to try to save his vision. His eyes were closed tightly, the inside of his eyelids still glowing. Then he realized he was moving.

The particle accelerator shot had impacted on the front of the debris pile, melting and vaporizing much of it and sending the rest flying around the room. Grax realized he was airborne, and an instant later he felt himself slam into the outer wall.

There was pain, and he felt the breath knocked out of him... but his veteran's discipline kicked in. He focused on his body, trying to decide if he was seriously injured. No, he realized. His armor wasn't punctured. None of his bones were broken. He was bruised and banged up, but nothing more.

He could hear yelling, his people shouting. The 'bot was down.

He felt a rush of excitement, and he started to get up. It was dark in his armor, and he thought to open his eyes. But they were already open.

"Captain, we've got another one of those things coming, sir."

He could hear his people shouting to him, joyous shrieks of victory replaced by terrified announcements that the battle wasn't over. That another 'bot was coming.

But Grax couldn't get his head around any of that. His mind was focused on one horrifying fact.

He was blind.

Coordinate Grid 20.2-42.8
Inside the Alien Vessel
Planet Gamma Epsilon II

"There are fighting sounds up ahead, Captain." Isaacs was in the lead, but Dawes was only a few meters back, and he could hear it as well.

"The Alliance forces must be fighting a 'bot." Dawes heart sank, but only for a second. Then he felt a rush of excitement. If the Alliance troopers were fighting for their lives they'd be distracted. His people had never had much of a chance, but the confusion could only help. It was a prospect that defied mathematics and probability, but it was something to grasp at, a faint hope that hadn't existed before.

"Let's go, boys." Dawes lunged forward, sliding past Isaacs and Ruiz, putting himself at the front of his tiny formation. "Keep an eye out for any of our people coming out of those other corridors, but otherwise, everything in there is an enemy."

He ran down the corridor, his rifle at the ready. He could see lights flashing ahead, the headlamps of the Alliance soldiers in the room at the end of the corridor. He let the anger take him, the rage at the Alphas who had been lost already. He was close now. Five meters. Three.

Damn!

The prayer. He'd said it every time he'd ever gone into battle, but this time he'd forgotten. The words flooded into his mind, but it was too late. He leapt into the room, his rifle spitting death on a cluster of Alliance soldiers ahead.

The room was chaos, an impossible maelstrom. There were Alliance troopers all around, scattered, disordered. And there were two of the 'bots, one badly damaged, immobile, returning fire with only two of its six weapons, and another, across the room, almost untouched.

Dawes eyes caught the debris of a third on the ground, unmoving. He'd seen enough of the 'bots to be cautious in declaring one completely dead, but he had no choice here. There were greater threats.

Two of the Alliance troopers in front of him fell under his fire. He'd taken them by surprise. They'd been focused on the terrible battle robots, not on human enemies. Even now, most of them maintained their fire on the alien combat unit.

Dawes understood. The 'bot was a far greater threat. He looked around the room. There were at least two dozen Alliance troopers down.

No, more than that…

The Alliance force was ragged, battered. The more Dawes looked, the more he realized their morale was failing. There were armored figures running down the corridors, especially the one leading back the way they had come.

They're breaking…

He dove behind a pile of boxes, swinging around and bringing his rifle to bear on the less-damaged 'bot. He fired, targeting the area where one of the appendages attached to the main body. His aim was spot on, and the arm—and the assault rifle it held—dropped limply to the 'bot's side. Then it fell off entirely, hitting the floor with a loud clang.

Dawes ducked down, behind one of the stacks of boxes. He saw Isaacs firing at a pair of Alliance troopers. The Alpha was focused, intent.

No…

"Robert!" Dawes screamed, but too late. It was the heavily damaged 'bot, down to its last weapon. The particle accelerator fired, a glowing trail of ionized air tracing a line from the weapon…straight through Isaac's body. The Alpha pitched backward and fell hard to the ground, a ten-centimeter hole ripped right through his chest.

Dawes leapt up, rushing across the room, firing as he did. He knew his scream had called attention to himself, and he could hear the fire of the Alliance troops, tearing apart the stack of boxes where he'd been kneeling a second before.

He was firing at the 'bot that had killed Isaacs, a pointless display of rage, he knew…but he did it nevertheless. His shots hit the 'bot right in the midsection, his rounds tearing into the vitals of the alien machine.

He swung to the side, moving to evade the fire he knew the Alliance troopers were sending his way…and he succeeded. For a few seconds. Then he felt the rounds slam into him from behind, in the back of the leg first, and then through his gut.

He stumbled forward, his arms reaching out to absorb the impact, even as his suit flooded his bloodstream with drugs, and the trauma control system began patching his wounds.

But the enemy wasn't done yet. There were at least five troopers firing at him now, and he felt the projectiles punching through his armor, and tearing through his flesh. He turned, trying to get up, but he slipped back down. He coughed hard, and he felt the thick blood bubbling up out of his mouth.

He pushed one more time, putting all that remained of his strength and will into a last attempt to get back on his feet, but he fell back down almost immediately, even as more shots riddled him.

He lay on the ground, miraculously not in pain, the result of his suit's futile efforts to save his life. Dawes had never been wounded in combat, not once during a twenty-year career that had seen him fight in some of the largest and bloodiest battles of the Second Frontier War. But it only took once.

He struggled to draw air into tortured lungs. He could feel himself slipping slowly away, the darkness closing in from all sides. The words of the old prayer drifted through his thoughts, the words he'd forgotten for the first time in a life of war.

He spat out blood, trying to clear his throat, to speak. But he only managed a few words.

"I'm sorry, mother…I forgot…"

Then he gave in to the darkness.

Chapter Twenty-Three

Coordinate Grid 20.2-42.8
Inside the Alien Vessel
Planet Gamma Epsilon II

Vandenberg raced back toward the main room, leaping over the piles of debris with almost reckless disregard. He could hear the sounds of combat ahead. He didn't know if any of the Alphas were caught up in the fighting, but he knew he had to find out. The jamming of his scanners and com meant he didn't have any real information on how many of his comrades were still alive, but his thinking had changed, from pain over who they'd lost to concern about who, if any of them, might survive. Half the Team, at least, was gone already, and the rest were scattered around, cut off from each other, facing the danger of more 'bots as well as the Alliance forces. He had no idea what he and his two companions would find up ahead, or whether they could make any difference if they found other Alphas surrounded and outnumbered. But he knew they had to try.

He thought for an instant he should say something, shout out orders or offer a few inspiring words. But he stayed silent. No orders were necessary…they all knew what they had to do. And he had no place trying to rouse these two veteran warriors, men who had seen a hundred times the combat he had. They were Alphas, and he knew they would behave that way. He hoped he would too.

He gripped his rifle tightly as he approached the end of the corridor. The sounds of combat grew louder as he approached, and he caught hints of light. Some were clearly the headlamps of armored troopers—either Alphas or Alliance forces—but there were brighter flashes too. He knew what they were immediately, and the realization made his gut flop. Particle accelerators. More alien 'bots.

"There are 'bots in there. Take care, both of you. Running in and getting yourself blasted isn't going to help anybody."

He halted a meter from the end of the corridor and crept forward, peering into the room. He saw a nightmare in full progress.

There were Alliance troopers, at least two dozen, and they were fighting two of the 'bots. There were at least as many of the soldiers down as still fighting, but one of the 'bots had also been pounded almost to wreckage.

Wait...the troops are firing at each other...

His eyes focused. There was an Alpha crouched behind a large structure of some kind. He was exchanged fire with a pair of Alliance soldiers. There was another figure next to him, lying motionless on the ground. Another Alpha.

Vandenberg felt a wave of rage take him, and he lunged forward, ignoring his own words of seconds before. He knew it was foolish, reckless, but he did it anyway, firing as he ran across the room.

He took the two Alliance troopers from behind, dropping them both with bursts of automatic fire. He kept running, heading toward the Alpha he'd seen from across the room. His comrade was wounded, he could see it now, the grayish-white foam of the trauma control system bubbling out of the holes in his armor.

He crouched down, dropping hard as he reached the cover and skittered to a halt. He could see the name stenciled on the armor's helmet. It was Ruiz.

"Jorge, it's Alex." He poked his head around the steel structure, looking out over the room. Jones and O'Reilly were moving along the outer perimeter, ducking back into each of the corridors and firing before moving on to the next.

"Alex…"

Vandenberg could tell immediately his comrade was badly hurt.

"Ruiz, we've got to get out of here." He turned and glanced over toward Jones and O'Reilly. They were moving toward the original corridor the Alphas—and the Alliance forces—had followed into the alien vessel. He gestured to Jones, pointing toward the corridor.

"Ruiz, what about the others?"

"The cap's dead. Robbie too. No sign of the colonel, the others…"

Vandenberg exhaled hard. He wanted to dive deeper into the vessel, to go in search of his comrades. But with Dawes dead and Reginald and Cho not around, he was in command. He might throw his own life away on a hopeless quest, but he was responsible for the others too. And for the mission.

"Can you walk, Ruiz?"

"I think so, Lieutenant."

Vandenberg looked around the room. It was chaos, but for a moment, it looked like neither the Alliance troopers nor the 'bots were focused in his direction.

"Alright, let's go. Back down the original corridor."

He reached around, pushing Ruiz gently and following along behind, his head turned back, watching for threats. They scrambled across the seven or eight meters to the corridor, moving past Jones, who was crouched just around the corner, covering them.

"Alright, boys, let's get out of here. The longer they…" He gestured back to the room with his head. "…tear each other apart, the better we'll be."

"What about the colonel and the others?" It was O'Reilly, but Vandenberg knew they were all thinking the same thing.

"I know, Sergeant…but there's nothing we can do to help them now. Even trying to get across that room would be the end of all of us. We need to get out, away from the jamming, and check if *Westron's* back on the air. Or any other Martian ship."

"But sir…"

"Enough O'Reilly. The lieutenant's right. The mission's first, always. The colonel himself would be the first one to say that. And if we can't raise the ship, we're all dead anyway." Jones' words were harsh, but Vandenberg knew they were nothing but the hard truth. And he was grateful for the sergeant-major's support.

"Let's move." Vandenberg gestured for the others to go, turning and facing back toward the room behind them. "Go. All of you."

The others paused, and Jones moved his arm in an indeterminate gesture, looking like he was going to say something about Vandenberg bringing up the rear. But then they all obeyed, moving quickly down the dark corridor.

Vandenberg looked once more behind him, into the room. Then he pulled up his rifle and followed his comrades.

Coordinate Grid 20.2-42.8
Inside the Alien Vessel
Planet Gamma Epsilon II

Crack. The sound of Elise Cho's rifle was unmistakable. Reginald hadn't been looking, but he had no doubt one of the Alliance troopers had just fallen. Then another shot…and likely a second kill.

Reginald was crouched down next to the sniper, his own weapon at the ready. He was on his last clip, and even that was mostly spent, just eighty-three rounds left from the original six hundred-thirty. He was fighting to stay alert, but the only thing keeping him going was the steady dose of stims his suit was injecting into his blood. His wounds were bad, but if this had been any sort of conventional battlefield, one with field hospitals and medical evac, they were entirely survivable. But there was nothing like that here, and he was beginning to realize he wasn't going to make it out of this one.

The thought was upsetting, though not at all how he'd expected it to be. He looked at it in an almost academic way, as though he was resigned to it. His pain was reserved for his Alphas, for the team he and Travis Warren had built. It was an odd coincidence that he would die his first time in command, on the very mission that followed Warren's death. But now he wondered if any of his people were going to make it through this one. It was painful enough losing Alphas…but the thought of the Team itself being destroyed was too much to bear.

Crack. Cho's rifle again.

Another kill…but it won't be enough. Elise will die too. There's no way we're getting through this room. This is where it ends.

The Alliance forces had the last 'bot surrounded. It looked like they had fought three of the fearsome things, and the horrifying scene in front of him spoke of the price they had paid. There were dozens of their dead strewn around, armor and bodies alike torn to pieces. It was like some nightmarish abattoir, perhaps the worst battlefield scene he'd witnessed in his long career.

But now they've finished off the 'bots. Which means the distraction that's been keeping us alive is almost gone…

Almost in answer, a burst of fire blasted the wall next to him. He ducked back, and as he did his eyes caught Cho. The sniper had taken a hit, a non-lethal one in the leg, but the injury made her stumble forward, and as she did she fell into a stream of fire.

"Elise!" But Reginald knew even as he shouted, it was too late. At least half a dozen hypervelocity rounds hit the diminutive sniper. Reginald knew she was dead, even as he screamed her name again.

He ducked back, as much by instinct as anything else, but he knew it was over. The 'bot was down, finished…and the dozen and a half or so surviving Alliance troopers were moving on him. He flipped to full auto. There was no point dying with ammo left.

He spun around, opening up on the troopers heading toward him. He fired a burst at one, at a second, dropping both. But then the return fire slammed into him, one round after another, tearing through armor, slicing through his body like a hot knife through butter.

He coughed hard, spitting blood all over his visor, and he felt himself falling to the ground. He heard the sounds of the Alliance troopers, but it seemed distant. The blackness was closing in on him, a single image floating before his tortured eyes, a view of the past. A little girl, six perhaps seven years old. A birthday party in the background, cake, balloons. But she wasn't looking at them. She was standing by the window, looking, waiting.

Waiting with a tear in her eye, hoping desperately for her father to come home.

Coordinate Grid 20.2-42.8
Inside the Alien Vessel
Planet Gamma Epsilon II

"Let's get the hell out of here!" Grax was screaming, forcing the words from his savaged throat. "There are more 'bots coming."

He was still blind, but his AI was controlling his movements, directing the servo-mechanicals of his suit to move his legs. He stumbled toward the corridor leading back the way his people had come. He still had teams deployed in the corridors, but he had no idea how many of those troopers were still alive. If *any* were still alive. But that didn't matter to him, not right now. All he wanted to do was get the hell out of this nightmare.

His rational mind cried out, reminding him of the fate that almost certainly awaited him when word reached Gavin Stark of the debacle. But there was no force in him now greater than the fear of this terrible, ancient ship, of the nightmare creations that lurked within.

His troopers were only too willing to obey his latest order. Many of them had run already, some back the way they had come, other blindly down the other corridors, deeper into the alien vessel. The few that remained—and he had no more than a dozen left—were the stalwarts, those who had stayed in the fight to the end.

But it's not the end. There are more 'bots coming.

He could feel his soldiers around him, some of them pushing past, moving far faster than his necessarily deliberate pace. He cursed them as cowards, but he didn't have time to get angry, to lash out. He was focused on one thing. Getting the hell out of the ship.

He stumbled again as another rush of fleeing soldiers pushed him aside. He'd have fallen for sure, save for his AI's control of his movement, but even with the sophisticated computer intervening, he bounced hard off the wall.

The sounds of the enemy 'bots were getting louder, closer.

They're too close…

His troops were all past him now, somewhere farther up ahead, fleeing for their own lives. It angered him, but he knew he'd make better time without the crush around him. The thought of the 'bots behind him, with none of his soldiers in between, pushed him to move as quickly as possible.

He felt his legs leap over something. *A pile of debris*, he realized. He was sure he'd make it out, at least reasonably sure. But the sound of the 'bots behind him still gave him a shiver between his shoulder blades.

Yes, I'll make it out. But what then?

Coordinate Grid 20-42
Inside the Alien Vessel
Planet Gamma Epsilon II

The intelligence was satisfied. Its resources were sharply limited, yet its defensive efforts had been crowned with success. Many of the invaders had been destroyed, indeed most. The survivors were fleeing, pursued by several of the security units. The enemy within the ship had been eradicated. The first force to enter had four survivors, and all had fled the vessel. The second force had originally numbered one hundred fifty-two.

Fourteen remained. Several had already exited, and the others were moving quickly toward their original entry point. Their intent was almost certainly flight.

The intelligence analyzed. What should it do next? After the first incursion, the intelligence had held its forces back… and the enemy had returned in greater strength. Indeed, two separate groups had come, forces that were obviously hostile to each other as well as to the vessel. Perhaps it should order a pursuit, send its units outside of the ship to attack and destroy the survivors.

It was a risk, yet perhaps one now worth taking. The Intelligence crunched numbers, its damaged processors evaluating millions of possible outcomes per second, assigning numerical probabilities to each potential action. But its findings were inconclusive. It lacked sufficient data to reach a definitive conclusion. There was no logical path, no next step derived purely from analysis, from data. It would have to proceed on alternative criteria.

Its files on the Ancients were sparse, many of them damaged or lost. But it had reviewed several concepts, motivations that had driven the beings that had built its predecessors. Intuition—making decisions seemingly at odds with a logical conclusion. Anger—motivation derived from perceived hostility. Vengeance—a sort of balancing effort, a response to return in kind an offensive action.

It analyzed the situation again, this time applying what it knew of the Ancients' decision processes. And it came to a conclusion. It would simulate anger, vengeance. It would send its 'bots out of the ship. It would attach the invaders, all of them.

And it would destroy them.

Chapter Twenty-Four

Bridge - MCS Westron
En Route to Asteroid Belt
Gamma Epsilon System

"Bring us into orbit, Lieutenant." There was urgency in her voice. She'd had to leave the Alphas behind hours before. She knew she hadn't had a choice, that she'd only done what she'd had to do. But that didn't prevent her from hating herself for it.

"Yes, Captain. Insertion in one minute."

"I want com on full power. We're going to send a transmission to the Alphas the instant we enter orbit."

"Yes, Captain."

Silver and her people had watched the fight as *Viking* destroyed one of the Alliance cruisers. The vessel had tried to escape from the battleship, but *Viking's* missiles had damaged its engines. After that it had just been a matter of time.

That left only one Alliance vessel in the system, as least as far as Silver could tell. By all accounts, *Viking* was more than a match for it, despite the damage she'd suffered in the previous fight. That was a good thing, she realized. *Westron* had won her own desperate struggle, but that had been by the slimmest of margins. The cruiser's engines had escaped any serious damage, but her reactor was at fifty percent, and two-third of her batteries had been blasted to scrap. She wasn't in any condition for another fight, at least not one where she was expected to make much difference to the outcome.

Silver stared intently at the screen, waiting for the scanner data to update. Intellectually, she knew she'd had no choice earlier, that she'd done what she had to do. And the victory against the two Alliance vessels had proven her correct. *Westron* wouldn't have had a chance if it had remained near the planet and faced all four hostile ships. But in her heart she still felt as though she'd abandoned the Alphas.

"Entering orbit now, Captain." Tomas sounded edgy too. *Westron's* crew and the Alphas had become close during their missions together, and Silver realized she wasn't the only one worried about the Team.

But you're the one who gave the orders, who left them here…

"Scanning now, Captain."

"Very well. Put me on orbit to ground com."

"Yes, Captain…on your line."

"This is Captain Silver calling Red Team Alpha. Captain Silver calling Red Team Alpha. Colonel Reginald?"

Silver sat silently, waiting. But there was no response, just soft background static.

"Red Team Alpha, this is Captain Silver. Any Team member, please respond."

Still nothing.

"Captain, scanners show no activity outside the jammed zone. No active energy readings. Nothing. Whoever is down there must be closer to the ship. Or…"

Silver took a deep breath, completing Tomas' statement in her head.

Or in the ship…

Or dead…

"Maintain scans, Lieutenant."

"Yes, Captain."

"Red Team Alpha, this is Captain Silver. Any Team member, please respond…"

MCS Viking
Gamma Epsilon System
520,000 Kilometers from Gamma Epsilon II

"Mr. Vance…we're getting a Gold Priority transmission from the Alliance vessel."

Vance turned toward the Captain's station, fighting to keep the surprise from his face.

That has *to be Stark…*

Vance was sitting at the same workstation along the periphery of *Viking's* bridge, but now he stood up abruptly. "I'll take it in your office, Captain." He turned and walked toward the hatch near the back of the bridge. Gold Priority was the highest designation for international communications, typically used in the direst emergencies or as a last-ditch attempt to avert war.

But can it be averted now?

He moved toward the captain's desk, sitting down and taking a deep breath. The tactical situation in the system had tilted to his advantage. He didn't know what was going on down on the planet's surface, but *Viking* had destroyed one enemy cruiser and, in a brilliant display of grit and tactics, Antonia Silver and her people on *Westron* had destroyed two Alliance vessels. Stark's ship was the last of the Alliance fleet, and there was little doubt *Viking* could win a final fight, despite the damage the battleship had taken finishing off the Alliance cruiser it had destroyed.

Vance was analytical by nature. People who met him even considered him cold, unemotional. But as much as he tried to hide it, he was a human being just like any other. He knew that his decisions of the last day, the actions taken by those he'd led here, had consequences, that war was a very real possibility. And he had no idea what he could do to prevent it.

He reached down toward the desk, picking up the headset, and putting it on. Then he paused a few seconds before he pushed the button to open the connection. "This is Roderick Vance."

The Alliance vessel was about 350,000 kilometers from *Viking*, just about enough to add a second's transmission time to messages sent in either direction. Two seconds wasn't a long time, but it weighed heavily on Vance's nerves.

"Mr. Vance, this is Gavin Stark, Alliance Intelligence. I'm afraid I must protest in the strongest terms the unprovoked attack on our exploration fleet."

"Unprovoked? Are you suggesting that you are not here to seize control of this system? That your forces did not constitute an invasion fleet? That you do not currently have ground forces on the planet's surface?"

"That is precisely what I am saying, Mr. Vance. Our ships came here on a mission of exploration. I will remind you that no internationally-sanctioned determination of ownership of this system has been made. The Alliance has every right to send research missions here to evaluate its position on supporting Confederation control…or asserting our own rights."

Vance sighed. He doubted Gavin Stark had ever uttered honest words in his whole miserable life. But he wasn't about to underestimate the master spy, and there was no doubt, his own actions could be made to look damning.

"Mr. Stark, do you expect me to believe that a fleet of Alliance Intelligence warships was sent here on a mission of exploration?"

"Of course, Mr. Vance. The ships your force destroyed had been converted to research vessels. Your suggestion that any other motivations are at play is offensive to say the least… though of course of far less import than the deaths of over one thousand Alliance naval personnel."

"Those were well-armed research vessels."

"Space is a dangerous place, Mr. Vance. As you have done your part to prove."

"If you are so convinced I am here to start a war, you should be concerned for your own safety. My vessel is between yours and the warp gate…and we still outgun you. Indeed, your hope of survival hinges on my good will, does it not?"

"Indeed, Mr. Vance…though murdering me and the members of my crew will do nothing to prevent the war you have started here. Indeed, it will only make such a conflict a certainty.

The perfidy of your conduct here will only make it that much easier to keep the other Superpowers out of it. The degree of provocation might even serve to keep the other Powers neutral, even if we violate the prohibition on conflict within the solar system. A lightning strike at Mars could end the war in a matter of days. Your vaunted new fleet would be blasted to scrap in its cradles in the orbital shipyards.

"If you get out of this system to initiate such a course of action, Mr. Stark."

"No, Mr. Vance, I'm afraid not. Your problem will not be so easily solved by more aggressive action. My personal AI back in Washbalt has been programmed to issue a pre-scheduled communique, one stating that our exploration fleet has been ambushed and attacked while exploring the Gamma Epsilon system. It also includes my own personal log, where I noted that the Confederation had already explored the system...and expressed my concern that it appeared significant Martian military assets had been deployed there. A clear violation of the international treaty on warp line explorations, I might add." Stark paused. "I'm afraid my death will not serve you."

"It might not serve me, Mr. Stark, but that doesn't mean I won't kill you anyway." Vance was working on instinct now, abandoning the careful doubletalk of international relations. He figured whatever the spy said, Gavin Stark was a survivor, one with no intention of dying simply to justify an Alliance attack on Mars. Vance had the upper hand, at least here in Gamma Epsilon, and he knew he had to use it for everything he could.

"Spoken like a true aggressor." Stark's voice was still calm, but Vance thought he detected something. A ripple of fear, perhaps? This was a showdown, a high stakes power game, and Vance knew he had to play his opponent. He had to find a way to come out on top.

"I suggest we dispense with the acting, Mr. Stark. You are here for the same reason I am here, and your warships and soldiers have engaged my forces, killed my people."

"Defending themselves only, Mr. Vance."

Vance sighed. He was no diplomat, and he despised the

whole game of parsed words and nuanced statements. But he had no choice, not now. Stark was understating the complexity and danger of an Alliance declaration of war…but Vance also knew his nation would likely lose a fight if one started now.

"You do not strike me as a man ready to die to create a casus belli for your successors to use to their advantage. Shall we go back and forth with useless posturing…or should we try to find a solution to this problem?"

"I am listening."

Damn, he is good…

Vance had heard much about Stark, but now he was realizing the talk—about the Alliance spy's intelligence as well as his ruthlessness—was understatement if anything.

"We both know what is on the surface of the planet, Mr. Stark. And we both know what it means."

Vance paused a few seconds, but there was no reply.

"Perhaps we can find a way to share it between our two governments."

There was more silence, perhaps five or ten seconds. Then Stark said, "That is intriguing, Mr. Vance. Please elaborate."

"I propose we cease hostilities, that we order our forces on the planet to stand down. Then we will both remain here. We will draft a communique to both of our governments detailing what we believe we have found here, and we will propose that our two nations share equal access to this amazing discovery."

"And our destroyed vessels? Our dead crews?"

"Will offset our own, Mr. Vance. All fighting between our forces will be declared a tragic misunderstanding and not an act of war. We will both attest to such to our governments. There will be no calls for retribution, no further hostilities."

There was no response at first. Then Stark broke the silence. "Agreed, Mr. Vance. I propose we proceed to the planet and enter orbit together. We can then assess the situation on the surface and prevent any further conflict between our ground forces."

"Agreed, Mr. Stark. We will proceed at once." He cut the line.

Vance leaned back in his chair, exhaling hard. He was willing to honor the terms of the deal he'd just made. It wasn't ideal, but the Alliance and the Confederation had a history as allies. Perhaps they could cooperate on the development of the new technology.

He tapped the com. "Captain, reduce our status to yellow alert, and power down weapons systems."

"Ah…yes, sir…if that's what you want."

"All crews are to remain at their stations, Captain…but I want the ship to appear to be in peaceful status to any external scans."

"Yes, sir."

Vance turned the chair and looked at the gray metal wall, his mind in turmoil.

Yes, you're willing to honor the deal…but is Stark?

AIS Shadow
Gamma Epsilon System
520,000 Kilometers from Gamma Epsilon II

"Captain, I want all weapons systems shut down at once." The spy walked out of the private room onto the main area of *Shadow's* bridge.

"Yes, Mr. Stark." The officer's voice betrayed an obsequiousness that seemed somehow beneath the dignity of a serving officer. Fear of a man like Stark transcended rank and dignity, and it was clear the spymaster was deeply focused on something. Not a good time to risk his anger.

Stark moved wordlessly across the bridge, sitting in his chair. His expression was hard, but almost emotionless. "Set a course for the planet at once."

"Yes, sir." The captain snapped off a series of orders, relaying Stark's commands to the other officers.

Stark himself was deep in thought, considering his exchange with Vance. The Martian was intelligent, there was no doubt about that. One day he would no doubt be a dangerous adversary. But he was still young, inexperienced. His proposal to share the technology was a pragmatic one, a solution that made sense. One that seemed palatable to both sides. There was just one problem. Gavin Stark had no intention of sharing the power this historic discovery offered. Not with the Confederation. Not even with the Alliance government. It was his, and his alone.

He glanced down at the small screen to the side of his workstation.

Two days, eleven hours...

Stark was a planner. His operations typically consisted of plans within plans...schemes with all kinds of backups and emergency provisions. And this situation was no different. He'd expected to enter the system with his four vessels, destroy he Martian forces, and take control of the alien vessel. But Roderick Vance had deployed an unexpected reserve, and the addition of a Martian battleship to the mix had upended Stark's plan. But the Alliance spy had his own backup in place, more than enough force to crush the two Confederation vessels...and secure the ruins on the surface.

The task force was regular Alliance navy, and that meant their deployment would make keeping the secret that much harder. Stark had hoped to avoid the complexities, the inevitable difficulties that would result from utilizing forces beyond his own total control. But he had no choice now, none except to stick to his agreement, and to trust Roderick Vance. And he didn't even consider that.

No, Stark had no intention of honoring the deal he'd just made, not for any longer than two and a half days. Then he would destroy the Martian ships...and eliminate Roderick Vance before age and experience turned him into a dangerous adversary.

And he would find a way to maintain control of the artifacts on the planet, even after the Alliance naval forces arrived. He might have to spill some more blood, but to Gavin Stark, that was a regular cost of doing business.

MCS Viking
Gamma Epsilon System
520,000 Kilometers from Gamma Epsilon II

Vance sat silently at the small desk, grateful for the closed doors separating the office from *Viking's* bridge. He was known as a man who never gave his thoughts away, one who had so effectively kept his emotions hidden, it was widely rumored he didn't have any. But he knew the uncertainty was clear on his face now. He'd made a deal with Gavin Stark, a devil's bargain, and it was gnawing away at him.

He didn't trust Stark, not on any level. The Alliance spy was dangerous, he knew that for certain. Even his tight-lipped father had spoken with great frustration about his encounters with the deadly agent, the man who, it was rumored, had engineered the sequence of events that ended the Second Frontier War.

The fact that Stark was outgunned, almost doomed if it came to a final struggle, only intensified his worry. Stark hadn't had any choice but to accept the deal…but that didn't mean he would honor it.

Stark's reputation is as a meticulous planner. He has something up his sleeve. But what? And when?

Vance was a man of his word, though he was beginning to realize that a career in intelligence was likely to cost him that distinction, at least when dealing with people like Stark.

His mind drifted to the surface, to the wonder of the ancient ship half-buried in the dirt of this alien world. He imagined the implementation of the technology. Weapons that could secure the Confederation's future, give it the means to protect itself without navigating a perilous course of alliance and treaties with totalitarian Superpowers. But his thoughts were on more than just tools of war, of death. What advances in medicine, in energy generation? He envisioned an economy vastly larger than Mars' current one, with prosperity reaching every citizen of the Confederation. He considered the advances in computer technology, artificial intelligences vastly superior to those possessed now by humanity, robots taking over every dangerous job, sparing mankind from the risk.

It was wondrous, a miracle that promised prosperity unimagined. Yet there was another side, a darker one. His mind saw fleets, great armadas of war, armed with weapons heretofore unimaginable. He saw war, unending, brutal, devastating war... destruction on a scale never before seen. The powers would fight over the alien technology, a battle that would never end—could never end—until all possessed the amazing ancient technology, or until they were utterly destroyed.

He wondered about the Alphas, the nightmare he knew they'd been through. Were any of them still alive? He was responsible for sending them here, and if they all died, it was his doing. He longed to order *Westron* to send down the retrieval boat, to find any survivors and to get them off that deadly world. But he couldn't. He found himself hoping some of the Alphas were still alive for another reason, one that came before concern, before worry or guilt. He had one more mission for them to complete.

It was one order he didn't want to give, one he'd tried to find a way around for the last half hour. But there was no other way. Anything else was just too much of a risk. If Gavin Stark somehow managed to gain control of the alien technology, the Confederation would be through. And if he went back on his word, attacked Stark's ship, he knew it would lead to war, a conflict Mars couldn't win.

He shook his head, still not believing what he was about to do. He tapped the com unit. "Captain, send a coded communique to *Westron* at once. Captain Silver is to execute Order 11-A at once."

"Yes, Mr. Vance," came the slightly confused response. "At once."

Vance stared at the top of the desk, fighting the urge to recall the command before it was too late. But his rationality had clamped down hard, and he realized there was no option, not one with a risk level he could accept.

Chapter Twenty-Five

Coordinate Grid 20.2-42.4
One Kilometer From Alien Vessel
Planet Gamma Epsilon II

"Keep moving...we should be out of the range of that jamming any minute." Vandenberg was racing across the dense yellow clay, moving quickly, almost recklessly. He knew it was far from certain that *Westron*—or any other Martian vessel—would answer, but he was driven by an urgency to try. Whether that was some kind of gut feel, or simply a realization that he had no other options, seemed irrelevant now. As was the thought that if he couldn't reach help, he and the others were as good as dead.

"We've got something coming out of the ship, Lieutenant." Jones had stopped on the ridgeline, and he was staring back the way the four surviving Alphas had come. "Looks like Alliance troopers, sir."

Vandenberg and his comrades had encountered half a dozen Alliance soldiers as they ran out of the ship. For the most part, the enemy had been routers, fleeing in panic. That had made them easy targets, and the Alphas had gunned them down. But the troopers coming out now were those who had held their order, finished off the 'bots. They would be far more dangerous.

He stopped and turned back toward the others. "Okay, you three, find good spots along this ridge. We need to be ready if they come after us. I'm going to try to get clear of this jamming and see if I can raise *Westron*."

"Yes, sir." Jones turned toward O'Reilly and Ruiz. "You guys heard the Lieutenant. Dig in and get ready to hold this line." Then: "Jorge, how you holding up?"

"I'm good, Sarge." Everything in Ruiz's tone suggested otherwise.

Vandenberg stood, looking back toward his wounded comrade. "Jorge, maybe you should hang back behind the ridge, try to get a few minutes of rest."

"No way, Lieutenant…I'm good. I swear."

Vandenberg hesitated. He wanted to order Ruiz to drop back, but something kept the words from coming out. "Okay, Corporal. Carry on." There wasn't much chance any of them were getting out of this…and if Ruiz was going to die, Vandenberg was going to let him do it with dignity, as an Alpha fighting alongside his friends.

He turned and kept moving, listening to the static from his com. His eyes darted around, trying to remember exactly where it had been that the colonel broke clear of the interference. And then suddenly, a voice blared loudly through his speakers.

"Red Team Alpha, this is *Westron*. Any member of Red Team Alpha…this is *Westron*. Do you read?"

Vandenberg felt a rush of excitement. "*Westron*, this is Lieutenant Vandenberg…commanding Red Team Alpha." The last words almost caught in his throat, and they sounded strange to him, unreal. He'd been the rookie, the one who'd had to earn his place. Now he was in charge.

"Lieutenant Vandenberg, I'm so glad to hear your voice. This is Captain Silver."

Vandenberg expected Silver to ask about the other officers, but she didn't.

"Captain, we're relieved to hear from you. We thought…"

"Lieutenant, listen to me carefully. I have a priority one order directly from Mr. Vance. You are to execute Order 11-A at once. Is that understood?"

Vandenberg paused. He had no idea what order 11-A was.

"Request confirmation," he responded. "Order 11-A?"

"I can't discuss it over an open com, Lieutenant. Your AI can fill you in. I've got to sign off now. You are to maintain radio silence until the mission is completed."

Vandenberg could hear the discomfort in Silver's tone. *Westron's* captain was worried about the command, and the Team. She hadn't asked about losses, about the situation. She'd just given him the order and then shut the line.

"Order 11-A, explain," Vandenberg said to his AI. He stood, frozen and stunned as the computer read the order to him. He could feel the sweat sliding down his neck, his back, and he sucked in a deep breath.

Pull it together, Vandenberg...

"Sergeant Jones...you are to remain here and hold this ridgeline."

"Yes, sir." Jones was prone, just behind the crest, his rifle at the ready. "The enemy does not seem to be pursuing us, at least not yet." A short pause. "Are you going somewhere, Lieutenant?"

"Yes, Sergeant-Major. I will be back as quickly as possible." He didn't offer an explanation...he was still struggling with it all himself. Then he turned and took off, running as quickly as he could, risking high, soaring jumps to do it.

Coordinate Grid 20.2-42.8
Just Outside the Alien Vessel
Planet Gamma Epsilon II

"Captain, they're coming...they're coming!" The corporal was on the verge of hysteria as he ran out of the alien ship, screaming to Grax.

"Calm yourself, Corporal. What did you see?"

"Didn't see anything, sir. Heard them. Those blasted 'bots. At least two, coming this way. They'll be here any second." The non-com kept running, right past Grax, past the fourteen troopers standing around outside the alien vessel.

Grax struggled to contain his fear. The alien robots were a terror. And they just kept coming.

"We need to find some cover." He moved his head around helplessly, nothing before his eyes except darkness. He couldn't see his display. He didn't know who was still alive, still standing in the ranks. At least what the ranks had dwindled down to.

"Highest ranking trooper still in the line," he snapped to his AI.

"Impossible to determine while within the jamming radius."

"Damn!" He flipped the com back to his external speakers and jacked the volume to full. "Any officers remaining, sound off now."

He listened. For a second, he thought he might be the only surviving officer. But then he got a response.

"Lieutenant Robinson, sir." He heard the sound of boots moving in the dense yellow dirt, and then Robinson again, closer now. "What can I do, sir?"

"We need to get out of here, Lieutenant." He turned down the volume and continued in a hushed whisper. "I'm blind, Robinson. I need you to get us to a good location."

"Yes, sir." There was a long pause. "Captain, there's not much but open ground."

"Then take us around the ship…maybe there's someplace in the ruins, on the hull. But let's move. We've got more of those things coming, and if they catch us in the open it's over."

"Yes, sir." Then louder: "Listen up, everybody, we're moving around to the left. Hug the perimeter of the ship, and get into some cover. The best you can find…'cause this fight isn't over yet."

"Do you need help, sir?" Robinson was speaking softly now.

"No, Lieutenant. My AI can manage it." Grax didn't like having to rely on anyone else. He hated being helpless. The Alliance Intelligence service was nothing like the Marines or the other forces. It was far from unknown for an officer to advance in rank by assassinating a superior. It was against regs, of course, but subsequent success tended to dampen any interest in investigating such things. And Grax had led his force to ruin. He couldn't imagine Gavin Stark doing anything but rewarding the subordinate who took matters into his own hands.

"Very well, sir."

Grax stood still for a moment, almost as if he expected Robinson to shoot him down where he stood. He had no doubt he'd have done just that if the roles had been reversed. But no shots came, only the sound of the officer's boots moving farther away.

"Let's go," he snapped to the AI. "After them…around the alien ship."

"Yes, Captain Grax," the slightly machine-sounding voice replied. Then Grax felt the legs of his armor moving, carrying him along.

Coordinate Grid 20-42
At the Alpha's LZ
Planet Gamma Epsilon II

Vandenberg rushed up to the lander, tearing open the cargo hatch. He rummaged through the piles of supplies—reserve ammo, weapons, armor repair kits…and one titanium canister.

"Is that it, Nate?" he queried his AI.

"Yes, Lieutenant. The item in its protective container weighs three hundred eleven kilograms in standard Earth gravity, Two hundred ninety-four in the local environment. Well within your suit's lift parameters."

Vandenberg reached down, grabbing the package. He struggled for a few seconds, trying to get a grip on it until he found two handholds on the side. Then he grabbed hold and hoisted it out of the cargo bay and turned around, facing the way he had come. There was no time to waste. He had to get back.

He'd hated leaving the others behind, but his orders were clear, as was the course of action they demanded of him. He was in command now. It was a situation no one had likely foreseen, and if they had, perhaps they would have placed Sergeant Jones in his place on the chain of command. But no one had done that, and his rank stood. Vandenberg was a Martian officer, a member of Red Team Alpha, and whatever it took, he was going to do his duty.

He had images in his mind, of returning, finding the others dead along the ridge. Of running into victorious Alliance troops waiting for him...or worse, more 'bots from the alien vessel.

He moved as quickly as he could, but he was slowed by the large canister he held. His armor could carry the weight, but it was difficult to run with both arms wrapped around a large cylinder.

His heart was beating so loudly it sounded like a drum in his ears. He was scared, for himself of course, but even more so about what he'd find when he got back.

I am in command. Whatever happens now—whatever has already happened—it is on me...

He'd kept radio silence, but now he wanted to know. He *had* to know. His comrades were right on the edge of the jamming zone. With a little luck he might get through.

"Sergeant Jones, report."

Vandenberg's guts were twisted into knots, but he felt a wave of relief when the sergeant-major's voice blared through the static on his com.

"We're still here, sir. But all hell's breaking loose down at the ship."

"Explain."

"The Alliance troopers didn't come our way, sir...I'm not even sure they know we're here. They formed up outside the ship, and then they hightailed it around the one side. We weren't sure what was going on, at least for the first minute or two, but then three of the 'bots came out after them."

"Very well, Sergeant. I'm on my way back...and we're going to have to get close to that ship again."

"Yes, sir." Jones was the hardest veteran Vandenberg had ever known, but even the grizzled sergeant-major hadn't been able to keep the doubt from his voice.

Vandenberg flipped off the com. "Nate, how close do I

have to get this thing?"

"Unknown. Insufficient data on material of alien hull makes accurate prediction impossible."

Vandenberg sighed. "Best guess."

"I do not make guesses, I analyze data."

"Then analyze what you have, and tell me how close I have to get this thing to be sure of success."

"Assurance of success, defined as a probability above the ninety-ninth percentile, requires placing the device inside of the alien ship."

Vandenberg felt like he'd been punched in the gut. He'd been worried about getting back near to the ship…but going inside again?

He kept moving, bounding over the last rise and looking straight ahead. His three Alphas were right where he'd left them, looking cautiously over the ridge toward the ancient vessel.

How am I going to tell them we have to go back?

Coordinate Grid 20.2-42.8
Along the Port Side of the Alien Vessel
Planet Gamma Epsilon II

Grax closed his eyes tightly and opened them again. Yes, there *was* light. He hadn't imagined it.

The visor display was in front of him. It was a blur, and he couldn't read any of it, but he *could* see it.

"Increase visor projection magnification to 3X," he snapped to his AI. The screen became clearer, and he could make out the readings.

"Retract display."

The blue light of the projected words and graphs moved upwards, mostly out of his view. He stared through the visor, looking ahead. There was a shape, fuzzy, blurry, but man-sized. And another. As he stared they became clearer. His vision wasn't normal, nothing close to it. But it *was* improving.

He heard shouting, coming from behind. Then fire.

He spun around, even as the figures he'd seen in front of him reacted too, ducking down into whatever cover the ancient ship's hull offered. He dropped hard to his knees, and then to the ground, grabbing his rifle as he did. He slid to the side, hearing the clang as his armor slammed into the ship's hull. He wasn't sure his cover was all that great, but it was damned sure better than standing out in the open.

He saw more shapes now, larger ones. Three of them. 'Bots.

He aimed his rifle, at least as well as he could, and he opened fire in the direction of the alien combat units. All his people were firing, most on full auto. He knew they all had to be low on ammo, but if they couldn't take down those 'bots that wouldn't matter. He really didn't care if a bunch of corpses had any fresh clips left on them.

He flipped his own weapon to auto too. He knew his aim was rough, but the 'bots were big targets. He could see two of them slowing, one even stumbling down on one—knee? The 'bots were still firing, and he could hear the sounds of their auto-cannons, a steady rattle. And every few seconds, a bright flash of light, one of the particle accelerators firing. He knew the energy weapons had a short range, that the atmosphere quickly drained their power. But at this knife-fighting range, a hit from one practically vaporized a man, even a fully-armored one.

He could hear screams, his people getting hit, dropping. His best guess was that half of them were down already. The damaged bot was almost silent now, only one gun still active. But the other two were still up and firing. His people weren't going to make it. He wasn't going to make it. It was a cold realization, but one he couldn't avoid.

His rifle kicked back, and he heard the clacking sounds as the autoloader inserted another cartridge. The entire process took just over a second, but when he looked out again, the two functioning 'bots were closer. He glanced over to the side, just in time to see one of his people riddled with fire. The soldier stayed up on his knees for a second, perhaps two. Then he fell forward, almost certainly dead.

Damn these things to hell…

Grax hadn't left the Corps to die on this desolate shithole of a planet. He'd been attracted to Alliance Intelligence by the money, of course, but it was also the risk that had drawn him in. He knew the spy agency had no tolerance for failure, that the disciplinary measures of the Marine Corps seemed like a light rap on the wrists by comparison. But Grax had never had doubts about himself, about his abilities. And Alliance Intelligence's soldiers were typically deployed in overwhelming strength, not the kind of hopeless battles so common in the Corps' history.

And yet here I am, about to die in a battle the Marines would have turned into a song…

He was scared, and angry too. But all that seemed unreal now, somehow distant. He was nailed to his position, firing away at the attackers he knew he couldn't defeat. He didn't know if any of his people were still alive, but he was sure they'd all be dead in a few minutes.

For three years, he'd served Alliance Intelligence, and in that time he'd lost the soul of the young Marine recruit he'd once been. He'd done terrible things, killed on the orders of Gavin Stark and others like him. Part of him wanted to feel regret, to repent for his choices now that he faced his death. But he'd never been able to be lie to himself. He wasn't sorry for his choices, and he knew if he had a second chance he would have done the same thing.

But none of that mattered now. He just angled his rifle and opened fire again. They could kill him, but his death wouldn't come cheap.

Chapter Twenty-Six

Coordinate Grid 20-42
At the Alpha's LZ
Planet Gamma Epsilon II

Vandenberg raced across the open plain, his comrades at his side. The 'bots had followed the Alliance troopers around the side of the ship, leaving the access point unguarded. It was an opportunity, one he suspected wouldn't last.

He angled his head, looking around the canister in his hands. Still clear…

He felt strange, defenseless. His rifle was hanging from its harness on his armor, his hands occupied. If any enemy troopers appeared, he would have to depend on his fellow Alphas. His friends.

We're going to make it…

He pushed, moving his legs as quickly as he could, burdened as he was. And then he saw it. A shadow at first, almost the feel of movement more than any actual sighting. But then it burst into view. One of the 'bots, moving around from the ship's starboard side, heading toward the open section of hull. It took one step in that direction, and then it stopped abruptly, spinning around and opening fire.

Vandenberg set the canister down as quickly as he could, and he dove to the ground, pulling his rifle out as he did. He opened up on the 'bot, his shots ricocheting off the metal of the alien war machine. He took a deep breath and focused, moving the stream of fire, targeting the spot where one of the appendages connected to the main body.

He heard a yell to his side. Jones.

"Sergeant-major…"

"I'm alright, sir. The thing just clipped me."

Vandenberg wasn't sure he believed Jones, but the fact that the non-com answered at least meant he was alive and conscious. And right now, Vandenberg was willing to take that.

We can't stay here…we're too out in the open. But what can we do?

"Listen up, guys. We're dead meat out here, even hugging the ground. We've got to spread out, approach that thing from different sides." He paused. "We have to get into that ship and deploy this device. We *have* to."

"I'm on the left, sir." It was O'Reilly, his voice distorted by the amplification of his speakers. They were back in the jamming zone, so the scanners were dead. Vandenberg couldn't see where the sergeant was. He couldn't direct anything. He'd just have to trust his comrades.

"I'm on the left, Lieutenant." It was Ruiz, yelling from the other flank. He didn't sound good. In fact, he sounded like shit. Vandenberg almost ordered the wounded corporal to pull back, but the brutal truth was he needed everyone. The mission came first. Always. It was the Alpha's mantra, the first thing he'd been taught when he'd joined. And now he was seeing it in practice, watching wounded comrades pushing forward against the odds.

"Alright, Sergeant-Major…looks like the two of us are in the center. You swing around to the left, and I'll go to the right."

Nothing. No response.

Vandenberg cranked his volume to full and repeated his call. Still nothing.

He had kept himself calm, focused…pushed back the fear and uncertainty. Now he felt it coming on, testing his will, his ability to resist. He wanted to panic. He almost *did* panic. But somehow he held on.

He turned and crawled to the left, toward Jones. For an instant he thought the sergeant-major was dead. Then he saw movement.

He scrambled the rest of the way, putting his hand on Jones' armor. "Sarge, can you hear me?"

"Yes, sir. Sorry, I was out there for a few seconds. The suit gave me a jolt of stims."

"How bad is it?"

"Bad enough, Lieutenant. But I'm still in the fight." His voice was strange, a rattling fluid sound accompanying every word.

Blood in his lungs?

Jones rolled over, moving around and bringing his rifle to bear again. "Let's do this, Lieutenant."

Vandenberg felt sick. He knew Jones was badly wounded. His mouth opened, ready to order the sergeant-major to stay where he was, to find his way back to the ridge if he could. But just as with Ruiz, the words didn't come. He needed Jones. The mission needed Jones...and everything the veteran non-com had left to give. Even his life if need be.

Vandenberg looked up. The 'bot was just outside the great tear in the hull his people had used as an entrance. There was no way to get in while that thing was still functioning. And he was far from sure the four of them could take it down.

He glanced at his display, at the readout attesting to his dwindling ammo. He knew the others had to be in the same situation. But failure wasn't an option. What could he do?

He was still thinking when he heard the blast of fire from off on the left. It was O'Reilly. He was up, moving forward in a wild zigzag pattern...and he had an assault rifle in each hand, proving for all to see how he'd earned his nickname, 'Two Gun.'

Vandenberg felt the urge to shout out to his comrade, to order him to get down, but he just watched instead, horrified and amazed. O'Reilly's sudden charge had taken the 'bot by surprise. It had been busy firing at Ruiz, and at Vandenberg and Jones, but now it was caught in the double stream of O'Reilly's deadly weapons. The veteran sergeant held the rifles out in front of him, weapons that normally required two hands to handle, and his aim was uncanny. His projectiles slammed into the 'bot right at what passed for its neck, each hit weakening the amazing, almost indestructible alien metal. The fearsome war machine stumbled back under the relentless fire.

But it was still in the fight, and it reacted quickly, redirecting its weapons to the new threat. Vandenberg watched in stunned horror, and now he did shout to O'Reilly. "Get down. Ian!"

It was too late. Vandenberg watched helplessly as the 'bot turned two of its autocannons on the charging Alpha. The heavy rounds tore into O'Reilly's armor, shot after shot riddling the veteran soldier. But still he moved forward, his fire undiminished.

"Stay here, Sergeant…lay down some covering fire until I get close." Then he screamed, loud enough, he hoped for Ruiz to hear him. "Corporal, covering fire now…until I get up there."

Then he leapt up himself, running forward across the couple hundred meters between him and the 'bot, adding his own fire to O'Reilly's. He'd covered half the distance when his stricken comrade reached the alien creation. Vandenberg could see O'Reilly was grievously wounded, at least a dozen gaping holes in his armor. But still he was on his feet, and now the grizzled sergeant dropped his rifles. They might have called him Two Gun, but he entered his final battle with just his blade extended from his savaged armor.

The blade was the ultimate technological development of the sword, made from the hardest metal known to human science and honed to an edge no thicker than a few molecules. It was sharp enough to cut through the osmium-iridium alloy of the most modern fighting suits, and with the strength of an armored arm behind it, the destruction it could wreak was fearsome. And so it was with Ian O'Reilly's blade.

The sergeant slashed at the 'bot, and even that mysterious alien metal proved no match for the edge of O'Reilly's blade, a thousand times sharper than any razor. The nuclear power of the dying man's suit drove the blade deep into the 'bot, slicing at its neck until the head dropped off.

The robot staggered back, but it didn't fall. It was not a man, and even without what passed for its head, it still fought back. One of the arms lashed out, the power behind it even greater than that of O'Reilly's suit. The metal appendage smashed into the Alpha with such force it dented his armor. Then again, and again it struck, and finally, Ian 'Two Gun' O'Reilly dropped to the ground.

But now Vandenberg came rushing in, his own blade drawn. He slashed wildly at the alien mechanism, severing limbs, cutting deeply into the body. The 'bot tried to turn, to fight back, but even its almost unimaginable power and strength were gone. Vandenberg sliced deeply one more time, and the terrible metal warrior dropped hard to the ground, laying less than a meter from O'Reilly.

Vandenberg leaned down, slicing into the seemingly dead 'bot until there was no doubt it was nothing more than a pile of rubble. Then he moved toward O'Reilly, dropping to his knees next to the stricken non-com.

"Ian, it's Alex…can you hear me?"

"Alex…" Vandenberg could hear death in O'Reilly's voice. He looked down at his comrade, at the shattered mess of his armor, the terrible dent that must have crushed his spine. There was no doubt. The wounds were mortal. He didn't even know how the sergeant was still alive, even if barely.

"Yes, Ian. It's Alex. I'm here."

"I'll fight with you any time, rookie." He gasped for one last breath, and then Ian O'Reilly fell silent.

Captain's Office
MCS Viking
In Orbit Around Gamma Epsilon II

Roderick Vance sat quietly, staring at the screen on the captain's desk. He was waiting, for word from the surface, for scanner readers—anything to confirm his special order had been carried out. But so far there had been nothing.

His mind raced as to what to do if his latest gambit failed, or worse, if it failed in a way that alerted Stark to what he was attempting. The plan was crazy, costly...but it was the only play he could see that offered a chance to avoid war. Whatever Gavin Stark said, Vance was certain the Alliance spy would have his own schemes, moves he would almost certainly make to gain total control of the artifact. Vance's initial flicker of optimism was gone, replaced by grim certainty that any deal with Stark had to end in betrayal. His only other option, the only one that would remain to him if the Alphas failed, was to attack now, while he had the edge in firepower. But that was a choice that almost certainly led to war.

He had been second-guessing since he'd issued the order, trying to convince himself there was another way, one less drastic. But his mind was rational, and his analysis cold-blooded. He risked war either way, but if the Team could carry out this last command, he had a chance, at least, of reaching a deal with Stark, of averting cataclysm.

He stared at the display. Stark's vessel was in orbit, about three thousand kilometers from *Viking*, and *Westron* was another four thousand beyond the Alliance ship. He sighed. If the Team failed, he knew what he had to do. Stark's death would at the very least throw whatever secret plans he had into chaos. If it came to that, if he ran out of time to wait for the Team—or if he saw any hint that Stark knew what the Alphas were doing—he'd decided on his action.

He reached out and touched the com. "Captain, I'd like to see you in here for a moment."

"Yes, Mr. Stark."

A few seconds later the hatch opened and *Viking's* commander stepped into the room.

"Have a seat, Captain." Vance was sitting in Hinch's usual chair, so the officer walked over to one of the two desk chairs. He sat down, and looked at Vance expectantly, but he didn't say anything.

"Captain," Vance said softly, almost as if he was concerned someone would overhear, despite the fact that the two of them were alone in the room. "I have a plan in the works, one I hope will extricate us from this situation without further fighting…and without starting a war the Confederation is ill-prepared to fight."

Hinch nodded. "Yes, sir. What can I do to help?" Vance was impressed by Hinch's discipline. The veteran captain didn't ask for details, he didn't even act like he was interested.

"You can be ready in case I fail, Captain. If my efforts do not succeed, we will have no choice but to attack and destroy the Alliance vessel…as quickly as possible."

Hinch remained calm, but this time he was unable to keep all the surprise from his face.

"Yes, I know we made a deal with Mr. Stark, but I know enough about him to be fairly certain his agreement is little more than a ploy, most likely to buy time until Alliance reinforcements arrive. And if the balance of force in this system changes against us, there is little chance Stark will honor the terms. Nor will he hesitate at the prospect of war, at the potential of millions of casualties. Not if it serves his purpose." Vance paused, looking up, right into Hinch's eyes. "No, Captain…if my plan fails, we have to destroy that ship. We have to kill Gavin Stark."

Hinch was silent for a few seconds. Then he said, "We have the firepower, sir. But they have the speed. Now that we've entered orbit and given up our position between them and the warp gate, it will be difficult to engage if they attempt to flee."

"Which is why I want you to be ready, Captain…ready to move as quickly and as aggressively as possible when—if—I give the word."

"If we go to red alert, their scanners will detect the increase in energy output."

"That is why we are discussing it here, Captain. I want *Viking* to be ready to blast out of orbit at full thrust. If we can get enough of a jump on the Alliance vessel, we can cut them off from the warp gate…and destroy them.

"That will be difficult, sir, at least without risking detection. We will have to have the reactor prepped for a flash ramp up." He paused. "It will be dangerous, sir. I'll have to shut off the safeties. If anything goes wrong…"

"That's a chance we'll have to take, Captain. If the Team fails, we'll have no choice…and even if they succeed, a positional advantage will help my negotiation." Vance paused. "Be ready, Captain…as ready as you can be. The future of the Confederation may hang in the balance."

"Yes, sir."

"You have my every confidence, Captain."

"Thank you, sir." Hinch paused. "I'll do my best, Mr. Vance."

"I know you will."

"With your permission…" Hinch leaned forward in his chair, his eyes locked on Vance's.

"By all means, Captain. Go prep your ship."

"Yes, sir." Hinch stood up and walked out of the room, leaving Vance sitting silently.

Chapter Twenty-Seven

Coordinate Grid 20.2-42.8
Just Outside the Alien Vessel
Planet Gamma Epsilon II

Vandenberg knelt down next to O'Reilly. The sergeant had been his nemesis when he'd first joined the team, the most aggressive and vocal opponent of admitting the rookie into the ranks of the Team. He'd hated O'Reilly, he'd fought with him. But now all he felt was pain and loss. O'Reilly had eventually accepted him, as all the Alphas had, and he'd come to really like the crusty non-com.

Vandenberg wasn't a rookie anymore. He'd had his baptism of fire, and he'd managed to overcome his own fear of death. But the price had been too high, and the loss of his new comrades weighed down on him. He hesitated, looking at O'Reilly's body, the force that had been driving him gone.

"He's dead, Lieutenant." Sergeant Jones' voice was strained. It was obvious he was trying to ignore his wounds, and just as apparent that every step he took was an agony. "We're Alphas, Lieutenant. We mourn the dead later, after the mission is done."

Vandenberg pulled his eyes from O'Reilly, turning to face the veteran sergeant-major and staring back in amazement. He'd seen how close the Alphas were, struggled to penetrate that tightly knit structure and gain acceptance. He knew Jones and O'Reilly had been comrades for years, yet now the sergeant-major stood before him, a moment after O'Reilly's death, reminding him of the mission.

He stood up slowly, looking back one last time at the mangled wreck of O'Reilly's armor. Then he said, "Yes, Sergeant-Major. You're right." He felt some of his strength of will return, courtesy of Tyrell Jones and the example he was setting for his young commanding officer.

He turned and saw Ruiz walking up, staggering, dragging one leg behind him. The corporal was wounded, and his suit was badly damaged, but he too was still in the fight, dedicated to the mission. He shouted as he approached. "What do you need me to do, Lieutenant?"

Vandenberg struggled to answer, emotion threatening to overcome reason. He was choked up by the dedication of these two veteran warriors, at their refusal to quit, even as they saw the Team destroyed around them. "We need to get the package inside the ship," he said, his tone firming as he forced his own discipline in place. "And we've got to do it now, before more of those 'bots show up."

Vandenberg almost told Jones to retrieve the device, but he held his tongue. The package was heavy, cumbersome, and he didn't think either of his wounded companions could manage it, not without great difficulty. He ran over himself. Then he reached down and hoisted it up.

"Let's go," he snapped, rushing back toward the great rent in the hull they'd been using as an entrance.

He heard his two comrades fall in behind him as he stepped through the gaping hole and back into the eerie gloom of the alien craft. It had only been a short time since he'd been there, but as he crept forward, struggling to see the obstacles over the heavy canister in his arms, it seemed like a distant memory, some old nightmare revisited.

"Nate, how far in do we need to get this thing?"

The AI responded crisply, "Current location offers ninety-five percent chance of complete effectiveness. Analysis of the shape and structure of the vessel suggest moving an additional sixty meters down this corridor will provide a ninety-nine point six to one hundred percent chance."

Right.

"Sixty meters, guys. Then we can drop this thing and get out of here."

Before either of his companions could respond, shots rang out. Vandenberg reacted immediately, diving behind a pile of debris. Much of the corridor was open, with little in the way of cover, but he and his two companions were fortunate. A part of the ceiling had collapsed where they stood, and there were chunks of twisted metal lying all around.

Vandenberg pulled out his rifle, but he resisted the urge to open up. He was almost out of ammo, and he knew his comrades weren't much better off. They'd have to wait for aimed shots, and that wasn't likely to be an effective strategy against more of the fearsome alien 'bots. Massed firepower seemed to be the only way to bring the monsters down.

"We'll have to leave it here. My AI says we've only got a ninety-five percent chance of complete effectiveness without going deeper. And going deeper just became an impossible option."

"Yes, sir," his two companions snapped back.

"You two keep an eye on the corridor while I activate this thing."

Vandenberg moved back, being careful to stay low. He reached around, fumbling with his gloved hand as he opened the small control panel. Then he saw it. A section of twisted and blackened metal. One of the enemy projectiles had hit the device. It didn't look like the mechanism itself was damaged, and it looked like the trigger was functional. But the timer was nothing but a pile of useless junk.

He felt a coldness in his body as he realized the implication. Someone would have to stay behind and trigger the device manually.

That's my job, he thought, even as the dedication to duty within him struggled to hold off the fear.

He heard a crash, and his head snapped around. It was Ruiz. The corporal had fallen on his back, a fresh hole in his armor.

"Jorge!" he yelled, spinning around, kneeling over the stricken non-com.

"They got me again, Lieutenant." His words were soft whispers, even with his suit's amplification.

"You'll be okay, Jorge..." Vandenberg was looking down at the medical readouts on Ruiz's armor. He wasn't a doctor, but he didn't have to be to realize he was lying to his friend.

"Sergeant-Major..." His eyes shot over to Jones, who was still looking down the corridor, firing a carefully-aimed shot every few seconds.

"Sir!"

"The timer on this thing is gone. I need you to help Ruiz out of here. And then you both have to get clear of this ship...at least two klicks. I'll wait as long as possible."

"I'll do it, sir."

"No."

"Sir...you'll be killed."

"And you won't be, Sergeant-Major?"

"But sir..."

"No buts, Sergeant Jones. You've served for decades. Somewhere along the line I know you learned how to follow a superior officer's orders."

Jones was silent for a few seconds. Then he said, "Yes, sir," still not sounding totally convinced.

"I'll...do it...sir." It was Ruiz. His words were barely understandable through the rattling sound of blood in his lungs, his throat.

"No, Corporal. This is my job. The sergeant will get you out of here."

"No...Lieutenant...I'm done...I...know it. Let me...let me do this. Please..."

Vandenberg struggled to hold back the vomit trying to rocket up his throat. Part of him felt relief at the prospect of a reprieve from certain death. But the thought of leaving one of the Alphas—one of *his* people—behind was more than he could bear. He'd held it together, taken command when the other officers were killed, and he'd pulled it off. Until now. This decision was too much, more than he could take. And he sat there, frozen, even as the incoming fire moved closer.

"He's right, Alex." Jones' words were soft. The veteran non-com was almost whispering. "He's going to die, no matter what we do. Let him die as an Alpha, completing the mission, trying to save his comrades. He'd rather go that way than choking on his own blood running away."

Vandenberg hesitated another few seconds. Then he nodded clumsily.

"Ruiz, you're the bravest soldier I've ever seen," he said, struggling to hold back tears. "I'll never be able to tell you how much it meant to me when you accepted me."

"I was…wrong, sir. You're a…true Alpha. Always." Ruiz coughed hard. "Now go…quickly. I'll hold here…as long…as I can." He coughed again, struggling to keep his throat clear. "Then I'll blow…this thing."

Vandenberg stared at Ruiz, unmoving.

Jones slid over toward him. "Let's go, sir. There's no more time."

Vandenberg tried to answer, but he couldn't force out the words. He just nodded again. Then he turned and moved off down the hall, staying low until he reached a point where the ship had been twisted, blocking the line of fire from the approaching 'bots.

He could hear Jones right behind him. He knew the sergeant-major was badly wounded too, but the veteran was keeping up, moving quickly. It was reckless in the semi-darkness, leaping over the scattered piles of debris. But there was no time to delay.

He saw the light up ahead, finally. The tear in the ship's hull that led to the outside.

"Almost there, Sergeant…just a few more meters."

He ran, pushing, his eyes fixed on the rays of sunlight coming through from outside.

Coordinate Grid 20.2-42.8
Just Outside the Alien Vessel
Planet Gamma Epsilon II

Grax staggered forward. He was seething with rage, angry at the Martians who had fought his people so fiercely, at the terrible 'bots that had cut his troopers down…at anything else he could think of.

As far as he knew, he was the only survivor in his entire force. Indeed, he was only alive because the 'bot had left him for dead. It had moved right past him, hunting down the broken survivors from his force. His wounds were bad—and painful—but he knew they had saved his life.

For how long?

Grax didn't know what to do. The mission had been a debacle. He couldn't imagine a way to explain his way out of this, not to a man like Gavin Stark. Losing his entire command and surviving himself, perhaps the only trooper to do so? No, there wasn't enough bullshit in the explored universe to escape blame for what had happened here.

Still, he pushed forward. He wasn't sure why he was still struggling. Death here would almost certainly be faster and more merciful than whatever horrible end he would face at Stark's hands. But he wanted to live. It was a primal urge, one that defied the rational choice of the easiest death.

He bit down hard as a wave of pain swept over him. His suit had given him a massive dose of analgesics, but the injuries, the fatigue, the punishment—it was all too much. Still, he had to keep going. There was at least one functional 'bot still active out there, and when it had assured itself all his troopers were dead, he had no doubt it would be back this way.

He was almost back to the front of the alien vessel. Of course, 'front' was a relative term. It was the spot they had found a large tear in the hull, the place they had entered the hellish ship.

His head snapped around. He heard something.

His body tensed. Was there another 'bot up ahead?

No…not a 'bot. More Martians?

He held his rifle out in front of him. He didn't have much ammo left, but if it wasn't another 'bot, perhaps he didn't need much. He hated these Martians, blamed them for the failure of his mission. There couldn't be many of them left…and if he had his way, by the time he was through there would be none.

He crept forward, carefully, staring ahead as he moved around the end of the vessel.

Coordinate Grid 20.2-42.8
Just Outside the Alien Vessel
Planet Gamma Epsilon II

Vandenberg climbed out of the vessel. He was exhausted, devastated at the loss of his comrades, weighed down by the pointless guilt he felt for leaving Ruiz behind. But it was still a relief to escape from the gloomy confines of the alien ship. He knew the vessel was a historical find of almost unparalleled importance…but his hours on Gamma Epsilon II had turned it into a nightmare, the physical representation of all his people had suffered.

He tripped over the entrance, stumbling forward a few meters before regaining his footing. Jones was right behind him, clearly struggling with his wounds, but still moving.

Then a shot rang out. Jones fell to the ground instantly, landing with a hard thud.

Vandenberg spun around, reaching for his rifle as he did. He fumbled, nothing more than a second's delay. But he knew that was enough. Even as that brief time passed, he saw the Alliance trooper, his rifle moving. Vandenberg was trying to take aim, to fire back. But in that fleeting instant he knew he was too late, that his adversary get his shot off first. That he was dead.

Crack.

A shot. He knew what it was, and he waited for the pain, the realization that he'd been hit. But it didn't come. Instead, he saw the Alliance soldier lurch forward and fall to the ground.

There was a gaping hole right around the neck, and Vandenberg could see blood pouring out.

He was stunned, confused. He looked all around…and then he saw. On top of a section of the enemy vessel. Another figure, this one clad in Confederation armor.

He was confused at first, but then the trooper began to climb down from his perch. He was struggling, clearly wounded. But there was no question he was alive.

Vandenberg ran toward the ship, looking up as the trooper slid down last couple meters, landing hard and letting out a pained grunt. The trooper leaned back against the hull of the ship and popped his visor.

Komack.

Vega and Komack had manned the autocannon when the Team had first gone into the vessel to escape the Alliance troopers. But there had been no sign of them when Vandenberg and the others had first escaped, nothing remaining but the clearly wrecked weapon still in its position. He had assumed the two gunners were dead. Everyone had.

"Komack, it's Vandenberg. I thought you were dead. What about Vega?"

Komack shook his head. Then he took a deep breath and said, "I found another way in, but it turned out to be a dead end, so I turned back." He paused, clearly in pain. "I was over around the side of the ship, and I ran into those Alliance bastards again." Another pause. "I took two hits."

"How bad?"

Vandenberg was standing in front of the non-com, trying to get a look at his monitors.

"Pretty bad…but the suit's got me patched up and drugged to my eyeballs. I'm good to go." He looked up at Vandenberg with an expression that told the young lieutenant that 'good to go' was a considerable exaggeration. "Where are the others?"

Vandenberg shook his head. "They're gone, Komack."

He turned toward Jones' figure, lying motionless on the ground. He knew the sergeant-major was dead, but he moved over to check anyway.

Yes, dead.

"All of them?" There was shock in Komack's voice, and grief.

"Yes. We're the only two left…except Ruiz. He's inside, mortally wounded."

"We have to go get him." Komack turned toward the entrance.

"No."

"What? Sir…"

"No, Komack. We have to get out of here. Ruiz is done for, no matter what. He's buying us time. Time to get out of here."

"Lieutenant, we can't…"

"Just follow orders, Corporal." Vandenberg's voice was the pure tone of command, harsh, brooking no questions, no resistance. It surprised no one more than it did him, and he had no idea where it had come from. "Let's move. Now."

He turned and ran across the plain, racing for the ridgeline about a kilometer away. Two things would offer protection from what he knew was coming…distance and intervening ground. The ridge offered both.

He almost turned to see if Komack was following, but somehow he knew the corporal had done as he'd commanded. Vandenberg had pushed aside the fear. The confidence he felt now was strange, a wholly different thing from the cockiness that had accompanied his exalted performance at the Academy. This was *real*, and he carried the honor of the Team with him.

He knew he was almost out of time. Ruiz wouldn't be able to hold out long…and even if the enemy 'bots failed to attack, Vandenberg knew his comrade hadn't had much time. His suit would pump him full of blood substitute and patch him up as much as possible, but the corporal was too torn apart, too desperately wounded for any treatment, certainly any this side of a major hospital. Vandenberg was sure of just one thing. Jorge Ruiz would trigger the device before he died. No matter what.

"Keep moving, Komack. We've got to make that ridge." A flash of light went by, bright even in the light of day. Vandenberg looked back. It was one of the enemy 'bots, coming around from the starboard side of the ship. And instant later, an autocannon opened up, its rapid chattering the sound of death itself.

"I'm right behind you, sir."

Vandenberg could hear that his comrade was falling behind. He stopped and turned to go back, to help Komack. The whole Team was gone. He'd be damned if he was going to run to safety and leave the last other survivor behind. He was the commander of Red Team Alpha…and his trooper needed help.

He was staring right at Komack, and he took a step toward the soldier. Another step. Then it happened. Another blinding light, sending flickering streaks all across the afternoon sky. And in front of him, Komack virtually exploded. One instant the trooper had been there, looking at Vandenberg with a pained expression…and the next, the top two thirds of his body was just gone, blasted to bits by the enemy particle accelerator.

"No!" Vandenberg screamed, feeling the urge to charge the enemy 'bot. He was on the verge of giving in to blind rage. He had to kill that 'bot. He simply *had* to. He brought his rifle down and opened fire.

No, part of him thought. *This is stupid, pointless.*

He felt the struggle inside him, the desire—the *need*—to fight back, to destroy the thing that had killed his comrade, battling the cold reason of the combat veteran growing inside him. He turned away, hating himself for wanting to survive, and he ran for the ridgeline, zigzagging wildly, doing his best to give his enemy a difficult shot.

He was halfway there, the 'bot's fire landing all around him. He waited for the impact, the stream of autocannon rounds that would take him down. But it didn't come. He was almost there…one last push…

Then he was off the ground, taken by a force that scooped him up like a rag doll. He felt pain, sections of his armor rupturing, digging into his flesh. He was confused, for a second, perhaps two. Then he realized what it was, even as he slammed hard into the ground. Ruiz had detonated the device.

He was in pain, worse than anything he'd felt before. Tears

streamed down his cheeks, and he gasped for air, struggling to turn, to look back at the vessel. But the shockwave had thrown him clear of the ridge, and now the spine of high ground blocked his view.

He tried to get up, but he was too badly hurt. The pain was indescribable...then he felt the drugs pulsing through his veins, bringing relief from the agony. His suit was doing what it could, but he didn't have any hope of survival. He was here, alone, trapped. Abandoned. He was the last of the Team... and soon he would join his comrades. But first he had one duty remaining.

He rolled over and crawled slowly, pulling himself up the ridge, using every bit of power his damaged suit could offer. It was torturous, achingly slow. But he kept moving...and finally he could see. The 'bot was gone, no sign of it at all. The ship was gone too. Nothing remained but a deep pit...and a small mushroom cloud, even now rising over the spot that, until a moment before, had held the greatest discovery in humanity's history.

Vandenberg hadn't thought twice when he'd received Vance's order, but now he wondered what could have caused the Martian spy to command the destruction of something of such momentous importance.

Whatever it was, you'll never know. This is where it ends. On this sickly yellow dirt, the last of your unit to die. He took one last look at the cloud, at the utter devastation the bomb had wrought.

He thought about Ruiz, imagining the dying soldier reaching out, triggering the warhead.

You died well, Jorge Ruiz. You died as a hero.

He felt the weakness overtaking him, and he let himself fall back. He lay there for a few seconds, staring up at the fading sunlight of this alien world's day. And then he slipped into unconsciousness.

Chapter Twenty-Eight

Captain's Office
MCS Viking
In Orbit Around Gamma Epsilon II

"You destroyed the ship?" Stark's voice was strained. It was clear the spy was incredulous, that he was still trying to process what his scanners had shown him. "All that technology, thousands of years advancement sitting there for the taking. Do you realize what you have done?"

"I destroyed nothing," Vance lied. "The active defenses we encountered suggest a functional power source. Perhaps age eroded its safety features, and the demand for energy to sustain an attack against our forces put too much pressure on the system. An ancient magnetic bottle rupturing…or something similar." He doubted his lie would fool his adversary, but he wasn't trying to convince Stark. He was trying offer him an out to a path that was problematic to both of them. The Alliance had the advantage if war broke out now, but in the longer term, it would cost them a likely ally, and weaken their forces just when the prospect of wider war loomed.

"Do you really expect me to believe that?" Vance could tell Stark was trying to control himself, but at that moment he caught a glimpse of the frigid darkness within the Alliance operative.

"I sent a small team down to investigate the wreckage, Mr. Stark. You landed a large strike force, one that attacked my people. Have you thought about all those soldiers fighting each other, and the apparently still-active defenses of the ship as well? Perhaps we would have been better served by cooperating, instead of fighting. Now, we've lost an amazing opportunity, a cache of scientific advancement greater than any in human history."

"That is preposterous. You ordered that ship's destruction, and your soldiers on the ground carried it out."

"That is not true." Vance had always considered himself an honest man. Now he was getting his first glimpse at how often he'd have to lie to do his new job. "I did not have anything to do with that explosion." He knew he wasn't fooling Stark. He wasn't trying to, not really. He just wanted to give Stark time to get over his shock and anger. He was sure peace was the best course for both the Alliance and the Confederation, and he wanted his counterpart to realize that. Whatever else he'd heard about Stark, it was clear the man did not suffer from any lack of intelligence. He would realize...

I hope.

Vance paused, just for a second.

Now...now it's time to add some pressure.

"I am as disappointed as you that we have lost the alien vessel...and I firmly believe our best interests are served by peace between our two nations. I hope you will agree with me on this."

Vance's hand moved toward the com unit. He flipped a switch, muting the connection to Stark, and opening one to *Viking's* bridge. "Now, Captain Hinch," he said calmly, leaning back and gripping the armrests of his chair as he did.

"Yes, sir," came the reply.

An instant later, *Viking* lurched hard, and Vance felt the forces of acceleration slam into him, more than 12g as the Martian battleship blasted suddenly out of orbit, heading toward the warp gate.

Vance was silent, barely able to move. He could see the light flashing, Stark's repeated calls going unanswered. He suspected whatever progress he'd made in calming the Alliance agent had just been shot to hell, but he'd had no choice. If he couldn't get Stark to agree, he wasn't going to let him escape.

He reached out, struggling to move his hand against the terrible force pushing him back. *Viking's* engines were blasting hard, building velocity quickly, giving the battleship a jump on Stark's faster vessel. But he didn't want to wait too long. *Viking* still couldn't win a race to the gate, and he was hoping to avoid a fight.

"Cease acceleration, Captain. Arm all weapons and prepare to fire on my command."

"Yes, sir."

Vance felt the relief of free fall, and he dropped his hand to the com, flipping the line to Stark back on.

"What is the meaning of this action…"

Vance cut off the furious agent. "It is simply this, Mr. Stark. The alien ship is gone…nothing can change that. You can blame me or not, but I submit it makes no difference at this point. It cannot be undone. We have two choices now. We can fight here…and consign our two nations to a destructive war that will benefit neither. Or we can seek to maintain the peace. Whatever might have been worth fighting over is gone now. Any war would be pointless."

"No doubt you feel that way because the Confederation is so unprepared for war. After what you have done here, what you cost mankind, you expect me to simply look the other way?"

"I will not argue with you over how a war between our nations would play out, Mr. Stark. That is pointless. But I remind you, Mars and the Alliance have frequently been allies. Would it serve your ends to cripple a power that will likely be on your side when wider war breaks out? To weaken your forces as the CAC and the Caliphate continue adding to their arsenals?"

Hinch's voice came through on Vance's headset. "Mr. Vance, we're picking up energy spikes on the Alliance ship. They're powering up their engines." Vance didn't reply, but he nodded, to himself he supposed, since the captain couldn't see him.

Stark had been continuing his angry rant. "I am not sure I agree with your…"

"Power your engines down now, Mr. Stark. I cannot allow you to leave this system unless we reach an agreement. You have no doubt left arrangements behind sufficient to initiate war, but I can assure you one thing. You will not live to see it."

"I will not take…"

"Now!" Vance roared. "Or we will open fire in ten seconds."

Vance sat silently, staring at the com unit, waiting. In a few seconds, he would know if he'd stared down Gavin Stark…or if the Confederation faced a ruinous war.

He could feel the tension. He wondered how many times his father had faced such situations, waiting to see if a desperate gamble had paid off. He'd done the best he could to cut off Stark's escape, but he figured it was still fifty-fifty that the Alliance ship could outrun *Viking* before it was destroyed. When he'd formulated the plan, he'd relied on Stark's pragmatism, and his desire to survive. But now all he could see was the alternative, a desperate flight, an incensed Gavin Stark getting away, reaching the Sol system first, and rallying the Alliance to war.

He waited for a response, each second passing slowly, almost unbearably so. Then Hinch's voice was back on his headset. "The Alliance vessel is powering down, sir."

Vance exhaled hard, unable to hold back his relief. He stared down at the com unit on his desk, waiting for Stark's voice.

"Very well, Mr. Vance. I agree to your terms. We will both leave this system and return to Sol. We will report to our direct superiors that the alien vessel was destroyed…and we will both agree that the entire matter will be classified at the highest level. No public announcements will be made that any signs of non-human intelligent life have been found, that first contact has been made."

"Agreed, Mr. Stark."

"Then, as a show of faith, I insist you power down your weapons and return to orbit."

"I will be happy to do that, Mr. Stark…" Vance knew enough about Stark to realize the Alliance spy was just about the last person whose word he would take about anything. "As soon as you transmit an identity-confirmed affidavit attesting to the accidental destruction of the alien vessel."

There was a long silence. Vance didn't know if Stark was planning treachery—in fact, he suspected it was likely the Alliance agent understood war would serve no purpose. But he wasn't going to take any chances. If Stark tried to doublecross him later, he intended to have what he needed on hand.

"Very well, Mr. Vance. We will make a joint statement, with the same caveats…to be shared only at the highest classification levels."

Vance felt a wave of relief. "Agreed, Mr. Stark."

He leaned back in his chair and breathed deeply. He had handled Gavin Stark.

Sickbay
MCS Viking
En Route to Sol System

"You justified my confidence, Alex. I confess, I had my doubts when I agreed to admit you to the Team…but you have proven yourself to be your father's son." Vance had sent down search parties, despite what seemed like a virtual certainty no one had survived…and they had found one of the Alphas, unconscious, close to death. But alive.

Alex Vandenberg looked up from his hospital bed. His body was emaciated, an expected side effect of the radiation sickness that had ravaged him since the explosion. He had a dozen wounds, including a severed spine, but the latest scans suggested he would heal, that he wouldn't need any risky regeneration procedures. He was lucky, if such a word could be applied to a man in his situation. He had survived, the only member of Red Team Alpha to make if back from Gamma Epsilon II.

"Thank you, sir." His words were soft, and each one tore across his aching throat. He'd been told he was out of the woods, that he would survive, but truth be told, he still felt like he was at death's door. "I'm sorry, sir…the Team…"

"Sending the Team in was my choice, Alex. I wanted to

secure the wreck, to find a way to transport it somewhere. I suspected Stark knew about it, but I wasn't sure. And the technological possibilities were simply too remarkable to pass up. You are not responsible for the deaths of your comrades. I am."

Vandenberg turned his head toward Vance. He stopped halfway as a wave of dizziness took him, and he let his head fall back into the pillow. "But I survived…I am alive, and they are all dead." There was sadness in his soft tone.

"You fought well, Alex. You stood by the rest of the Alphas, fought alongside them. Fought *as* one of them. There is no shame in your survival…and Colonel Reginald and the rest of the Team would have been the first ones to agree with me on that. You're all that is left of them, Alex, the last member of Red Team Alpha. Will you move forward? Will your honor your comrades by making something of the chance your survival gained?"

Vandenberg looked up at the Martian spy. His impression of Vance—everyone's impression of Vance—had been of a cold, emotionless man. But now he saw the spymaster differently.

"I will, sir. I will do my duty. I will do it to honor them."

Vance forced a tiny smile, and he nodded. "I am proud of you, Alex. Your comrades would have been too. And your father."

Vandenberg gasped for air, struggling to hold back the tears he knew his dehydrated body could hardly produce. "Thank you, sir."

"I'll let you rest, Alex. We'll talk again later."

"Yes, Mr. Vance."

Vandenberg watched the head of Martian Intelligence walk out into the corridor. He didn't think he could sleep. There was too much…too much pain, too much regret.

He was still thinking about all of it when he drifted off.

Residence Block AR-117
Ares Metroplex
Mars, Sol IV

Vandenberg walked down the hallway, his eyes darting to the side every dozen or so steps, checking the unit numbers on the doors. He was still limping, but two months of treatment and therapy had put him back together. Mostly, at least. He still had a limp, and more than a few aches and pains, but the medical staff of *Viking*, and later those of the Military Hospital, had gotten him more or less back in working order. They'd helped him put his psyche back together too, but that was still a work in progress. And this errand was part of it, something he'd promised himself he would do.

He stopped abruptly in front of a door. There was a small plaque on the wall reading '1707.' He stood silently for a moment, collecting his thoughts and taking a deep breath. Then he pressed the small button.

A few seconds passed, and then the door slid open. A young woman stood behind. She was tall, clad in civilian clothes suitable for almost any professional job. Vandenberg knew she was a computer technician, but that wasn't why he was there.

"Yes, Lieutenant," she said softly, her eyes darting to his uniform. "What can I do for you?"

"Are you Lina Cavenaugh?" He knew she was before he even asked. He saw it immediately, the resemblance. It was a young woman standing in front of him, but the eyes looking back into his were Colonel Reginald's.

"Yes, Lieutenant. What is this about?"

"I'm Alex Vandenberg. A friend of your father's."

The pleasant expression on her face faded away, replaced by an angry scowl. "I don't mean to be rude, Lieutenant, but I'm really not interested in anything from my father." She shook her head. "Did he send you here? Didn't have to courage to come himself?"

Vandenberg paused, swallowing hard. "I'm sorry, but your father is dead."

She stood still, looking almost dumbstruck. The angry gaze was gone, replaced by a blank stare. "I knew this would happen one day. Since I was a little girl I knew. For years, every time the com buzzed, every time someone came to the door, I just knew it was somebody there to tell me he was dead. You can only live that way for so long…and then you stop caring." But Vandenberg could see that, in spite of her anger and resentment, she *did* care.

"I'm very sorry. I looked up to your father, and I respected him greatly. That is why I am here."

"I'm sorry, Lieutenant…"

"Vandenberg."

"Lieutenant Vandenberg…but my father chose his course years ago. He had a wife, and a daughter who loved him…but he left us behind." She paused. "I may be a bit—surprised—right now, but that doesn't change anything. My father has been dead to me for a long time." She sighed. "Now, if you'll excuse me, Lieutenant, I…"

"Please…I just want to talk to you for a moment." He paused. "I know how you feel."

"Do you?" There was a flash of anger in her voice now. "Do you know what it is like to sit and wait for your father to come home for weeks, even months at a time? To listen to your mother in the next room crying because she is lonely? Abandoned?"

"Yes, as a matter of fact I do. My father was your father's best friend…and his closest comrade. The two of them served together for many years. I daresay I have as many stories as you, and I suspect they are shockingly similar. But there is much you do not know, much you cannot know. Our fathers were part of a highly secret military unit…one that has saved countless lives over the years."

"So, you are saying my father, the man I can barely remember, was a hero?"

"Yes, he was. A great hero. And he did most of the good he did in the shadows, without fanfare, without even thanks. He did a lot to make Mars safer. He died to protect it."

Lina stood still, but Vandenberg could see the confusion on her face. She'd hated her father for years, indeed, she'd used hostility as a coping mechanism. But now she seemed unsure, the solid wall of her anger cracked now, even crumbling in spots.

"Where did he die?"

Vandenberg shook his head sadly. "I'm afraid I can't say. You will have to take my word, but he died a hero. He died for Mars."

"He died for Mars? All I ever wanted him to do for me was come to a birthday party, or just sit home with me watching movies. To be there. But he almost never was. Now you're telling me he did it all for Mars?"

"I know that sounds strange, but it is the absolute truth. I didn't come here to lie to you. I came here because I like to think your father, in the short time I knew him, was my friend. I don't know if it serves any purpose now, if he will rest easier with your forgiveness...or if it will help you in some way. But I promised him I'd come. And I had to follow through on that."

She stood for a moment, looking down at the ground, not saying anything. Finally, she looked up at him. "I don't know what to say, Lieutenant. Whatever good my father did, it doesn't change the fact that he wasn't a part of my life, not really. I wanted him to be, but he never was. Perhaps he did important work. You seem like an honest man. But I'm not sure what that changes. What do you want from me? To absolve him? To say I am fine that I grew up without a father, that my mother was left alone to raise me? I'm sorry, Lieutenant, but I just can't do that." Her expression had hardened again, but Vandenberg could see a fragility that wasn't there before.

"I understand. Perhaps I would feel the same way in your shoes. I had my own resentments, but my father and I reconciled before he died, at least after a fashion." He paused. "I just felt I had to come see you." Another pause, then: "I don't want to intrude any further. I will be going now. Again, my apologies if I upset you."

She nodded slowly, turning away as she did. Then she hesitated. "Lieutenant?"

"Yes?"

"This is a lot for me right now. I need time. I can't forgive my father, at least not now. But perhaps another time, when I've had a chance to think about all this."

"Of course," Vandenberg replied softly. "You can reach me at Metroplex Base if you ever want to talk. If I'm on assignment somewhere, they will see the message gets to me."

Lina nodded again. "Thank you, Lieutenant."

Alex smiled. Then he nodded and turned toward the hallway, walking back the way he had come.

Well, sir…I don't know where this will go, but maybe I can help her to understand. To forgive.

He didn't know if any of it mattered really. Colonel Reginald was dead. But Vandenberg figured his commander—and friend—would rest easier. Perhaps he was just telling himself what he wanted to hear…or just healing his own wounds by reaching out to the colonel's daughter. But whatever combination of factors had driven him to come here, he decided to believe John Reginald would rest easier because of it.

From the Personal Journal of Alex Vandenberg

I came home alone, the only survivor of the Team. I left them behind, my brothers and sisters, the honored dead, killed on a mission the importance of which they could barely imagine as they died one by one on that strange world.

My comrades died without fanfare, without any honors or even the gratitude of the millions whose lives they had almost certainly saved. It was one of the hardest things to accept about service on the Team, something that still fills me with admiration for those men and women who have served so selflessly. They fought some of the most dangerous enemies to threaten mankind, faced the deadliest threats. That work was invariably done in secret, the Team's adversaries and missions highly classified.

There were no parades for those on the Team, no fanfare, no recognition, no memorials, not even when nineteen out of twenty combatants died. Those we fought for, died for, never knew who we were. That we even existed.

I was no longer a raw cherry when I returned…indeed, though I'd only spent a few brief hours in battle, no one who had seen what I had would dare to call me a rookie. And any who did would find out just how capable I was in a fight.

I was burnt out, distraught at the loss of my comrades, ready to leave the Team, and the service itself. Even my father's shade visiting me in my dreams was too little to dissuade me from embracing civilian life. But in the end, Roderick Vance somehow convinced me to stay. I still don't know how he did it, what combination of guilt, logic, manipulation he employed. Those who consider the head of Martian Intelligence to be a cold fish don't know the man, not really. There is coldness in him, certainly, an unwavering devotion to what he sees as his duty. But that day long ago when I walked into his office to resign my commission, I saw the real Roderick Vance. We talked for hours, and he told me things about my father I hadn't known… and then he spoke of his parents as well, for he had been compelled to succeed his own father far too early, as I had mine.

In the end, he convinced me to stay…and to rebuild the Team. "We need you," he said simply. "Mars needs you. And there is no escape from duty, from the calling of your birth. As there is none for me." I still remember that last statement, and I think that is what truly got to me. Suddenly I realized. Vance didn't want his job, indeed, he detested his life as Mars' top spy. But he had accepted his duty…to Mars, to his parents, to the thousands who answered to him and the millions whose lives depended on his vigilance. And I knew I could do no less. In the end, I accepted with a single condition.

Red Team Alpha would never again take the field. It was gone, sacrificed on the rocky plains of a distant world. That designation would be retired, it would lay with the spirits of the dead on Gamma Epsilon II. The new force would be Red Team Beta, and I decided then and there it would be a tribute to my lost comrades.

My friends hadn't died for nothing, indeed, their sacrifice

had almost certainly saved millions of lives. Gavin Stark wasn't done with his plots, not by any measure, and by the time he was done, he had wrought more destruction on mankind than any monster in human history. The Fall, the cracked domes of Mars' great cities, the devastation wrought by the Shadow Legions...all of that lay decades in the future, but all of it was his doing. I have wondered often if Roderick Vance made the right decision at Gamma Epsilon II, if averting a war was reason enough to allow Stark to survive when he might have died so many years ago, before he wrought the devastation he did upon mankind. In retrospect, the answer is clearly no, and for a while I blamed Vance. I was one of the very few who knew what had happened so many years before, and watching so many millions die at Stark's hands had simply been too much to endure without lashing out.

I think Roderick knew how I felt, that he could detect the coldness in my behavior toward him. But I eventually came to regret all of that. Whatever happened decades later, there was no way Vance could have foreseen it. He had saved lives, perhaps millions of lives, and to hold him responsible for the unimaginable calamities Stark would ultimately unleash defies any sense of fairness. My anger was at his lack of clairvoyance, and I came to see the absurdity of that. He and I spoke late one night, not too long after the Fall, and we made our peace. And I came to realize no one was angrier at Vance for allowing Stark to survive than he was with himself. After that night, we never discussed it again.

Lina Reginald didn't forgive her father the day I first visited her, nor the second. But she did shed tears for him, and I saw that as a start. Forgiveness in vids and books is so often immediate, and we forget that things are rarely so simple in real life. It took her a long time to forgive him, but she eventually did...and years later, once the First Imperium War had begun and the old records were declassified, I was finally able to tell her the truth, all of it. Whatever resentments she'd still harbored, I am sure she let go of that day. I hope John Reginald rests easier today, that the affection of his daughter somehow reached him.

I knew Lina Reginald for a long time, though I saw her infrequently. The wars that engulfed the Martian Confederation kept me busy, and often away from Mars for months or even years at a time. I think John's daughter came to think of me as a friend, at least of a sort, one with similar experiences. Or perhaps as a conduit to her lost father, the only one that remained to her.

Lina died during the Fall, when the domes of the Ares Metroplex were broken. I didn't find out for some time after—and when I did, it was her son Graham who told me. John Reginald never got to meet his grandson…but I think he would have been proud to see his daughter's son take up his legacy. Graham Reginald is the commander of Red Team Beta, a post I assigned him to myself, my last official act before retirement. The first time I saw him address those twenty men and women, it was as if John had been reborn. I knew that wasn't the case, but I could almost see my old commander smiling back at me.

I served for many years, and eventually I became as much a veteran as any of those I served with on Gamma Epsilon II. I lived through the First Imperium War, and I came to truly understand the deadly threat that ancient vessel had represented, the terrible capabilities of that advanced technology. I survived the war against the Shadow Legions as well, and I shudder now to think of what would have happened if Gavin Stark had obtained First Imperium technology decades earlier. The horrors his bid for power caused were unimaginable. Had his forces been equipped with First Imperium technology, there is little doubt that he would have prevailed…and that all mankind would now be living as his slaves. Preventing that, even with all the death and horror we have endured, is a fitting epitaph to my comrades. My friends.

For fifty years, I kept the tradition, drinking my toast to them, on Mars, on battlefields far away, or in ships on the battle lines. But wherever I was, whatever cataclysms were occurring, I've never missed that anniversary. And I never will. Not until that day, far closer now than years ago, when I finally go to join them, the finest comrades and friends I have ever had.

Red Team Alpha.

Red Team Alpha Duty Roster
(classified at highest level)

Colonel Travis Warren (previously deceased)
Colonel John Reginald – KIA
Captain Clark Dawes – KIA
Lieutenant Elise Cho – KIA
Lieutenant Alexander Vandenberg
Sergeant-Major Tyrell Jones – KIA
Sergeant Samuel Jacobs – KIA
Sergeant Robert Isaacs – KIA
Sergeant Justin Thoms – KIA
Sergeant Darren Covey - KIA
Sergeant Aaron Vega – KIA
Sergeant Lin Ming – KIA
Sergeant Ian O'Reilly – KIA
Sergeant Douglas Morgan - KIA
Corporal Jorge Ruiz – KIA
Corporal Janet Wagner – KIA
Corporal Thomas Simms – KIA
Corporal Anthony Venno – KIA
Corporal Vincent Komack – KIA
Corporal Eliot Benz – KIA
Corporal Steven Brown - KIA

Free Martian Confederation
Capital: Ares Metroplex

In the years just before the start of the Unification Wars, several small U.S. colonies were established on the surface of Mars, followed by similar settlements from China, Russia, Japan, and the U.K. While the nations of Earth fought decade after decade of increasingly savage and destructive war, these colonies survived, prospered, and grew.

Millions wished to escape from the cataclysm occurring on Earth, and the Martian colonies had their pick of immigrants. Consisting almost entirely of the highly skilled and educated, the Martian Exodus, as it was called, created somewhat of a "brain-drain" on Earth, but it fueled the expansion and prosperity of the Mars colonies.

When the Treaty of Paris was signed and the nations of Earth again focused on space exploration, they found that the Martians, as they'd come to call themselves, felt they were independent of any Earth authority. They banded together into a loose confederation and demonstrated that Mars was quite capable of defending itself, possessing what was at the time the largest fleet of spacecraft of any nation.

While the population of Mars was tiny compared to that of the superpowers, it was almost entirely comprised of productive elements. Where the superpowers had crime ridden, poverty stricken, and useless cities, the Martians had a well ordered and highly educated society. Where the powers of Earth were devastated, exhausted by war, and plagued by crumbling infrastructure, Mars was a high-tech and productive society. The superpowers had no viable choice but to accept the Confederation as an independent power, one that controlled most of the extra-terrestrial resources of the solar system.

By far the smallest of the powers, the Confederation relies upon small, well-trained, and superbly equipped ground units to maintain its position in the interstellar race. The Confederation is the least expansionist of the powers, and while it dominates the moons and asteroids of the Sol system, it has a very small group of interstellar colonies. Mars rarely intervened in the wars between the other powers, preferring to maintain a policy of armed neutrality, until the First Imperium and Shadow Wars pulled every power into a desperate fight for survival.

Also By Jay Allan

Marines (Crimson Worlds I)
The Cost of Victory (Crimson Worlds II)
A Little Rebellion (Crimson Worlds III)
The First Imperium (Crimson Worlds IV)
The Line Must Hold (Crimson Worlds V)
To Hell's Heart (Crimson Worlds VI)
The Shadow Legions(Crimson Worlds VII)
Even Legends Die (Crimson Worlds VIII)
The Fall (Crimson Worlds IX)
War Stories (Crimson World Prequels)
MERCS (Successors I)
The Prisoner of Eldaron (Successors II)
Into the Darkness (Refugees I)
Shadows of the Gods (Refugees II)
Revenge of the Ancients (Refugees III)
Winds of Vengeance (Refugees IV)
Shadow of Empire (Far Stars I)
Enemy in the Dark (Far Stars II)
Funeral Games (Far Stars III)
Blackhawk (Far Stars Legends I)
The Dragon's Banner
Gehenna Dawn (Portal Wars I)
The Ten Thousand (Portal Wars II)
Homefront (Portal Wars III)

www.jayallanbooks.com
www.bloodonthestars.com
www.wolfsclaw.com
www.crimsonworlds.com

Made in the
USA
Middletown, DE